PAPER PROMISES & PUNISHMENT

X_____

Author: Payne

Copy written @2014 Payneless Publishings
ISBN 10: 0988173719
ISBN13: 987-0-9881737-1-2
LCCN NUMBER: TBD
Typesetting by www.21StreetUrbanEditing.com
Cover Design by Donna Osborn Clark at
CreationByDonna.com
Photography by CEO Snipes
Cover Model: A very special woman whom chooses to stay anonymous.

THIS NOVEL IS NOT FOR THE FAINT AT HEART. IF SEX- VULGAR LANGUAGE- RACIAL SLURRS OR URBAN DIALECT OFFENDS YOU. THANK YOU FOR WANTING TO SUPPORT ME BUT I UNDERSTAND THE CONFLICT.

Praise & Props

This is truly the most difficult page of the book to write. If I omit a name, please place the blame on my head and not my heart. I am only human. Even though I have not produced a Christian work of fiction. I know nothing is possible without God's blessing. For His mercy, grace, and guidance, I am more than grateful – I am humble.

Beamon Paul Jackson and Lawanda Elizabeth Payne, in your absence I celebrate the life you have given me. Every ass whippin', punishment, hug, kiss and tear nurtured and molded the person determined to complete and promote this book. Every fiber of me is a direct reflection of the love of you. Saundra Pearson, for the three years of hell you endured, not sure if this acknowledgement even scratches the surface. You are my Claire Huxtable, my role model MOM. If I never said it, you did the best you could with what you had and I thank you.

Josephine Cook and Maggie Rex, from the depths of my soul, between you two my mother rests easy.

Atiana Najah Payne and Jovon Daeshaun Payne, I know love and pain because God saw fit to bless me with two of the most challenging children to raise. You have been my rocks and reasons for wanting better and never quitting. I know unconditional love because I have been privileged to raise you.

For all the poems, stories, spoken word, and complaining my family and friends have had to endure. Valentina "Cookie" Dugan, George Irby, Mike "Havoc" Smith, Marcus Camper, and Thadd Gaskins for a lifetime of friendship and love, I thank you...

Tatia M. Payne-Moore and Carolyn D. Boone-Payne for not allowing me to quit and reading the "sloppy copy".

Asia Baines and Cee-Cee Irby your support love, and encouragement is bigger and deeper than I could ever pay you for (good, cause I am broke). Who says you cannot meet an angel on the internet; Cherell L Eutzy with the magical red pen. Your faith and support is limitless, thank you will not be enough. Your wedding poem will be epic. Donna Osborn Clark the magician for taking my basic photos and turning them into something the world can enjoy. More than a graphic designer, she is a blessing.

To my small, yet special circle of friends that I have learned to call family: Fantastic 4 plus two more, Nia-Jen-Big Ash-Lyn-Tey Tellem. Momma E, Big sis Christie, Aunt Neicy, Raymond Jackson aka Brah Man, Lamont R, Lisa H, Brian Daniels, Gavin, Darlene M and team turn up, Sandy L, POOKIE, Addie aka Red, Mona C, Rabbit, Myra M, Jamillia, Albert B, D.J. Mahhd, Claw (806), Ms. Chocolate, Officer Corbin aka Smash, Starr, Faye, Monique, Trecee, and my reconnected friend Elizabeth Bulter- Owkena.

My children of choice, God and adopted, Jomira and Joniece H, Richie Roe {R.I.P}, Kaliem, Kahiem, Bryan, Bob, Jazz, Yaz, Gi-Gi and Jai, Shay-shay, Shara, Shabani, Shawn, and my new baby CYA.

To my III-J crew {Jovon, Jovonnah, Jayon } and their mothers. Family is priceless....My new arrival Mekhi.

Tamara Murphy, aka Momma, for the long, hard and uncertain road you have challenged me like no other and for daring me to write something better. Hope I did just that!

Richard Gibbs, Saudlita Roberts, Doreasa Barker, Martin Stephens, Desiree Mansfeild, Tena Smith, La'Shawnta Hargrove and Ty-Isha Harris. For being honest and helpful sounding boards and motivators. I have a support team like no other I am grateful to have you all pushing for me.

To my role model Lisa Smith aka Vytiman Voyce, if the ones you expect to love you don't, know that someone on the outside admires, respects and supports you for no reason other than you are amazing. Now if we can find out how to market your crazy, we can both get rich.

Paper Promises & Punishment was a huge leap of faith so many people believed in me enough to purchase, read and respond to my work. So here is how I say thank you. {random}
Belen D, Eileen M, Barbara D, Cushawn S, Quiyana S, Alisha E, Andrea G, Leander M, Lakeith K, Michelle W, Dilana L, Samaya J, Tuashey G, Sonia Massie, Doris D, Bernie, Latarsha M, Latoya C, Jayden & Javar, Monique P, Al Fuller, Clara M, La'Shawnta H, Tracy R, Diane H, Catrice T, Kathy H, Lyn R, Sakeenah D, Lou H, Ms. Nina B, Mona T, Kenya D, Lucrezia S, Summer S, Terri S, Vickie J, Kayla S, Joyce M, Mr & Mrs. Tyler, Neecy, Troy N, Sharifa D, Tameka C, Breyonah, Niema F, Lesley J, Brittany T, Deyonka G, Thick Princess, Buddha, Ni-Ni R, Jen H, Kera S, Tajuana White, Poppie, Marisol, Yoshie V, Tyke, Lori L, Patti, Chuck G, Casino Dar, Joey M, Big Rich, Ms. Carol P, Big Shirley, Jeren, Icky-W.O.S, Tommie, Ava, Frenchie, Brandon, Emily, Kelly, Terri, Lisa C, Reggie, Linwood, Ms Brunnie, Jiggy, Robin, My Lu-Lu, Caroline Sandra, Margerita, Ms. Roe, Pete T, Jan Hoffman, Nikki G, Ms. Miles, Asia D, Donna D, Brunnie, Jackie-Immacannon, Phil, Desmond Harris, Angie, Cherell B, Parker, Miss Kim check cashing, Sandra R, Juan N, Lanitra B, Shirley G, Khadijah R, Phil, Tozine T, Shamia M, Banana, Rollie, Mom Kathy, Shantel aka Magnet, Tamara, Lamont W, Chris Troila, Ms. Natalie scheduling, Big Shawn, Matah, Angie & sister, Ms. Sherrie x-3, Big Rich, Velencia, Monica H, Jahlanda N, Sharon, Big Mike, Raheem, Rollie, Tamara, Shade`, First Lady Philly RR, April, Free, Heff, Snicker, Jenna, Milly, Physco, Magnet,

and Juspreme. If I forgot someone I apologize. Monk Marsh & Michael Mixon I still have your book!!! These are the people who took the leap of faith and supported me just because. I am so grateful. Book two your feedback and encouragement. Thank you.

Much love for having my back Shannon Phillips, Raquel Clark, La'Shawnta Hargrove, Saedah Mixson and Sakeena Davis. Ladies I am so happy to have you in my circle.

For the detailed conversations about part one for inspiring me to put a sick twist on part two. Khadijah Rollins {cuzin'} it meant so much to be listed as one of your favorite authors. Ty-Isha Harris, Didi Belen, Kadidra Nonpareil {cuzin'} that grounded straight talk no chaser or filters. Please don't stop.

To my Instagram & Facebook family. Thanks for always being cheerleaders on my team even when I did not want to be on the field, your applause kept me going.

Jesse Calloway IV I may have wrote the words but the technical support and saving my computer when I down loaded a virus. Hours of understanding I needed to write. I may not say it often but I love you. You are priceless thank you for being on my team.

AFFAIR

It's hard to juggle two lovers,
I hope you understand...
One pays my bills and the other
delivers me to promise land.
Necessity and fantasy tug at the strings of my thong.
Both daring me to choose the other,
and see who won't last long?
Turn your back on me and let's see how you will eat?
How you afford those nice clothes and those pedicured feet.
Desert your desires and life will surely beat you down.
So I bend over for one.
And suck the other until I drown.
Death would be too simple.
I'm carrying the curse of the damned...
Fighting for who I want to be... but living as I am.
Being true to oneself is a battle rarely won.
Someone always losses the outcome seldom fun.
Oh what a thrill when I am in that light,
The looks on their faces, when I kill the mic.
When the applauses cease to be heard.
When no one is watching.
It's the other that sustains me and keeps me plotting.
The hunger never fed and the need eating me alive
This is a Poet who works to survive.
This is my Affair

~ PAYNE~

Prologue

Zylar

"Happiness" is a drug. One most of us chase with every dollar and emotion we possess. Retail, social or financial happiness are the most common. However, desiring the companionship of another to aide in your happiness is a dependency all of its own. Do you really want to hold onto someone who, wants someone else?

I had dreams as tall as the Empire State Building, before I met Lamar. With the talent and motivation to back it up. I never fathomed him not being a permanent piece to my forever. Least of all pregnant and single, how quickly life changes. I reluctantly, let my goals subside to be the lover, companion and partner that he so desperately needed. I smoothed out his rough, Paterson, edges. Refined and molded his mannerisms and speech to be taken seriously in the very same industry that over looked me and embraced him. Why be a "Princess", when by his side I was Queen!

Giving another woman my prize was never part of the plan. If she wants him she will have to pick him up from the rubble I leave him under. Anyone can love you when you are doing well and shining. Who will love you, when you are tarnished and damaged?

"Even the beauty of birth, bares its own scars". Amir Sulaiman, Poet. Love is no exception. Life, is about beating the person that beat you. Even if that person is you (we are our own worst enemy). Some take the road of least resistance and persevere, allowing their success and accomplishments to speak for themselves. While others gloat, boast and brag about how they defeated the odds and

made a mockery of their opponents. Lamar, doesn't even know that he has made me into an adversary.

"Do you believe a man can truly love a woman and constantly betray her? Never mind physically but betray her in his mind, in the very "poetry of his soul". Well, it's not easy but men do it all the time."
— Mario Puzo, Fools Die

Sheed

How much loyalty is too much? I feel like I am repaying a debt with my life. Haneef's drama is 24/7 – 365. The New York City sewage system has less shit coming through it. Following orders have become impossible. As a man there is just no way that I can risk my freedom and life to make others comfortable; not anymore.

Every day that I watch my own child grow inside of Fatima's belly I know that I am not the same. I question my own worthiness of the opportunity to be a Father? How has Allah continued to over look my transgressions? From reckless adolescent to man-hood, my mistakes are just as blatant as they ever were.

I have not been to Jumar since Haneef has been incarcerated. Not that I do not have so much to be thankful for. I've been shot twice, stabbed and hit in the head with the butt of a gun. So many fist fights that I can't recall. Two car accidents and one crazy ex-girlfriend that threaten to poison me.

Kalief, has been deceased for more than ten years and I swear he was the lucky one. Living with my own regrets has become a life sentence. Countless nights I wondered why that bullet grazed my right bicep and hit Kalief in the lung. His blood drenched my velour sweat suit. Cold sweats and nightmares are my constant reminder that I made a promise that night Sept. 11, 2005. "Take care of my brother Shawn my mom's can't lose us both."

Today is like every other day, vague and uncertain. But my love for the Mason family perpetuates my progress, or is it my guilt?

"The more sinful and guilty a person tends to feel, the less chance there is that he will be a happy, healthy or law-abiding citizen. He will become a compulsive wrong-doer."
Dr. Albert Ellis Devin

Mo'Najah

I chose to stay in his shadow. My own comfortable and familiar Hell; created and controlled by the one person I loved more than myself. Living for years with the excuse, I did not know. Ignorance was my bliss. When I became knowledgeable, my crutch was fear. Once I grew stronger and wiser, my finances and accommodations justified being silent and stupid. The love that I had for Momma M and Lil' Neef kept me cemented in my own destruction.

Where does a weak woman find the courage to be strong? Was I somehow intimidated by Tanya's life-long connection or her sense of entitlement to Haneef? Did I intentionally provoke him? Maybe, being assaulted was the push I needed to break free of mister jail...

"There is a wonderful mythical law of nature that the three things we crave most in life- - happiness, freedom, and peace of mind- - are always attained by giving them to someone else."
Peyton Conway March

Tick, Tick
Tanya!

Dear Haneef,

I never got a response from the letter and photos I sent. I want to say that I'm surprised, but I'm not. What I can't understand is how another bitch that walks, talks and bleeds just like me, has so much control over what you do, how you think and what goes on with our family???

You think she is better because she is mixed or maybe because she was a virgin when you met her. She is a North Philly, hood rat no different and damn sure not an exception.

I will give her props for not turning into a full fledge whore however. Even after she started to get confirmation about all the bitches you fucked and tricked up on. See on the strength of that alone I may have emptied your damn accounts out. I may have even taken your lifetime rival in the streets on an all-inclusive vacation. But that's just me!

As I sit here and think, I birthed your mother fuckin' son. I was the one on the team when you were barely moving ounces. I was the one that had the cars and cribs in my name. So now that I need you most you gon' shit on me? Over a piece of pussy?

Mo'Najah, ain't even legally married to you. At any time that bitch can jump ship. Leaving you assed out! That would be what you deserved. But at the end of the day I am raising your son. I am cooking his food and helping with his homework. All of that is me. Your priorities and loyalties are fucked up. I know I have done some dumb shit in the past. None of us are perfect. With that said, I never turned my back on you. Even after you chose to start a new life with her. I was always there, a phone call away. If you needed me to handle something you never had to ask twice. If you wanted to fuck you never had to ask at all.

The bond between us was supposed to last until the grave Hanz'. I guess I am dead to you now?

Since you refuse to give me this money for the plastic surgeon to repair my face. I feel like there are too many bad memories here. My family will be moving out of the state as soon as I can transfer my section eight. You will always be Lil' Neef's Father, but your definitely not his Dad.

I never thought that I would grow to hate my first true love. The father of my son. The man that I believed in more than my own Father. I gave up my entire life just to be a memory in yours. Now you will get a chance to replay those memories, of what you had and how you lost it.

You know that old saying; "keep your friends close and your enemies closer". Well you are too far away to do either. So a lifetime of dirt is about to collect around your ignorant ass. I hope you have your Quran handy because it will take a lot of prayers to remedy the secrets I am about to expose.

An estranged lover with an axe to grind, will stop at nothing to watch the shit you love and cherish crumble. If I have to wear this khimar {muslim woman head wrap} the rest of my life. So be it. But the shit I know about you and your business partners will body your little fuckin empire. No, I am not threatening you, it's a motherfuckin' promise.

"Until you do right by me everything you think about is gon' fail!"

30 grand will be the least of your worries...

Locked & Loaded
Mo'Najah

"Mo' dis text message shit… Not cool it's been 5 days since u sent me the photos of ur face. Either u cum c me or u gonna need to worry about da other side of ur face! Where have u been and wtf is goin' on? Sheed has even been past here!"

I guess ya'll wanna know to?

Parking lot of the jail…

I was so furious, that I could not find the rental car. Fumbling through the bag I was carrying I pressed the panic button on the remote. I felt like every camera was on me. My Bluetooth was dead so, I connected the phone to the stereo system in the car. Did I want revenge or freedom? Mentally all I could comprehend was revenge. I allowed, Haneef the opportunity to hurt me again, this time in fuckin'public. The swelling of my eye was bearable, but the throbbing of my head and the five shades of blue, blacks and reds. I stared in the visor mirror for at least ten minutes. Which only validated the answer to my question but it also generated a few others.

"Serie call China."

She did not answer; I drove directly to her townhouse in Camden, after my drama. Only to find myself alone, in her empty apartment, I went into her bedroom and stole a pair of her Carrera Champion aviator shades that covered most of my face.

Ashamed and embarrassed, I wanted to go straight home. However, hiding from my problems was not going to make them disappear. How could I hide in the house Haneef had paid for? In addition I needed to secure my personal investments. Before Sheed, Snipes or Goldman had a chance to react to the recent fall out between Haneef and I. Haneef's off-shore accounts could not be touched until Monday. I called the 1-888 number and changed his codes. Locking out Goldman and Momma Mason. Hurt me physically, I will heal with financial compensation.

The fucked up part about that was Haneef, was never phased by money when I was concerned. Every time he got caught doin' bullshit, money or elaborate gifts would quickly follow to appease me. Back then it worked. This time I was takin' the severance package.

I made a trip to three of the four stash spots. Removing, half of everything in each safe money and product. The only reason I missed the one on the west, off of Haverford, was because Sheed was there. Resolving our partnership without everyone knowing was to my benefit. Yes, I could have been greedy and emptied out everything. The shit I had contributed to was what I was walking away with. No more and I refuse to take anything less…

Roughly every flip Haneef got close to 50 grand. With the average re-up being every six- eight weeks. The way I figured it, the 28 months Haneef has been down. Sheed and I deposited close to a million dollars into Haneef's off shore account. This was separate from the money from the barber shop, detail business and the two afterhours. I felt as though I was entitled to at least a third of those funds. Not to mention if Pennsylvania did recognize common law marriage which they did not… I would be entitled to half of everything that was acquired during my time in this dysfunctional relationship. For my pain, suffering, public humiliation and adultery I would be paid accordingly. Who needed a divorce attorney!

The next step was to find a place to lay my head. Returning to the house in Ardmore, was not even an option. Haneef's house, his rules. I called Buddah and told her I needed a moving van for a few hours for personal use.

By the time I collected my half of all the money and the product I had close to three hundred grand. Barely concealed in the trunk of a fuckin' rental car, talk about ridin' dirty. Parking the 2013 Buick LaCrosse in a secured lot, I had Buddah scoop me in the van. Removing the few things I knew I would not be able to replace. I had the van damn near full. I parked the van in front of my neighbors crib. Pulled out of the three car garage in my Acura.

Looking at the time and the gas gauge, my next stop was B.B.W. When I arrived at the club, Powder (the manager) was not there yet. But Bella the owner was, in full swing, makeup flawless, high heels on, giving orders like the Queen he was. When I walked in, she paused, looked at her Cartier Pasha watch.

"Darling, you had me thinking I had lost three hours. What's up Moet?"

"I really need to speak to you in private."

Bella escorted me to the office. Sitting me down, she instantly noticed my face.

"Oh, I need a drink! Bitch, do I need to make some calls? Who did this to you?" She went into her stash and pulled out a $1500 bottle of Louis XIII with two snifters.

Bella and I never really talked before, but I felt as though I did not have to lie. I felt like whatever I said was not going to go any further, so I told the truth. It felt wonderful to cry. I had not let anyone else know my burdens. Bella, spoke to me in Spanish most of the time, telling me not to worry and that things would be fine.

"As long as I own this bitch, you have a job. Take all the time you need. Girl, you need a thick, raw, cold steak and some rest. If anyone knows about taking a beating, trust me, mami, I do. The boys in Florida did not always play fair, especially the ones in the closet."

"Thanks, Bella. I am gonna go to the market and then to bed."

Soon as I got back from NYC.

The time I sat in the parking lot deciding how I would get my freedom and my revenge opened the gates to several other unknowns. The first one being that Hanz had three accounts in the Caribbean the total of all three did not have what I had in my one Cuban account. I choose Cuba to hide my money knowing that they did no extradition and would not cooperate with the Feds or any other US government. So either there was another account that I had no idea about or Goldman was stashing money for Haneef. The second question was the New York, connect?

There had never been an explanation to how Haneef suddenly had a connect in NYC. Neko's name was never mentioned or heard of until shit got tight for the family. With the price being slightly higher than Florida, why wouldn't he use this connection earlier? If he had, Hanz would still be on the streets. I needed to know if Neko would do business with me even if Haneef and I were no longer on the same team?

When I arrived in Brooklyn, I called Neko directly. He agreed to meet me at the hotel I had checked into. Neko was a very well-connected and protected guy. With good reason I was sure. His appearance was always immaculate, as if he was just leaving a business meeting briefcase and entourage in tow. When he arrived he wore slacks freshly pressed and a button-up with platinum and black diamond bezeled cufflinks complemented with Ralph Lauren butter-leather open toed sandals. His cologne, Armani, fit his dark skin and smooth hair. He commanded someone to make sure the room was clear. Once his people returned, we went upstairs to talk privately.

Sometimes you never know the power you possess until your back was up against the wall. Once we entered the suite, Neko said, "damn, it took you all this time to decide to make love to me?"

Turning around to face him, I removed my Carrea shades, displaying my bruises. Neko cringed as he gently touched my face. After telling him the entire story, from Lil Neef to the slap, he snapped!

"My nephew has me doing business with a fuckin' faggot! Any man that has to beat a woman to control her is a fuckin' homo! You're too beautiful to be mistreated, Moet. Just stay here. Allow me to take care of you?"

I was flattered by the offer, but men like Neko and Haneef have a lot in common. Women are garnish to their already-full plates. I desired to be a man's only dish for a change.

"Neko, that is not why I came."

"Okay, then tell me why your here?"

"I need to know if you only did business with me because of Haneef?"

"Haneef? Do you know what I sell my product for in Brooklyn?"

"No, how would I?"

"Twelve grand more than what you pay per brick. Do you know why I sell it to you for wholesale?"

"Neko, no I don't, that's why I am here."

"The connection between Haneef and my nephew is the only reason we ever met, but not the reason why I do business with you. Let me explain."

"Emmanuel, a.k.a. Manny, was in Allenwood for some white-collar crimes he had committed: fraud, money laundering, and theft by deception. Manny is my sister's first born, not to mention my favorite nephew. When Manny came home from jail, all he talked about was how Hanz looked out for him. My nephew boasted about Haneef endlessly, saying things like, 'Hanz made sure nobody fucked with me. Uncle Neko, he's just like you. From the time Hanz stepped foot on the tier, things changed. There were about three convicts he sent to the infirmary. He took his spot; he did not ask for it.' Manny also admired the females that clung to him, even with a double-digit sentence."

"So as a favor to my favorite nephew, I agreed to do business. Goldman, received a name, number, and the stipulations. Mo'Najah, Haneef means nothing to me."

The stillness in the room was deafening. Haneef, did not even know who the fuck Neko was. All this time I thought I was riding his coat tails when I was actually standing on my own.

From the first interaction, Neko was direct and blunt about how he felt and what he wanted from me. Time tamed all animals. However, after over a year, Neko still let his interests be known, but never on a level that was offensive. He admired my devotion to Haneef and made mention of it constantly.

Neko turned and retrieved his, Zero Halliburton Aluminum Attache` case from by the door. After he opened it removing three large piles of money and his I-pad, tossing them all on the king size bed. I stood there completely baffled about the contents of the briefcase or the relevance to our conversation. Quietly I stood and watched as his wavy hair danced around the collar of his Hugo Boss collarless shirt. As he pulled out a large white envelope which contained photos. Laying them all on the bed. He motioned me to come closer with his well-manicured finger. I stood speechless as I stared at the photos. Recalling where I was on those particular days or nights almost six months ago. Each photo was my life under a fucking microscope. From the club to meeting Sheed at the barber shop, running through the park, and leaving my classes. At least several weeks of activities.

"At first it was because I thought you were beautiful. Then it was because I wanted to fuck you. But then I saw how hard you work. You're trying to make something of yourself. You take my advances as physical, but I actually know a lot about you, Ms. Harrison, as I do with anyone I meet by referral. A man of my stature needs to know who his enemies are. Even if it benefits others, how could I take your money? I wish my lazy ass sisters had half of your ambition and courage. My people even say you go to the firing range at least once a month."

"Damn, how long have you been watching me?"

"Long enough to know I did not have to kill you."

The hairs on the back of my neck stood up. For the second time, in this game I was being watched, instead of doing the watching. A feeling I definitely did not care for.

"After we did business for a few months, I took some major losses. I needed to know if you or your team were a factor. Obviously you were not – you're still alive." He said with a chuckle.

"How come you insisted on someone who speaks Spanish? Your English is perfect."

"I feel more comfortable speaking and conducting business in Spanish. How many Spanish cops do you know?"

"Good point, not many. But anyone could be taught to speak the language."

"Yes but the dialect is innate, not something you can get from an instructor or Rosetta Stone. Listen, you already know I would make you my love slave, but I respect your grind and loyalty. I did the favor for Manny. Now I just look out for you, Mo'Najah. If you reward me with some sort of sexual favor, I will be more than receptive. Would you like me to take care of your Haneef situation?"

"No, Neko, that is sweet, but he has screwed himself. They will ship him out to another facility for acting out. I will take my revenge in cash."

"Smart woman. Dead men don't pay no bills. If I am not doing business with you directly, then your boys are going to have to pay retail."

"Then that they will find out on their own. I need to start looking out for myself."

"Damn, where were you twenty years ago?"

"Pre-school, Neko. I know I have taken up enough of your time. Thanks so much." I walked over to Neko and gave him a hug.

Just by embracing me, he became erect. Grabbing his bulge, he warned, "You better stop." Neko, proceeded to leave the room, but I had to admit, his dick was huge.

"Neko if I decided to fuck you would you respect me after?"

"If you fuck how you dance… You might not respect me. Every man has a weakness, mines is pretty women wit' good pussy and paper with the faces of dead presidents."

Apologetic
Haneef

Love,

I am really trying to fix shit between us. Me not being able to call you is really driving me crazy. They have shipped me to Virginia. I have to wait for my funds to clear from Allenwood, before I can buy time for the phone. I had to borrow an envelope and stamp from another Muslim brother that's here. I don't have anyone on my list but you Mo'Najah. I am sorry. Babe' tell me what I need to do to make it right? I can't eat I am barely sleeping, and I lost 8lbs since I been in this fuckin' place. I lost all my good time and they are trying to hit me with an assualt charge. Mo' I need you to at least talk to me. You are my ride or die. Everything a man could ask for in a lady, partner, and a friend. How the fuck am I suppose to function without you?

I can't... My entire life moves with you in the center of it Mo'Najah and with you gone I am less of a man. Even to write this shit is scary as hell to me Mo'. I can't make it through this shit without you.

I believed you when you said Tanya brought all of that on herself. I even respected the fact that you attempted to get Wise out the way without getting your hands dirty Ma'. You a fuckin' thinker, a problem solver, the remedy to what is reckless in my life. I know I would not be the man that I am today If I did not have you in my life all those years....

Mo'Najah remember you use to thank me for taking you out of your mom's crib. Buyin' you the best my money could afford. Taking my time to teach you certain shit about the game and this life. I guess I should have been thanking you. You taught me how to do more than just fuck. You made it okay for me to love a woman with my heart and my soul. You made my mother and my son so dependent on us that you are irreplaceable. I knew that then. But I am a nigga' flawed and fucked up mentally.

No matter how many times I pray and go to Jummah I will never be blessed because I keep hurting the one person in this world that loves me unconditionally.

After all this I could give a fuck about Tanya's face. If you ever loved me, then these words would somehow get into your heart. You were meant to be mine forever. Until my last breathe is taken I will fight to keep your love, Mo'Najah.

Ya' Husband,
Hanz

Return to sender addressee no longer lives here!

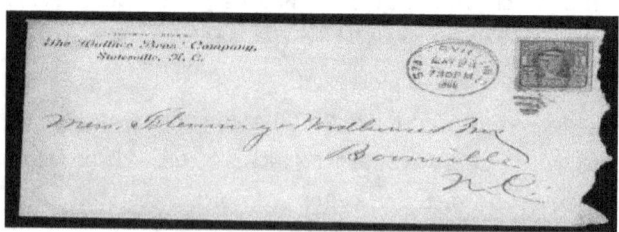

I.O.U.
Ofc. Saunders

When the paper work came across my desk to have Haneef Mason's medical records transferred. Fear and panic owned me. What if they found the drugs that I brought into the prison? What if they somehow figured out the number he was calling belonged to me? Maybe someone knew that his trips to the infirmary were bogus. What the fuck was I thinking? As if I don't have enough issues with men, that are not incarcerated. At least not physically.

Months of compliments, day after day of being mentally seduced weakened me. His Philly boy charm noticed everything from a change in my perfume to the color of my nails. After missing a few days of work due to car and man trouble. Haneef inquired about my absenteeism.

"Damn, gorgeous you just taking vacations and not saying bye. I thought we was better than that. No tan, no big smile what's up?"

Recalling how attentive he was after me and my ex had a huge falling out over Facebook. I don't know why I confided in him. My heart needed to be mended. Every woman wants to feel like she is appreciated and loved. Even if it's fake. Shit his game was better than most of the free motherfuckers that tried to approach me. He did not press too hard, or come on too strong. Before I realized what was happening I desired to see and talk to him just as much. When he sent me five grand I was impressed, not by the money, but that he was a man who kept a promise. His word meant something to him. After I received the money and moved into a new apartment and repaired my 2010 Chrysler 300m, he did not demand shit from me. I thought I would be able to repay the money back in a timely fashion. Taking a loan against my pension would have been an option but I already had one out.

We talked on the phone, I wrote letters. Before I could stop myself, feelings developed. I started to ask personal questions? Things that I had become extremely curious about. Things like how often do you masturbate? Did he perform cunnilingus? One of the many things my EX did not enjoy. As he assumed I should be happy with the standard dick performance. I wasn't.

Remembering how it all began... Haneef, had cut his hand playing basketball in the yard one evening. The scar was very deep and transport was going to take him to the local hospital at 06:00. I was the duty officer in the infirmary on watch that night.

When I read his name on my manifest sheet for list of inmates in the section my panties got wet. My intention was to take the fire that had been sparking on paper and in our conversation into something I could feel. Too many mornings I would rub my clitoris and wish it was him that I was cummin' for.

After I got relieved for chow there was no other officers passing through the infirmary. Being as thou there were basic drugs to administer you needed to be buzzed in and out of the corridor for security purposes. Talk about an opportunity presenting itself. Assured of one thing, I knew that Haneef, was HIV negative and disease free. What kept him coming to the infirmary on a regular was to check his blood sugar. He had discovered since his incarceration that he was boarder line diabetic.

As I radioed into command for a 10-7 (personal break). I went to my locker and freshened up. When I returned I did my routine head count. Which should be done hourly (but no one ever does). Purposely leaving Haneef's cell last to be checked. As I unlocked his door. He was wide awake laying on his back with gauze wrapped around his left hand. Staring aimlessly at the ceiling.

"I smelled you hours ago." He said in a voice barely above a whisper.

"A Dozen Roses, blends wonderful with your chemistry. At least you liked the gift I sent you."

"I was hoping maybe I could return the gesture with a gift of my own." My heart raced with adrenaline. Anticipation and curiosity ran rapid through my sexually repressed body. Standing directly above Haneef as he laid in the bed he muttered one command.

"Unbutton your pants."

Between the shank proof vest, utility belt, hand cuffs, baton and radio. I had more accessories than Barbie. But I did just what he asked.

With his right hand he slid my lace cut panties to the side and gently rubbed the tip of his fingers against my swollen clit. Pleased with my facial expression he continued to travel further south until he found my wetness. He teased my vaginal opening with his fingers. Making my muscles contract I stood perfectly still not wanting to interrupt this pleasant surprise. As he inserted both fingers into my wetness until I felt his knuckles. I gazed down into his brown eyes he stared at me intensely. As if the response on my face, meant more than the cum on his fingers. Slowly he started to maneuver his index and middle finger into my dripping and throbbing pussy. The radio chirped and blared as the other officers got relieved for breaks. None of which distracted me my high was unfathomable.

Haneef removed his hand, that was dippin with my vaginal juices and slowly licked each finger. Until all of the white cream disappeared.

"Let me taste dat."

Before he could ask twice I had my left leg out of my pants. He tore the crotch to my lace panties with very little effort. One leg on the metal frame of the bed and the other barely holding me stable on the floor. I watched in amazement as he squatted down to the right position to feast on my goodness. His tongue moved over my clit so many times I wondered if he possessed a second set of lips. Orgasm was at its threshold. I wanted to moan. I found myself biting my own bottom lip to muffle the pleasure that was brewing between my legs. Without warning, Haneef re-inserted three fingers into my pussy and sucked on my clit simultaneously. Convulsion and muscle spasms occurred in multiples as he probed barely inches into my vagina with a slight bend in his finger he summoned a wave of thick creamy fluids that had me vibrating.

The tent in his sweat pants could not be ignored. I wanted to experience the stroke that followed a head game that serious. Haneef, exposed one of the prettiest two toned penises I had ever seen in my life. With thick, proturding veins and girth. His dick had a place in my mouth.

"You can look but you can't touch. Tonight is all about you." he whispered.

Flattered and disappointed I was at a total loss for words. Not only did he eat my pussy like it was Campbell's soup wit' no spoon. But he finger fucked me until he found my G-spot causing me squirt all over his face. Something that never happened especially from an oral performance. After all of that he did not complete the mission! Haneef refused to fuck me.

He devoured my pussy on more than one occasion and would not put his penis inside of me. After a few weeks I was so open. Meeting Sheed at the gas station was how I leveled the playing field. I wanted him to know he could trust me. But I also wanted to feel him inside me. I was willing to do whatever to make it happen.

The fucked up part about this entire thing. He never asked me to return his money, or to meet his boy. The most he ever asked was to use my cell phone. Everything from the sex to me bringing in over 20 ounces of cocaine into the facility was all my dumb ass idea.

When he tried to pull back and not call or find a reason to visit the infirmary. I flipped the fuck out. I was strung and the shit was good. He kept money flowing into my pockets; I was having multiple orgasms on a regular. He was state property, no competition and all his attention. Even a chick in a visit could not get closer to him than I was. Talk about having the dick on lock down. Damn I had just started gettin' the dick now it was gone. Shit!

The reason for his transfer was not in the file I had. However the rumor mill at the prison is worse than the streets. From a fight to an incident in the mess hall the officers talked more about the inmates than the other way around.

"Assaulted a female during visitation, Officer Burton explained."

Parts of me was relieved. After I stopped worrying about my job and if I was under investigation, I got pissed.

Haneef always told me that if something ever went down that he would take care of me. I had instructions to follow to the letter. I guess I owed him at least that. When I got off work that morning I had several calls to make.

"Hello, Mrs. Mason, I am one of Haneef's friends. He asked that I call you and several others to let you know that he has been shipped to another prison." I spoke nervously into the phone.

"Baby, who am I speaking to?" the older woman replied in a stern tone.

"I would rather not tell you my name. I could get into trouble for calling you in the first place. They have very strict rules on fraternizing with inmates. He just did not want for you to make a trip up here for nothing or worry if he does not call for a week or so."

"Okay, dear, you have a nice day."

Damn, why did I agree to make these calls? None of these people even have a clue who I am. Shit, I wish I never spent his money, then I would not feel obligated. There were six names on the list…Five to go! Using the Metro-Pcs phone that Haneef paid for, I dialed the second number.

"Hello, Ms. Harrison, I am a friend of Haneef's. He asked me to call you and some others to let you know he has been shipped to another prison."

"Oh, is this his guard friend?"

"How did you know who I was?"

"Let's just say Haneef and I work for the same company. Do you know where they are shipping him to?"

"No ma'am I don't"

"Oh, okay, did he say anything else?"

"Just for y'all not to worry. He will be able to make contact in a week or so."

"Did Haneef compensate you already for these calls?"

"Yes, I have been taken care of."

"Have you already called Mrs. Mason, Mr. Goldman, Snipes and Sheed?"

"Just Mrs. Mason and you so far." Her accuracy of the names on the list amazed me. But after all if she was his business partner, she probably had instructions to follow also.

"Okay, just call Sheed. I will call Mr. Goldman and Snipes."

"There is another name on the list though, a Ms. Lewis. Can you call her also, please? I would really appreciate it. Like I told Mrs. Mason, I could really get into trouble if they find out I'm making calls on his behalf."

"Oh sure, let me get a pen."

"Ms. Lewis, 1-856-555-1111. Girl, it's too hard to find a job these days!"

"I completely understand. Call me Moet, Hanz spoke briefly about you last time I was there."

"Really?"

"Yes, he told me that you are a loyal friend. Which is obvious, you're risking your job to help him out."

"Awwww, how sweet! He puts on this tough demeanor. At least someone knows his softer side. Okay, Moet, let me make this final call."

Hustle Harder
Sheed

I did not realize that hurricane Haneefa was brewing in my own camp until two days after it had occured... Mo'Najah refused to answer my calls. Haneef could not have visitors. The chick from the prison was my only hope and the number I had used to reach her was going straight to voicemail. When she did finally reach out, I had already figured out the basics.

Money and product was missing from every safe but only half so I know I was not robbed. When I arrived at the house in Ardmore everything appeared to be normal until I got to the bedroom. All of Mo's shit was gone. From her lotion to her baby photos, only Haneef's clothes hung in the closet and he had been gone for years. Someone or something had lit a match to the flammable fabric of their relationship. My only question was who needed medical attention and who needed the coroner? In order for Mo' to cut all ties and roll out. I already knew the bullshit had just begun. Lighting the tip of a chocolate Black and Mild I inhaled deeply. How was I the only person that knew the outcome of this saga?

I had to let the cabinets get close to empty before I could make that trip to Brooklyn. You never want to tell a customer you're out, because a fiend has no fuckin' loyalty. Dudes buying weight will spend their money on sheet rock just to keep their flow coming. Cats will take a chance on getting straight beat or caught up in a damn sting before they waited on me to flip. Timing was critical. If I didn't take more than 250 grand I could easily be making a second unnecessary trip. If I took too long, my major money clients could find alternate sources. The hustle is more flocculating than the stock exchange. I reached under the mattress for my rainy day money. With Mo' taking half of the product and the profits, give her what? She took her cut off the top!

Summer was almost over but the heat in NYC made Philly's heat feel like an ocean breeze. The air was dry and stagnant. Like a million motherfuckers had exhaled at the same time. The hustle and congestion never amazed me. Just the fact the a million people lived and functioned in a city where no-one could give a fuck less about the other. Traffic accidents were over looked as busy business men made their way into Manhattan. Homeless woman is curled up on a packed bus stop and no one gives a fuck if the lady is dead or makes mention to how badly she smells. So much shit happened in this city, because no one gave a fuck about what occurred in a place where saints, sinner and salaries come to engage in poverty, prosperity and progress. Money definitely spoke volumes. Can you hear it aloud thru the cement, on the billboards as you moved throughout the boroughs? Even people from other countries knew NYC was the place to make, break, or escape to.

Since this was my first trip as "Da Boss", I wanted to make sure I did not spend anything less than what Mo'Money spent the last time, so I had to cut a few corners. There was no transport team, no room in Brooklyn. The longest we ever waited was an hour before Papi, sent someone for us. We did travel in two cars however. Mario would drive the packages home. The routine was the same, I had it down packed. I needed Mario to negotiate the deal. We hit the cellular number. You would not believe Mario's code: "slow screw".

Total, I had three hundred thousand in the black duffle bag to work with. I had to make sure everything went smoothly. A few grand could keep a cop off my ass on the right day. Especially since I did not use any of our connections on the force for traffic or random stop locations. A lot of the precautious Mo' tactics were expensive. This trip was high risk for higher stakes.

When we arrived at the stash house, everything seemed cool. Mario did not do business with the same dude however. This cat wore a blue Yankee fitted, white- tee and cargo pants. But they all look so much alike I wouldn't have known the difference, if he did not say anything. The entire conversation was in Spanish.

Mario came over to me and said, "The price damn near 30% higher. They want thirty-five for a brick of that girl and the boy is forty. Pills are the same though: three a pill, 250 minimum."

"Ask him what's up wit' da change in the price and where is the other dude Neko?"

"Qué pasa con los nuevos precios?¿Dónde está Neko?"

Mario translated the guy's response. "He said something about retail, favors are over, and everyone deserves a day off."

"What? Look, we really can't afford to go home empty-handed. Just get half of what you wanted 'til we can get a better deal." Mario whispered into my ear.

"I spent 200 stacks for half the product we usually brought."

We were given the keys to the rental and the product was loaded into the trunk, usually in the spare tire.

Once we got inside of the rental car, I exploded. "Yo! Papi just did some bullshit! We never paid that kind of money for a key! Retail? What the fuck was that all about! Dude was looking at us all the way out. Shit, if I gotta pay retail, I can go anywhere!"

"But at least you know his quality is correct," Mario reminded me.

"Yo, there is no way in hell I can get this money to flip right with what we just paid. Dude just fucked us hard with no lube and no foreplay."

"Look, let's swap the cars and get the product back to Philly. What's done is done, unless they have a return policy?" Mario said sarcastically.

"Naw, you're right, let's just get back home."

Meeting Mario at one of the drop spots, he had all of the product in one fuckin' grocery store bag. "Mario, dis shit ain't adding up. When you and Mo' took the last trip everything was smooth right?"

"Maybe the other dude got locked up. Maybe they had a shipment problem. You know like I know, ain't no guarantees in this business. Man, we could what if' all fuckin' day. The reality is, you're paying twelve grand more per brick than what you're used to. Either we gonna start shopping around, or you gonna pay it."

"You right, I really need to get in touch with Haneef. He has not called me since he got shipped out.

"Damn, for real? He talks to my mom's like three times a week. I think he is kicking himself for that shit with Mo'."

"I told the nigga to leave shit alone. Things were going fine. Now he wants to stress. I can't deal with his personal shit. I just need to find out what other routes I can take."

"Man, what have you been doing all these years? You been in this game for more than six years. You should have your own fuckin' connections and resources."

"I refuse to deal with motherfuckers I don't know. That's how you get all jammed up. I'm damn near thirty-one. I have not been in anything more than a holding cell and I like that. My driver license is in my name. I still have the fuckin' right to vote. Yo! Man, my freedom is priceless. Fuck a connect! I got a kid coming."

"Damn, nigga, you pick a fine time to take over an empire. Seems like ya conscience is kickin' in!"

"Listen, I don't want to be a king pin. I just want to be able to give my girl and my seed the same shit Haneef gave Mo' – security."

"Sheed, maybe you forgot how that fairy tale ended."

Grinding
Lamar

As I paced the well padded carpet of my office. I am on a conference call with the Young and Reckless Records; who seems very interested in Menace collaborating on a single for a new artist they have. Placing the call on mute I noticed that my desk phone has three lines lit. Waiting in the lobby is my main mission. Maurice aka Menace.

"Mrs. Palmer, can you please send Menace in?" I chimed in through the intercom system in my office.

"Yes, Mr. James, right away."

"Menace, Lamar will see you now, go right in."

To the left of my desk was a 20 x 30 poster of what the album cover was going to look like.

"Yo! The cover is fire!" Menace screamed as soon as he noticed it.

"I think so also. It just came in this afternoon. Both singles have done really well. The radio stations are giving you some serious rotation and the album release party is gonna get you mad publicity. I want to shoot the video before the party, that way we can get a world premiere of your talent at the release. As long as you and Alashia make that shit hot, I see platinum in our future baby boy. This charity event in Philly is only going to keep your name on people lips. I got some big plans for you Menace. Are you ready to get this paper?"

"Lamar, man, I just really want to thank you for pushing me. Good lookin' out for not bailing on a nigga' when I got a little cocky or off-track. If it weren't for you and Zylar,

I'd be fucked up in the game, probably signed to raping-you records or some shit. I'm even taking your advice about the Alashia shit. Professional, it's all about the paper. Just because we freaking in the song don't mean I have to fuck her in real life. It's a job, you almost never like the people you work with -except for you, man. Truth is, the song is hot. Maybe us not liking each other adds some flavor to the track. Just like 50 said about Kim: it was a business decision, no more, no less. I want to be a king in the business, not just a pawn. You teachin' me the game Lamar, I really appreciate it, man, real talk."

"Listen, teaching you makes me a better man Menace. The 40/40 is going to be blaze! Just make sure you are at the hotel on time; Mrs. Palmer reserved two suites for you and your guest."

"Where you staying at man?"

"Harrah's. I'm trying to line up a party at The Pool, so I will be there the night before to make sure all things go as planned. Menace, you staying on your pen game, right?"

"L baby, I got so much shit written down, adult diapers could not hold it."

"Okay, 'cause I wanna do some underground stuff with you, push them off the Juicee website and I-cloud."

"What time is the limo picking me up?"

"At 11:40 p.m. sharp. I want you to make your grand entrance at midnight.

Reggie already told me the wardrobe is sick. Have you decided what way you gonna play it?"

"No, but I am gonna take most of the stuff he picked out. Now for that cat to have so much sugar in his tank, he can dress a man."

"Listen, Juicee hires talent, not appearance or personal preference. What you do in your personal life is fine as long as it don't fuck with my paper."

"I can dig that hot shit."

"Menace, don't drink too much before you get to the 40/40 just in case you get an interview or something. Your boy is calling in some major favors to make this shit pop off. Just in case, be ready to give them what the people ask for. It could be freestyle, a few bars from your single, you never know."

My tone was meant to be fatherly; however my mind set was always financial. If Menace slipped up one-time between now and the album release the media would have a field day with whatever drama he publicly displayed. Menace is not Miley, not everybody can bounce back from bad media coverage. Shit, ask Chris B.

"Lamar, don't worry, man, I will not let you down. So what's this charity thing about?"

"Everyone in NYC knows you because you're a local based artist I have a beautiful friend that is looking to put together a charity showcase in Philadelphia, Juicee Inc. will be a sponsor. We need more than just World Star to get our name out there."

Giving Menace a brotherly embrace I watch as he leaves my office.

Speaking of the beautiful friend I have in Philly, it has been at least three days since I have verbally spoken or face-time with Mo'Najah. Even thou her text messages are consistent, she normally does not go a day without demanding to see me smile. Removing my I-phone 5 from the breast pocket of my blazer I call her phone. As the ringtone plays "Bad" by Wale & Teira M., I find myself distracted thinking about how fitting this song is for Mo'Najah. She does not answer, I don't leave a message.

 As much as I complain about Glide-Ovoo-Facetime. I miss seeing ur smile. 3 days 2 many. No texts, no calls, face 2 face !!! A.S.A.P.

Sabotage
Tanya

I had taken 676 East across the Ben Franklin Bridge into South Jersey. Traveled on route 42-South until I reached the Atlantic City expressway. This had been my third Friday with the hopes that he still attended the Mosque on Atlantic Ave. An entire hour before Jum'uah began I sat in my Maxima and watched as men and women entered the building of worship, as the women used the front door the men used another entrance. My stomach did hella' flips. Dressed in all black with an over garment and a head wrap, I did not stand out at all. Being greeted by brothers and sisters as they walked passed in traditional Islamic fashion. "As-Salaam-Alaikum" "Wa-Alaikum-Salaam." With my head down I mumble the greeting back out of sheer respect. My conscience was making me second guess my plan. How far was I willing to take this with him being the running force? Was I prepared for the aftermath? As I turned to my left, tempted to walk away, the window from the convenience store mirrored my image. Reminding me loudly why I was here. Twenty-nine grand for the surgery and the muscle therapy that would follow the procedure. Money could make my life normal again. Not that it was ever perfect. But I never looked in the mirror and cried before this. Most of my scars were internal, until recently.

I had not seen him in close to five years. Which I thought was a sheer hallucination. After all, I had attended the massive funeral. Watched as teachers, friends and old lovers stood in front of life size photos and cried. Shit, I was one of them. I happened to be in Baltimore at the seafood festival, seated close to the water; when I saw an image that resembled a lover I would never forget. Chills ran down my body. I am a firm believer in everyone has a twin. But, this sensation did not allow me to dismiss the thought. As I excused myself from the table I made my way in the direction of the ghost I had just seen. I chose to stay a safe distance, wondering why he would fake his own death? But the voice would confirm it for me. As we grow older things change. His thin build was now full muscular even. Chiseled chin now had a full sunnah. The thick corn rows I remembered braiding had been chopped off. A cream fedora and Carrera shades. Before he passed away we had not spoken our history was explosive. In fact, it was almost deadly. If it were not him I had nothing to lose and if it was. Kadir, had managed to make himself disappear.

I never feared Kadir, even with his reputation and deadly temper. He knew, he was alive only because of my son. Shortly after the rumors of Mo'Najah started to surface I needed proof. Kadir had no problem providing me with pictures and the address. Haneef warned me, drilled into my head repeatedly about how grimy and manipulative men would be after they realized I was single. Parts of me thought Haneef was being controlling; wanted to have his cake and eat it too. Haneef never revealed to me why he had such repugnance towards Kadir. Only that he better not see him around his son. A warning that I passed on to Kadir out of concern. Only to be hit with the million dollar question, does he have your son around other females?

Kadir was tall and thin. Not chocolate but a smooth hazel nut complexion, chiseled chin and deep brown eyes. His Islamic mannerisms and soft spoken demeanor added to the attraction. His intelligence turned me on as we discussed political views, woman in the work place, the missing element in today's household. Even thou he held the reputation of a monster; he approached me like a gentlemen. Treated me like a lady and fucked me like he had something to prove.

However the more I tried to avoid Kadir the more his charm, persistence and generosity had no limits. Not to mention how accurate his information was about Haneef and the female he had lied about for months. That was the icing on the cake. We both knew that we were running with scissors. Kadir had a way of making the pain feel good back then. Kadir never told me why he loathed Haneef so much. Between the money and the attention I can honestly say I didn't give a fuck. Haneef gave me money to stay away from him. Kadir made it worth my while to defy Haneef.

Haneef Jr. was about to turn three at the time, Kadir had sent a pony for a day package to the house for juniors' party. Not to mention the five hundred in cash he gave me the night before. Haneef's face crumbled as the children ran from the inflatable castle and the face painting artist to the Pony that was out front. Kadir arrived shortly after the elaborate gift in a white stretch limo wearing all white. As he passed out money to the kids, according to their ages, Haneef was livid. I had found him hours later in Jr.'s room with two semi-automatic guns placed on his chest one, was a Glock 9 and the other was a Berretta PX4.

"Don't leave, come in and close the door. Bitch I don't give a fuck about what you do with your life. That is my son, my life, my world and next time you allow another man to take my shine in his eyes. I will do life behind bars to teach you and him a lesson. The only reason you are still standing is because my Mother is sitting out there. The bad part is you were raised with a mother and a father. Why shouldn't my son have the same family structure? You have the intelligence to comprehend what dat' bitch nigga' just did. Nothing he can offer you will be worth the drama you have just started. It could cost someone their life; I hope the dick and the dollars was worth it?"

Tears leaked from the corners of Haneef's eyes, he never looked at me or changed position on the bed. "Call my phone when it's time to sing happy birthday to my son."

After that I made sure Lil Neef was with Momma M anytime I had plans with Kadir. Never did I mention or ask for money that remotely involved my son. The grace of God kept Haneef from snappin' that day. Even thou Kadir took the threat idly, I saw a hurt in Haneef's eyes that I knew I would forever pay for.

Kadir took great pleasure in flaunting me in Haneef's face. I would be more of a liar if I told you I did not enjoy giving Haneef a taste of his own medicine. Kadir and I were never exclusive, partly because of the religious differences and he really was not my type. We both knew that outside of amazing sex we were both seeking payback. It took about a year until finally we saw Haneef with Mo'Najah, by then the seed was already planted. If heads could do a 360 I don't think he would have stopped staring at her. I had only heard of the little girl Haneef was fuckin' wit. I even had someone I know bring me a yearbook picture just so I could know what the chick looked like. When I saw her in person she looked like a thick version of Lisa Raye. Jet black hair flowing down her back, small waist, big breast and a gorgeous face. I don't know who watched them longer me or Kadir.

Once Kadir realized I was old news his attentiveness came to a screeching halt. When I found out I was pregnant, I had no choice but to tell them both. Fearing for my life if I had chosen to abort either one of their embryo. Yes, I was fuckin' them both!

Haneef had the paternity test fixed so that Kadir would never know that Taliah was his biological daughter. But that was only the beginning. Haneef never got over the stunt at the party, anytime he saw Kadir in a public place, it was a brawl. If either was strapped up it was gun play.

Haneef even went as far as having a pimp by the name of Styles turn Kadir's only sister, Khasmere, all the way out. Haneef had orchestrated several sting operations to level the score with Kadir. After the cops confiscated the drugs and money, they left thousands of dollars worth of jewelry behind purposely. Haneef placed on the foot of my bed King- Kadir's crown piece that hung low on a 45 inch platinum chain. Deadly was the game that Haneef and Kadir played with one another. However Kadir had way more to lose than Haneef did. With Haneef already having a criminal history, prison was of no consequence. Kadir had businesses, real estate, connections and a bachelor's degree. Kadir wanted revenge but he was not willing to give up his freedom to get it.

As the custom painted 2013 XJ Jaguar parallel parked in the spot I knew it was him. My heart pounded with anticipation, would Kadir actually help me? Closed mouths don't get fed.

"Kadir, can I speak with you privately?"

"Sorry sis' do I know you?" Kadir responded, leaning in slightly not at all aware who I was. As he waived the other brothers to go ahead. I slowly lowered my niqab, revealing my face and my scars.

"Tanya?" He said with surprise and confusion, looking around in a paranoid manner. "How did you know I was here and when did you become Muslim?

"Kadir, I am not Muslim I wear the khimar & niqab to cover the marks on my face and neck."

A look of total disbelief settled on his face. Kadir began to look around uneasily as if someone was watching us. Noticing the change in his behavior, maybe this was a bad idea?

"I thought I could ask you for help with a delicate matter but I should not have come. Sorry for wasting your time enjoy your Jumu'ah."

As I scurried to my car, sweat drenched the top of the khimar. My heart raced, once he realized who I was he instantly thought he was being set-up. I did not see fear but his instincts told him I was the enemy. Body language speaks louder than words. Within moments I was paying the toll to get back on the Philadelphia expressway.

When I pulled into my drive way I notice my neighbor's had a sign posted for a yard sale. Something instantly went off in my head. Between the jewelry, pocketbooks and the expensive shoes. Maybe I did not need Kadir or Haneef. The old stuff that Lil Neef never played with and all of the secret gifts Hanz brought for Taliah.

My very first stop was the basement. After three failed attempts at the combination I finally was able to open the safe. I pulled out the old small lock box, that now held my jewelry, passport and everyone's social security cards. As I shifted through the box I had thousands of dollars worth of shit I had forgotten about. Gucci link bracelets, massive rope earrings, with my name going across the center. Not to mention a custom made Hello Kitty charm that Kadir, got made for me when he purchased his crown. Most of this stuff came from Jeweler's Row. Maybe with the price of gold being so high right now I could get most of the money on my own. If I get close to twenty grand I could apply for a car title loan for the rest.

"Keema, can you make sure the kids get in the house safe? I have to make a run real quick, here is a few dollars for your trouble." I said pushin' a twenty into my neighbor's hand before she could say no.

Money Talk
Devin

There was a light tap on my office door.

"Mr. Davis, Mr. Sanchez and Mr. Ramirez are waiting in the lobby to see you."

My receptionist was always so pleasant. However, with my recent personal issues, I had been avoiding most of my face-to-face clients and only having phone consultations. Sleeping on a futon and truly not being sure about my future was fucking with me big time. Luckily, my ability to invest and advise had not been compromised. If anything, I was better at work than I had ever been. When all else failed, use your talent to mask your misery. Mr. Sanchez sudden visit had caught me off guard, however he was not one for appointments. Money makes busy people available.

"Mr. Sanchez, how have you been? When did you arrive in NYC?" I extended my hand to greet one of my largest personal finance clients and his assistant. Sanchez had a translator to interpret the conversation for us. "My associate and I just arrived this morning. I am doing well."

"Good, what brings you to town?"

"I think that it is really important to support Juicee's next star, considering how much money we are investing into this album," the translator responded.

"True, true. I'm sure Mr. James would be nothing but delighted for you to share in the success of Juicee Inc. Menace is very talented." The delay in the conversation allowed me to read Mr. Sanchez's body language, as they spoke in Spanish to one another.

"Looking at the expense account, we are investing a pretty penny into this artist's career Mr. Davis."

"Is this a subtle way of expressing some concern with Lamar's business decisions?" I asked with my fingers laced while settling further back in my chair.

"No, not at all. I just wanted to see how my money is being spent. As long as we stay in the black, there are no concerns. Trust, I understand that it takes money to make money." The translator relayed the message in a language that I understood.

"Good, because I have the utmost faith in Mr. James and his ability, not just as a businessman but as a friend."

"So will you be attending the event at the 40/40?"

"No, sorry, not my scene. I will be taking the boys from Juicee in the hood camping that weekend. After all, someone has to hold down the fort."

"Funny you should say Fort. Yes, I also wanted to speak to you about increasing my holdings in certain areas."

"Now is actually a great time. I can cancel lunch and we can look into some things. How much are you looking to invest?"

Two and half million dollars. But I am looking for a short term investment. Mr. Sanchez is very interested in some quick returns.

"Quick returns come with large risks. The market is very volatile right now."

"Without risk, do you think Donald Trump would have the building downtown? Like I said earlier, it takes money to make money. So, Mr. Davis, let's see what you can do with a million dollars?"

Within the hour I had 1.5 million dollars of Mr. Sanchez's money in high risk trades. As I told him about company's I had been watching, he picked three and dove in with a half a mil each.

As I walked Mr. Sanchez and Mr. Ramirez to the limo they had double parked out front, the glare from sun strained my eyes. I would be glad when summer was over. Just as I reached for the door handle, Lamar calls my name.

"Devin wait up."

"What's good, Lamar you just missed your business partner Sanchez and Ramirez?"

"Really, damn, man you look like shit."

"That's great, 'cause I feel like hell. Shit is an improvement."

"Devin, when are you going back home?"

"LJ, I don't have a home, I have a house. Home means a family's permanet place of residence. There is no family, so why should I even be there?"

"3D, because that is where your heart is. Brianna has tamed and claimed you since day one. Are you really prepared to leave your wife?"

"Man, every day I ask myself a million questions. The only answer I am 100 percent sure of is that I want to be a father. Diaper changing, sleepless nights, first steps, father. Adopting means I'm shopping for a kid that the fucking parents did not want."

"You're not being fair. Those kids don't ask to be born or abandoned. What about the kids whose parents have passed away? 3D, you're really being an ass about this."

"Lamar, you are living your dream. Every day you make music, you find artists you promote and produce. You walked away from a woman who was fucking perfect for you. Let's not even mention how rich her family is. It's cool for everyone else to have their dream, but I am supposed to suffocate mines? Fuck that shit! If I have to deal with four different women to equal up to Brianna, fine, so be it. Nobody can judge me for wanting what I want. I want some fucking babies, and if Bri can't give them to me, then - "

"Look, man, you're still mad. Maybe you need to go talk to your mom or get some professional help."

"Man, I don't need my Mother, you or a shrink to tell me that a man's purpose is to PROVIDE, PROTECT, PRODUCE. That shit was written a long time before I was born. If mankind is too ignorant to play its position, fine. But trust and believe, I know my place in life. As fucked up as you may think I am being to my wife, I love her enough not to waste anymore of her time. Being a father is the only thing worth living and dying for. When you get there, then we are on the same page. Deuces LJ, I'm out."

I grabbed my brother, best friend and all around dude by the shoulder.

"Changing girlfriends can't be compared to divorcing your soul-mate. Brianna is everything you are not. She is the balance, the reasoning in your irrational life. When you and Bri got married, I remember one of your vows to her. You said, "A man that knows himself knows when the right woman has entered his life. Everything has a value, a place, as long as Brianna is by my side." Devin, some shit is just irreplaceable. What you and your wife have is one of those things."

"Did my wife send you here? If I stay married and have ten kids or I get divorced and have two you will always be my brother. Good – bad or indifferent. But this longing; a man without a child cannot understand a man who wants one. How about I let you have the stripper and you let me live my life?"

"Have you seen or heard from Zylar?"

"No, why would I? Zylar is not my friend; she is my wife's friend."

"Zylar has basically disappeared, quitting the choir, returning the car. She has disconnected herself from anyone that we know, almost as if she is hiding. I just want to make sure she has not reverted back to that depression state."

"Lamar, what happens to Zylar is no longer your concern. She is a big girl, she can take care of herself. Just in case you have forgotten, Zylar's family can afford to fix any problems she has. If you're really that curious, why don't you call her?"

"Listen, this break-up was smooth and clean. I got back the ring and the Benz. I'm concerned, not crazy."

"So I guess that chick is keeping you busy?"

"3D, her name is Mo'Najah."

"Ho'Najah?"

"Ha fucking ha. You will get to meet her at the 40/40."

"Man, I am not going."

"Why not?"

"I volunteered to be a chaperone on the camping trip, remember?"

"Damn, that's the same weekend?"

"Duh, yeah, someone has to think about the kids we mentor. You're really serious about this broad? You're about to flaunt her in front of all the who's-who of the music industry? Make sure there are no poles around."

"Damn Devin, if I did not know better, I would think that you had stock in Haterade."

"Listen, I am not going to pretend that I understand what you see in this female. Since I have known you, women have flocked to you, from registered nurses to marketing executives. But if you like it, I love it."

"Dancing is what she does, not who she is…Good lookin' out with the Juicee-in-the-hood boys. I will make sure you guys have everything you need. Cool man, I am going to get out of here." Giving my brother from another mother a hand shake- hug. I turn to leave.

"My futon is calling me away, later LJ."

Hushhh Little Baby!
Zylar

I had been home for almost a week, tiptoeing around my parents, telling them my version of why Lamar and I were no longer engaged. My Father was furious; Mother just cocooned me, keeping my spirits high, painting a picture that all of this was a bad dream. Facials and spa days would cure what a shopping spree wouldn't.

Their house was huge. This was home; I was raised here. Hardwood floors stretched throughout. There were cathedral ceilings, elegant chandeliers, marble columns, and high archways. My brothers used to run and leap to touch the tip of the one in the foyer, the truest sign that they were getting taller. The sweet smell of lavender and pine soil filled the air. Mother still cut her own roses from her garden. I turned in the playroom, which was now a study, as I remembered the click-clack of my tap shoes on the floor. There was no place like home. So much had changed. The entire house had been renovated since I left for college. The basement was now a cigar room with a full bar for my Father's monthly poker night. Mother's garden had been replaced with a huge in-ground pool with a built-in waterfall. They hired people to do the gardening and lawn these days. Growing up, I remember Jr. and Lawrence spending the entire morning cutting the grass. The estate sat on an acre and a half. Mom planted the most beautiful plants and flowers. We always had the best house on the block.

Both my brothers were older than me, at least ten years my senior. Laura was determined to bring a female child into this world and the third time was the charm. There was nothing that was too good for their only daughter. I couldn't remember a beating or a punishment, maybe a stern lecture here and there. When I said I wanted for nothing except to sleep in their bed, that is where father drew the line. But I had it all: Cabbage Patch, Nintendo, gymnastics and tap. You name it, Zylar Wingate was there. Prom queen, cotillions, beauty contest, I was even the number one seller for the Girl Scouts. *My child will grow-up here also, in the same love and comforts I thought to myself.*

My father was home from the hospital today. We enjoyed a light breakfast of fresh fruits and toast. My Father was sitting in his study with the paper when I was summoned.

"Zylar," he said in his distinct voice. I swear he should have been a preacher. "We need to talk, dear. Men will never take a woman seriously if she allows herself to be to open or loose. Lacking direction, personally sends signals to men. Do you understand what I am saying, darling?"

"No, Dad, I don't."

"Your mother was a prize when I found her. Pure, driven, from a good strong, solid family. Laura's beauty captured my eyes, but her spirit kept my attention. Her intellect and willpower kept me humble and hostage for months. My manly advances fell on deaf ears until she was sure my intentions where marriage. The other gentlemen that tried their hand for your mother's attention only made the prize that much more worth winning. Wingate woman are delicate flowers. NYC has hardened you. But you're home now, where there is love and understanding. We will overcome this obstacle."

"Daddy, I'm so glad you feel that way. I have some great news to tell you.

Daddy, I am pregnant!"

"Zylar, please tell me you're joking. A bastard child in this house is unacceptable. How the hell did I send you to New York in the first place, only to become some random baby mama? I have a friend in North Charleston. The procedure should only take a few hours. Your mother will never have to know. Let me make a few calls."

"Make a few calls for what? If it is not for prenatal care, then I am not interested!"

"Zylar, how, when, and who is going to take care of a baby? You can barely cook, let alone raise a child. If you thought for one fraction of a moment your mother and I were going to raise another child, you're mistaken. We planned on cutting you off after your wedding. Zylar, your mother and I never intended to support you forever. It is past time the fairytale came to an end. Lamar marrying you was our relief. Your break-up is your wake-up call, dear. This luxury ride is at its end. If you so choose to factor an unborn child into your equation, then let the choice be yours. We have paid for your education, demos, studio time, and voice coaches. You have had a lifetime of designer labels and endless funds. You have no true bills or obligations. It's time for a little – no, a lot - of independence and sacrifice."

"Mom would never let you throw me out on the street."

"Throw you out? Heavens no! But cut you off? Yes, dear, it was her idea."

"Mother and I have a great relationship. If all of this is true, she will give it to me straight." *Damn, did I really expect for them to support me forever? What was I waiting for? Oh, to be a multi-platinum recording artist. Then I was waiting on Prince freaking Charming to marry me. Is a baby the motivation I need in order to stand on my own? Is that why Lamar chose someone else?*

All of a sudden the room started to spin. My heart was pounding like I just got off the treadmill. Perspiration covered my forehead. My legs were giving out. Hands shaky, I attempted to grab the wall to stop my fall.

"Zylar? Zylar?"

"This is 911, what is your emergency?"

Vanishing Act
Mo `Najah

The last two people to see me face to face were Neko and Buddah. My attempts to send text messages and talk to people that needed to know that I was fine was not as sufficient as I had hoped. Lamar had called three times and sent several text messages that would have been alarming if I did not move out of the house in Ardmore. It's amazing how much information someone can get from a credit card receipt these days. Note to self: Cash is best. Somehow the tickets I purchased to take him to see the 76'ers vs the Knicks had my credit card info on it and the address to the home I shared with Haneef.

As I looked out of the wall to ceiling size window, my view from the 12th floor suite captured an amazing mirage of what Philadelphia was supposed to be. Only obvious to someone who lived here or that dared to venture off the tourist path... My five star accommodations did not shield the crime infested, unemployed, dog eat dog world that I knew to be just a short L ride away. I guess a city holding the world with so much history should have just as much misery to balance out the natural order of things.

The swelling had gone completely down thanks to Bella's advice, plenty of rest and pure vitamin E. However the vessel in my eye that erupted had not healed a bit. I dreaded telling Lamar about the incident. Not wanting to alarm him about things that I had under control. At least I thought I had. Avoiding the confrontation completely I decided that this paradise was only making it harder to return to my real life. I needed a place to live.

"Thank you for calling Perfect Purchase Reality how may I direct your call?"

"Hello may I speak to Mrs. Davis please?"

"Let me see if she is available, may I ask who is calling?"

"Yes this is Ms. Harrison."

"Please hold. Ms. Harrison I am connecting you to Mrs. Davis have a good afternoon."

"This is Mrs. Davis how may I help you?" Her voice was so upbeat and chipper.

"Mrs. Davis this is Mo'Najah, some things have transpired out of my control and I need a huge favor ASAP."

"I am not going to make any promises but I will do the best I can. What do you need?"

"I need a cash deal on a four bedroom- two and half bath- two car garage home like yesterday."

"Mo'Najah I don't know about yesterday but let me make a few calls to see what I can do. How much do you want to spend and is there an area that you don't wanna be in?"

"As far away from Philadelphia as my money can take me. Three hundred thousand if it's perfect 200 if it needs work."

"Dwight out of my Philadelphia office and Cheryl out of my New Jersey office will be getting a call, let's see what they can find us. Cash deals are tricky they almost never come with inspections or any reassurance for the buyer."

"I just need a place to lay my head and not worry who is watching for at least a little while." Ending the call with Mrs. Davis I took a deep breath. I command Serie "to call Lamar."

After three rings on my end of the phone I thought I was getting a pass. Just when I was about to swipe the phone to end the call.

"Mo'Najah, something is wrong I can feel it."Lamar's statement aimed directly at my neck.

"Your right… I am just not in a position to talk about it over the phone. I am staying at 'The Sofitel Hotel' in center city Philly."

"I will be there in three hours to come get you."

"Mar, that's not going to resolve my issue either."

"Mo'Najah are you hurt?"

"Not anymore."

"Accept my face-time request!"

Every muscle in my neck tensed up from the tone of his voice I already knew how this was going to end.

"How about I just give you the address; see you in a few hours."

"How about you trust that my concern for you is genuine and allow me to be the MAN in this relationship!"

With the swipe of my index finger his face is on the screen of my I-phone within moment mines will be on his. My hair was a mess, no shine to my skin. I had basically been secluded in this room for days waiting for my eye to clear up and plotting my next move. It took exactly six seconds for him to see the clott in my eye. His jaws tightened, the nostrils on his perfect nose started to flair. He looked around his office as if someone could make what he had seen go away. What seemed like forever had passed before a word was said.

"I already know it was not an accident because you would not have hidden from me all this time. Tell me if this was business or personal, Mo'Najah?"

"Personally the result of something I tried to handle like it was business."

"Pack your things I am sending a car for you."

"Lamar I have a car."

"Then get here I will meet you at the penthouse in three hours!"

Every ounce of my body was turned on by the possessive, protectiveness, and dominance that man just displayed. Controlled, but angry concern but cautious. My panties were drenched as I packed my bag. Butterflies rumbled in my gut I was actually looking forward to having daddy spank me. As I showered and got ready to leave my rented paradise, I thanked God for sending me a man strong enough to handle my drama!

Speaking of drama... I had almost forgotten about Ms. Lewis. *These bitches are gettin' too easy to manipulate*, I thought as I carefully mapped out my plan to call Ms. Lewis. I needed to get as much information from her as I could without seeming too obvious. The scared guard had no idea that she had just given me the missing link that I needed in order to confirm my suspicions. Haneef would only reach out to key people in his life. Ms. Lewis was a name I had never heard of. If she was indeed Kay-Kay's mother, Haneef should only pray money was the only thing I took. Using caller ID faker, I made my number appear to be one of the numbers Haneef had called from when he was in the medical unit.

"Hello, may I please speak to Ms. Lewis?" I sang into the phone, almost nervous to find out who exactly this woman was. Knowing Hanz, she could be a mule, a female that he had money invested into or someone from his past that he wanted to remain part of his future. Either way, my stomach churned with anxiety. Ignorance was every woman's bliss.

"She's not in right now. May I take a message?" announced the very young voice on the other end of the phone.

"This is Mrs. Parrish from Allenwood federal prison. I was wondering if Ms. Lewis had a recent shot record for

Kay-Kay? We had a recent outbreak in the jail and we are asking for all the parents to submit shot records."

"I would have to ask Ms. Yolanda. Sorry, miss, I'm just the babysitter."

I now knew why Ms. Lewis's number was given to the guard at Allenwood. His best-kept secret was leaking out. "Oh, I apologize for any inconvenience," I softly said into the receiver. "Can you just verify the address where Ms. Lewis and Kay-Kay reside at and I will let you get back to your duties?"

"I'm not exactly sure of the house number but it's on Chestnut Place, Lindenwold, NJ."

"Thank you, have a great day. What time should Ms. Lewis be available?"

"Any time after 8pm you have a good night Mrs. Parrish"

As the rage bubbled in my gut, I felt a strange sense of validation for taking his money. As passionate as I was about finding out the truth. That very moment I realized I had something better. Kayla and Yolanda Lewis were only nails in my relationship coffin. The shit was dead years ago I just refused to bury his ass!

Before I left town I had China and Buddah meet me at Starbucks. I had two bricks of cocaine, half a kilo of heroin and more pills than I could count. If these broads was on deck then it was time to build my team from the ground up.

411
Haneef

"You have a call from an inmate in the Virginia State Federal correctional institution. To proceed with the call, please do not use three way calling or your call will be terminated. To continue with this call please press one now." Instructed the automated system.

"Hello Mom, how are you?"

"Other than worrying about you and my grands I am fine."

"Ma when was the last time you actually saw Mo'?"

"It's been a while come to think of it. Is she okay?"

"When was the last time you spoke to her Mom?"

"Haneef, I have not seen or heard from Mo'Najah! Did you call to talk to me or about her? Last I checked it was not my turn to watch her. Who in the heck is the woman you have given everyone's name and home phone number to? I swear even from a prison cell you're still a freakin' handful. The damn lady never even told me her name she was so terrified."

"Mom, I called to check on everyone. I had an associate call everyone so that no one would worry. It took five business days for the funds to get transferred from one spot to the next."

"Well, Sheed has been past here constantly. He really wants to talk to you. Your son is doing great in school. Things are very quiet over there at Tanya's now. Kayla is starting kindergarten in a few weeks. She reminds me of a little princess Haneef. You should be very proud."

"Mom, does Mo'Najah know anything about Kayla being my daughter?"

"How am I supposed to know what that child knows? What you need to be worrying about is how your son is going to react to having a sister. That is what you need to be thinking about. As we can already tell, Neef acts out when he is not happy. Tanya is already going through enough. I am not sure but I think she is taken too many of those pain medicines. So are you going to help her with the surgery?"

"No, Mom, I am not."

"But why not?"

"Look, Mom, I know you are tryin' to keep the peace. But you don't have all the details. Let's just say Tanya was not innocent in what happened."

"It's your money, so you can do what you want with it. But what good is having money if you can't help someone who really needs it? So how long is Mo' going to stay in the house in Ardmore?"

"What?"

"How long is she going to live in your house? Ain't I speaking English, Haneef!"

"Mom, Mo' is not going anywhere. As long as she is still there, I know we still have a chance."

"A chance at what, Haneef? Do you hear yourself? If that young woman does not want to be in your life, you can't force her! You may want to definitely call Sheed."

"Mom, Mo'Najah loves our home, from the plants in the garden to the tile in the rooms. As long as she is there, we are still connected. Mom, I fucked up. This is worse than Kayla and Tanya put together. I don't know what to do to fix it. I've offered her money, I begged for her forgiveness. She won't take any of my calls, she has returned my letters. For the first time since I got locked up, I'm stressing. My appetite is fucked up, I have insomnia. I can't lose her. Mom, I will call you in a few days."

"Haneef, your family loves you. We will never leave you. Your son and daughter are what you need to be concerned about."

"Yeah, okay."

"Haneef Ellis Mason, please don't do anything reckless!"

"I'm not, Mom. Can you call Sheed from your cell phone? Find out when he will be home."

"He is home now, I love you son.

"Love you more Mom."

"You have a call from an inmate in the Virginia State Federal correctional institution. Blah, blah, blah…"

"How the fuck are you gonna just disappear?" Sheed barked into the phone

"Man, I'm locked up, where the hell am I disappearing to?"

"Goldman, Mom…nobody has heard from you. You break up with Mo' and divorce the rest of us? Shit is real out here!"

"Oh, and I must be on the fuckin' set of OZ. There is nothing - and I do mean nothing - more real than bein' locked da' fuck up 24/7 for the next sixteen years. Man, I did not call you to play twenty-one questions. Mo'Najah and I are not broken up, we are just going through some shit. Sheed, you wanted to be a King. The shit ain't as easy as I made it look, huh? Damn, you gotta be willing to lay your freedom on the line, your morals in a safe at home, 'cause out in dem' streets, that shit will get you shot, nigga! So what is so fucking important, Sheed?"

"Damn, I will be glad when you and her work that shit out. Check, D, I'm in the grocery store last week - not the Shop N Bag, but I go all the way to Shop Rite. When I get to the meat department, all the meats are priced, three nickels higher than normal - no heads up, no notice in the paper. Nuttin'! If I keep paying these prices, a nigga gon' need a second job."

"So how long had the increase been in effect?"

"Since the liquor store stopped carrying Moet."

"Do you think there is a connection?"

"Hanz, I don't fuckin' know! Last trip they made to the market, it was Mario. The sudden price changes have me fucked up. I had to cook less, and the kids are hungry. Is there any way you can reach out to your uncle and auntie down in Miami?"

"I have not talked to that side of the family since I got knocked. However, I think Mo' may have a trip to Disney coming to her from that side of the family."

"Maybe you can tell me how to reach them?"

"Mo' knows how to get in touch with them who remembers numbers these days?"

"Somehow I don't think she is going to give me their number."

"Why the fuck not?"

"Shit's been tight out here. I had to make some cuts in the budget - no bonus checks."

"So you tell me that since our talk, you have not fed her?"

"Nah, I needed all the money to go shopping."

"Yeah, you really fucked up. Come at her wit' your checkbook out."

"Are you serious?"

"Either that or start looking for a new meat market! Real talk, I don't know any of these convicts, and I ain't trying to know them. You're gonna have to figure this shit out for yourself. You wanted to be the chief delegate, allocate and compensate!"

"Haneef, you started this shit. You told me to retire Mo'."

"I also told you to fucking compensate her. You did not listen to that part. Why the fuck are you blaming me?"

"Hanz, I didn't pay her because she came through like hurricane Sandy! Took half of every beach with her on her way out. Just in case you have not found out yet she left the crib too."

"Sheed call this number from you cell phone right now…

1-888-555-0000. Put the phone on speaker."

Carribean Savings in loan to access your account please press 7, please enter your 10 digit account number followed by the pound key. Now enter your 5 digit pin number followed by the pound key. Your account balance is 135,000.00 USD. Please press 1 to continue.

"Haneef! Haneef!"

Rescue
Lamar

What the fuck was I thinking? Talking to myself as I pace the men's room at the studio. Mo'Najah is not Zylar or any other woman I had ever dated. Mo'Najah is not in Philly eating $50 boxes of gourmet chocolates and sippin' $300 bottles of wine. Days without hearing from her could mean anything death, jail, or hospital. I don't even know where the fuck she lives at. Just when I thought I had pinpointed an address for this chameleon, she tells me she is in a five star hotel. If something were to happen who would even think to call me? *Is it too soon for me to be feeling this way?* I ask myself. With every scenario I have played in my head all I vision is me sitting by a phone that will never ring. This can't be happening. *This connection can't be this strong.* I'm in ma' feelings right now. Too much Drake'n and Drivin'.

As I glanced at the time on my Breitling Navitmer, she had a little over an hour. Wrapping up the concerns that could not be postponed I had Mrs. Palmer forward all my calls to my cell. I wasn't doing nuttin' but stressin' any damn way! As I walked out of the studio the heat slapped me first. Unloosing my tie with my briefcase in one hand, my phone in the other. From the Google bar on my phone I looked up 'blood clots in the eye.'8-12 days for them to heal but you can try warm and cold compresses and plenty of rest. After reading that I think I got pissed off all over again.

When I arrived at the penthouse Jim the doorman was on post. "I am expecting a lady visitor within the hour can you call upstairs when she arrives. Gently placing $20 in the palm of Jim's hand I continued to my apartment. Between the Chinese food from three nights ago and the heat my place smelled like rotten broccoli and ass. Bleach and hot water in the garbage disposal and five burst of Febreze. As I grabbed the trash can I ran to the incinerator. Laughing the entire way down there; this is the shit Zylar would be pissed about.

When I returned to the apartment right outside of my door was a large box that read "Portable Pole".

Seated on top of the marble island in my kitchen wearing a full length grey and black mink coat, thigh high black leather boots with a grey studded chocker and silver chain dangled from her neck falling perfectly between her D cup breast. As her curly hair swayed just past her shoulders. Black lip stick and sexy circular shades only made the outfit even hotter.

"You might want to bring that box inside before your neighbors get the wrong idea of you."

"Fuck what they think my issue is what are you thinking Mo'Najah?"

"I am thinking your upset…You have every right to be. You want an explanation I can respect that. You want to save me but don't know how. I am also thinking I don't want to fight with you. This is me being submissive, obedient and subservient."

Slowly she slides her body off of the countertop never taking her now bare eyes off of me. She had this speech down before she got here. The fucked up part is my dick is so hard I don't want to be mad. I want to give her nine and quarter inches to sub- serve to.

But in my heart I can't. I walked away from my weakness and retrieve her box from the hallway. Closing the door behind me. I proceed to the bathroom where I grab a robe and a hot wash cloth. I hand them both to my now speechless guest.

"This is not a babe' I lost my phone and I forgot to call situation. This is not ummmm I got drunk and I crashed my car incident. This is me rearranging my life to have you in it and you not doing the same in return. This is you holding on to your past and second guessing your present. Yes, I would love to take you in that room and make love to you until I forgot what day it is. But if you can't or don't see me as man enough to be by your side then we both are making a huge mistake. Not even sex will fix it."

Silence falls on the room the rays from the sun cast a shadow on her beautiful face. I love her but I refuse to be weak, that is not what she needs. I don't care about her wants right now.

"What the fuck do you want from me?"

"Let's start with three addresses, your mother's name and for shit and giggles an emergency contact. Then we can go into why I have not seen you in days. Followed by why, you think the only thing you have to offer is a pretty face and good pussy."

"Lamar, sometimes I wonder what do I really have to offer? The one person I devoted my life to cheated and lied so much that even I started to believe I was the cause. Maybe if I would have sucked his dick more or was freaker he would have been faithful. Maybe if I was not so young he would have had his babies with me. Maybe if I was as strong then as I am now Haneef would have respected the woman that I was. Everything I have learned for most of my adult life has been influenced by him. So yes, I figured fuckin' you would shut you up... But since you need something more than my body, you are going to have to be patient with me. I will tell you anything you want to know. But I need a week to wrap up my business and personal past. Can you give me that?"

Exposed
Zylar

As I lay in the hospital bed with an intravenous drip, running from my right arm. I had no idea of what had happen. The left side of my head hurt like hell. I tried to force myself to open my eyes. But my parents not so soft whispers made me re-think that decision. My father was definitely in control of everything in our family with me being the one exception. Deciding against the miracle recovery routine, I laid there with partially opened eyes to observe my parents reaction.

"Zachary, what is going on? I was in the middle of a seminar."My Mother complained in her most exhausted tone. As her completely grey covered head shook with dismay. She adjusted her handbag, brief case and cell phone.

"Honey, its Zylar. She passed out this morning. The doctors are running some tests."My Father explained in a calm, but compassionate tone.

"She has been fine all week. As a matter of fact, her mood has been the total opposite of a woman who just got jilted weeks before her wedding. Her demeanor is pleasant, upbeat, and cheerful. The mere fact that she chose to come home and tell us in person displays that she is maturing, dealing with life and its disappointments. Not hiding in her room or turning to pills. What happened, Senior?"

"We were discussing her future - her plans, or lack thereof. Now that she is not about to marry Mr. CEO, it's time for Zylar to become an independent, self-sufficient, strong black woman. The exact words we discussed were JOB and RENT!"

"Zachary Wingate Sr., did you tell Zylar we have been discussing terminating her living expense account?"

"Yes, Laura, I told her."

"She is still our daughter, our fragile and delicate baby. So is there a chance that your little conversation triggered this attack?"

"No, her being pregnant and husbandless provoked this episode!"

The gasp from my mother's lips pierced my heart. Even thou I could not see her facial expression I knew that she was flabbergasted. The words did not leave father's lips with pride. He stuttered for the first time ever. As his left hand rose slowly to my mother's quivering shoulder.

"Laura how about you go home? I will keep you abreast of the situation as it transpires."

"I cannot leave my baby Senior, not when she needs me most!" Mother said with pain in her heart and what I assumed to be tears in her eyes.

"Laura, I am not asking you to go home, Zylar is my daughter also. I have allowed you and her to navigate this mess- she now calls a life without any input or objections. Today is the last day of that. Zylar needs her father now. I will see you at home. As he gently kissed my mother on her cheek. The weight of her shoes on the cold hospital floor echoed in my head.

Moving On
Devin

"Welcome to the building." Imanni said, extending her well-manicured hand. "When do you think you will be moving in, Mr. Davis? I can block off a time for your furniture and major items with the service elevator. If you have a specific date and time or will Mrs. Davis be handling those details?"

I was twirling my wedding ring around my left hand; I realized that I was still show-boating my wedding band.

"No, we are no longer together, she's deceased. I just can't seem to grasp the reality that she is gone." I said as I gazed at the sparkle from a tarnished promise.

I found myself being way too deceptive with this stranger as I turned my ring nervously. This apartment was the first step I had made towards my new bachelor lifestyle. The lie flowed off my tongue so smoothly. The glimmer in her eye and the change in her posture spoke volumes.

"I'm so sorry to hear that. Well, I am here to make your transition as smooth as possible. May I call you Devin?"

"Please call me 3D. All of my friends and frat brothers call me that."

"Well, 3D, I am on property Monday through Friday from 8 a.m. to 5 p.m. You already have the office and maintenance numbers. Here are your keys. Let me know if I can do anything else to help."

"Well, as you already know I'm from Jersey. I work in mid-town, but can you tell me some good restaurants in the area? I won't be cooking for a week or so."

"Well, what do you like Mr. Davis, excuse me, I mean 3D?"

Each time we made eye contact was more suggestive than the last, flirtatious but professional, teasingly tasteful. We exchanged personal numbers before I left the building.

Imanni, was from Nigeria, 5'8" tall, coffee-bean black with almond shaped brown eyes. Her strong cheek bones gave her that Robin Givens look. She sported a short, sharp haircut. Her thick hips filled out her skirt to capacity. Her blouse was conservative, but not enough to hide the double D's. She was nothing like what I had at home. Her accent was intriguing, and the way she said my name sent instant surges through my groin. Yes, I could foresee a warm, wet welcome.

Holding the keys to my new apartment in my hand I decided I would need a few things from the house in Jersey. Living out of my office had filled me with such discontentment. The weight of my world had started to feast on my sanity. Navigating my Camry into the drive way I wished things could be different.

To my surprise as I placed my key into the top lock no entry was granted. Certain that I had the correct key I attempted the task once again. Boom- boom- boom! Ding-ding- ding! I found myself assaulting my front door. As I began to cause quite the disturbance my lovely wife decided to save herself the embarrassment of being the spectacle of the neighborhood.

"To what do I owe the pleasure of you company Mr. Davis?" Brianna asked from the other side of the locked door.

"Brianna, I am in no mood to argue with you. I can't believe you changed the locks on the house. I am entitled to anything we have bought together. I only want my clothes and the contents of my office. I will continue to pay the mortgage until you can sell the house. I believe I am being more than fair. Please let's not make this any more difficult than it has to be." I shouted from the exterior of the home we shared. Once I started to act a fool in front of the neighbors she rushed to open the door.

"Devin Dickerson Davis, is that all you really care about? Some clothes, your computer, and the fucking PS3? It took you a month to realize that the fucking locks are changed? You selfish bastard! I have cried widow's tears over not being able to birth your children. My heart has crumbled a thousand times as I have worried and wanted my husband to recognize that our marriage is worth salvaging. Every night, I have prayed to a merciful God that you will honor your promise before Him and our families. Our lives may not be perfect, but I thought with time, you could love me in spite of it all. If that is all you wish to walk away from this home with, so be it. I'm too good of a woman to want a man that has already left. Loving you is like holding onto ice with a warm hand - impossible."

I was so elated the weekend that me and the boys went on the camping retreat was fast approaching. A change in scenery was really what a brother needed. I reminded myself to call Lamar to ensure all of the arrangements were made for Hunter Mountain. Between the apartment, business, the facade with this adoption and my separation. Life, love, and losing are playing for keeps with my piece of mind.

Imanni…just the thought of spreading her mahogany legs…It had been months since I had touched Brianna. Lying beside another woman would mentally put the nail in the coffin of my already-dead marriage. My body had left her, but my heart and my soul were rooted so deeply that every day hurt more and more. But when I saw her, I owned a rage and confusion that I couldn't control. Punishing her for what was real just seemed like torment to the damned. Hurting her was more painful than hurting myself. Leaving was the lesser of the evils.

Acceptance Not Tolerance
Mo'Najah

Goldman and I were on a plane early in the morning. We had to be at the Virginia federal correctional institution by noon. After departing the plane, we took the shuttle provided by Enterprise, where I had reserved a rental vehicle.

"Mo'Najah, are you sure you want to do this?" Goldman asked after hours of silence.

"Yes, and after I do, I will have to hire my own legal representation. Can you refer me to someone?"

"Mo'Najah, you are walking away from a few million dollars in property and cash, at least a third of which you have contributed to. Whatever you and Haneef are going through, I am sure you can work this thing out."

"Goldman, you are going to make this drive longer than it has to be. If a woman does not have self-respect, then she is not a woman at all in my book. Haneef has done everything imaginable to push me away. There have been countless women, not to mention another child that will never know her father's love. Silence and ignorance have brought me so much pain. Forgiveness has made me tolerate things a real woman would have abandoned a long time ago. Holding on to his memory is only hindering my progress. I have to amputate the disease so that the body can live."

"Maybe you should go to school for law. That was a wonderful argument, one I will not dispute any further."

"Before we get there, I should tell you that I have taken half of the money. Not off the total, but half of what I helped him earn since Haneef has been incarcerated. I took $283,000 and transferred it to my own off-shore account. Ten percent is in a trust for Lil Neef. I believe I am entitled to at least that. If he would like me out of his house, I will be out by the end of the month. I don't want anything except my jewelry and the art we have collected."

Haneef, had been granted a supervised visit with Goldman and myself so that our partnership could be officially dissolved. After being searched and escorted through the building, the room appeared to be a renovated cell. It reeked of old coffee and stale Marlboro cigarettes. The windows had bars on them and the door was made of steel. The guard removed Haneef's hand cuffs. He sat in the chair farthest from me. A perplexed look on his face he stared in silence.

Haneef and I listened as Goldman explained the recent monetary transactions. What it meant if I was no longer his power of attorney. The papers were placed in front of me to sign then slid across the table for him to do the same.

"Haneef, either your mother or I can be made the executor of your estate. That can be done with a phone call." Goldman explained while he extended a gold pen to Haneef.

"Mo'Najah, where is your ring?" He inquired finally, breaking the silence.

"In a safety deposit box with a few other things I am keeping for your son."

"Mo', you promised you would never take it off."

"Haneef, you promised never to hurt me again. So much for promises. I guess they are truly made to be broken."

"I know you don't want an apology. Just tell me what I need to do to make this right. You want more money? Tell me what I need to do to make you love me again?"

"Haneef, loving you and enduring your mirage of love are two very different things. You raised me better than my mother and father ever attempted to. For that, I will always be grateful. You taught me more than I could learn in any classroom. I guess you have become my version of Tanya. Hanz, you're everything I no longer need. As your lover and friend, I am done. If that somehow reflects on my partnership with Mr. Anderson, then fine. But when I leave here today, I am concluding all of our ties, personal and business. I ask that you no longer contact me, directly or indirectly. If there is a true matter that we need to discuss, please go through Goldman. Can we please wrap this up? If we leave now, we can catch the 3 p.m. flight back to Philly."

"Before I sign, I just have one question. Just tell me who he is?"

"Excuse me?"

"Mo'Najah Maria Harrison, I have watched you breathe for almost seven years, known you for damn near eleven. That attitude, this demeanor, is me in a female form. I am only battling the monster I created. If I don't know anything, I know there is someone in your life now. You would not leave me to be alone."

"Newsflash, Hanz: I have been alone since way before you got locked up. I was just too young or dumb to know. But it is what it is."

A woman's worth is not hidden under her skirt,
The bubble in her jeans or the cup of her bra.
None of that my friends will get us very far.
The length of your hair or fairness of your skin.
Your worth my worth it's deeper and lies within.
Her education or occupation has no relation,
*   to how she is relating to life situation.*
To busy being lovers we have over looked becoming
wives.

Our struggles and stains to maintain.
Collectively leaving us victims to the same damn thang.
Neglect, abuse, and ridicule, finishing school.
Still made to feel like we're the fools
For simply following our hearts.
Inconsiderate lovers...you would think they were born
Without mothers
The way they disrespect, disregard, and disappear.
Leaving families and children here with no remorse
And most of the time with no support.
Our tears water the paths to strength
Your ability to heal just to be torn again.
Each promise broken a constant reminder
That we have survived.
Some, punishments passed down in the name of love,
Heartbroken, manipulated and emotionally spent,
We as woman are often left without a cent.
And I am not referring to money.
Lonely makes you a different type of prey,
Wanting to correct the mistakes of yesterday
Has us hanging on to fractions of a man
Parts of lovers, friends, or providers
Just to say we had that someone to lay beside us.
Living daily with the misconception that part of a man,
Is better than no man at all.
A woman's worth is in her ability to keep trying.
Being alone does not make you less of a woman,
It simply means that we have stopped settling
For less than what a real woman deserves!

TABLES TURN
Tanya

How many times do you see those damn cash for gold commercials? Or better yet the "we buy any car" advertisement that comes on the television so much you actually play with the idea of finding out how much your vehicle is worth? I had so much jewelry; I knew that I could raise half of the money I needed. Wrong! They barely offered me four grand for close to twenty thousand in jewelry. I was desperate not dumb. We buy any car will only give you a fraction of what your car is worth. In the event they need to repo ya' shit they can still make a profit. I actually got a better deal from sum internet cash for gold company. I dismissed the car title loan thing all together. Let's not even talk about the personal payday loans. Fuckery!

With the few dollars that Wise had left here and the money I got from the jewelry I had close to eight grand. *How was I gonna' get twenty G's was all that I could think of. Bitch, get a job! Shit at $10.00 an hour I would have to work two fuckin' years to get the money I needed, and pay someone to watch my kids.*

Hopelessness and aggravation started to settle in. The few hours in the house alone would do me good Lil Neef and Taliah were enrolled in a summer program in west Philly on Parkside. I dropped them off and Momma Mason would pick them up in the afternoon. When I entered the house I went straight to my room to take a Percocet. Removing the Nasiq from my face I took the pain medicine and drank some water. As I laid across my queen size bed, the tears started to collect in the corners of my eyes. My breathing had become rough. Eventually the pills kicked in ushering me into my own calm-sleep.

Jolted awake from my drug induced sleep I heard the alarm from my maxima blaring in front of the house. Without thought I found the keys in the bottom of my Michael Kors bag and press the button to silence the alarm. I glanced at the screen on my Galaxy 3 not one text message or Face Book notifications. How suddenly things had changed. As I rushed to the bathroom, I avoided the mirror at all cost, these days. Just as I flushed the toilet and headed back to my bedroom. The alarm on my car was activated again. As I grabbed the keys, I swung open the front door to the house agitated.

Just as I crossed the threshold of the door frame. The click of a .38 millimeter gun caught my attention. With the gun pointed directly at my temple, moving my head to see the gunmen was not an option. Within seconds Kadir, gracefully strolled up to the door way.

"Tanya, may we come in?"

Not wanting to make a scene for my neighbors to gossip about. I slowly walked backwards into my house. Never taking my eyes off of Kadir's dark & deadly face. Our eyes stayed locked for what seemed like forever. As his assistants stood like guards at my front door, only now the guns were put away.

One surprise deserved another I tried to reassure myself. But coming to my crib with goons and guns was not cool. Kadir, could give a fuck less about what was cool. As we stood in complete silence our eyes telling one another thoughts.

Kadir lowered his head and moved slowly close to my face. I stood statue like not wanting to give his boys a reason to draw their weapons. So close that I could smell the coffee on his breathe and the Azzure, cologne on his neck. Kadir's slim but muscular build fits perfectly into my tall, shapely mold. His chest grazed my breast my heart pumped a 1000 times a minute. His left hand grabbed my face, which caused me to re-act I attempted to pull back from his tight grip; unsuccessful.

"That is one of the things I miss about you Tanya. That feisty, sassy, sexy spirit. Muslim woman don't get to display that once they become married." Kadir spoke barely above a whisper directly into my left ear. Never loosening his grip on my jaw. Suddenly I felt his wet, thick tongue on my cheek. As he traced the length of my damaged face with the tip of his moist tongue. Chills ran rapid through my body as every sensory nerve was disturbed.

"Imagine my surprise to see you at the one place a man's enemy should never be. My job, the bars I patronize maybe but never in a hundred years did I ever think Haneef's whore, would remember where I prayed at. I definitely underestimated Ms. Thompson. That I will not do again.

Kadir released my face from his firm clutch. Noticing the fury in my eyes he smiled. Calm and in control his stance, clothes and cologne reeked of superiority.

"Do you still wet up half the bed when you have an orgasm?"

"What?"

"Come on now Tanya, it's been awhile but you can still remember unless your accident affected your memory as well as your face?"

"Oh, is that why you stopped pass to take a stroll down memory lane? You miss the way good ole' Tanya would drench that dick in thick white cream until you could barely see the veins in ya' shit. Or better yet you miss the taste of this pussy? Because the way I remember it my pussy stayed in your mouth!"

"Actually, no I remember vividly your skillful bedside manner. I recall you had a nigga' open for a minute. Haneef taught you very, very well. So well that you could not stop fuckin' him. Even after you knew he had another lady. Let's just say sloppy seconds was never my thing."

"Listen, I thought I could ask for your help on a money matter. However after seeing your response outside of the Mosque. You clearly are not the same man that you were several years ago. My presence had you shook. I saw the change in your body language. You quickly turned your back to oncoming traffic to see if I was alone. Your shoulders hunched as you looked around in a panic. I may not have a fancy degree. But I can read between the lines. Shit you don't even carry your own guns any more, you pay these motherfuckers to do it for you. It's okay to mature, Kadir"

"Your right, I am a business man these days. Playing street wars with Haneef was a long, long time ago. Before I knew my worth, when I believed he had something that made him better. It all ended when you found out that your daughter was his actually. Allah had given me yet another chance to be the type of man, father, leader he could use in the community. There were plenty thugs and baby daddies."

"Your visit rehashed a lot of old memories and posed questions to a lot of things I had almost forgotten to follow up on. See I knew Hanz was locked-up and his fine ass wife was running shit along with Sheed. But imagine my delight to find out by the time that Kat comes home, my son will be graduating from high school. All these years I thought I needed to get revenge on my childhood bully. When all I had to do was sit back and watch him self-destruct."

"So since you have allowed karma to settle things between you and Hanz why the fuck are you here? I only have a few hours before the kids come home. You and your squad are taking up my 'me time'."

"Tanya I know you... Better than I care to admit. Whatever had your ass in Atlantic City is about payback. It could be about the chick that cut your face up. Which, ironically Mo'Najah posted bail for. It could be about Haneef, dogging you yet again or it could actually be a monetary come up. I am here so you already know my interest is piqued."

"I need 25 grand and I know where **WE** could get at least five times that amount from. But I don't trust you, I don't see this as working to my benefit."

Kadir, began to laugh hysterically, the sound filled my living room bounced off the walls. Holding his left side he found my dilemma painfully hilarious.

"Personally, I fail to see the humor in anything I just said."

"You want to betray the father of your fuckin' kids for twenty five grand. But you don't trust me? Bitch you need to be on stage with the material you got. Because I had not laughed that hard since Kevin Hart's, 'Let Me Explain'."

"How do I know this is not a setup Tanya? How do I know that after you get your punk-ass money you won't flip on me like you're doing him? Betrayal always comes from the person you trusted the most. I have been a ghost for more than five years."

"The scars on my face is how you know I am not going to cross you. I want my fuckin' life back Kadir. You would think being the mother of his kids he would want that for me. That is why I am making the moves I am making. Why should I suffer while everyone else lives the life style of the rich and ratchet. Haneef, Sheed, Snipes and Mo'Najah. Help me get my life back and I will give you the satisfaction of beating your childhood rival."

My eyes watered as I spoke to him. A deal with the devil. What other fuckin' choice did I have?

"Prove your loyalty to me and I will help you."

"Kadir how do I do that?"

"Wess, give me your trash piece." Kadir barked at the shorter goon standing by the door.

Wrapped in a zip-lock bag Wess, handed Kadir a pistol. Kadir placed the gun on my dining room table.

"You do a favor for me. I'll do a favor for you, whatever I get from Hanz's people we split 60/40 your favor. Just to show you how trust worthy I am I will give you this."

Kadir reaches into his billfold and pulled out a wrapper which contained five thousand dollars in a bundle and tossed it on my dining room table. Standing up he adjusts his penis in his linen pants. Cole Hann sandals, diamonds in his left ear sparkled so much every move caused the light to reflect. Glancing at his watch he stretched almost touching the ceiling standing at 6'3.

"Someone will be in touch with you; about my issue and yours. Just promise me when you stick the knife in me; let me see you coming."

Soldier or Sinner
Sheed

How can God- Allah or whomever controls this toilet of a universe. Keep taking the people that have the potential to make a difference. You hear all these miraculous stories about people being shot 8 times and living to tell the story. Cars flipping over four times and the driver does not have a scratch. Shit even Magic Johnson is living proof that someone has a cure for HIV. It's more money in the crusade than the fuckin' cure. Health care, prison, and the judicial system if the powers that be can't find a way to get rich off the shit I swear it buried so deeply in plain sight that us ordinary folk. Just live to die.

Please don't label me a 'NIGGER' because of my life choices. My moral code has been saturated into my skin with blood. I stopped dreaming when my best-friend died. Why make a plan only to have karma come and snatch that shit right from under you. Death, despair and drugs; are more common that success, happiness and hope. More profitable also. Seems the people that are doin' fucked up shit get more than 5 seconds of fame. Lock three women in your basement and become a legend. Help save the victims and become a target.

At times I swear my life stopped when Kalief died that night. Not one move I have made since, has not been directly linked to that event. How do you hold the head of your best friend as he bleeds to death and stay the same? Impossible. Fuck the bullet that was lodged in my bicep. The gut wrenching screams and stampede of people scared that they too would be shot. Three bullets were found his upper torso that night. Three bullets changed my life.

I don't know if I tolerated Haneef's bullshit to mask my guilt or to smother my own. I tried to separate Haneef's chaos from my money! However the fine line of hoes and hustlin' crossed continuously. Mo'Money was just the main female I had to deal with. There was a total of five women in Hanz's stable. From a Neo-natal nurse to a supervisor at Wal-Mart. The promises and bullshit never cease to amaze me.

Haneef's drama with Mo' however had affected my pockets, deeply. Dude from Brooklyn changed the prices and Mo' wiping out Hanz off shore accounts had me perplexed. Not that I could ever count dat' mans money but Mo'Najah, was not to be underestimated-anymore. Sitting back I can't say I would have done anything differently except taking everything. But she knew that would have caused a war. Cunning, calculating and vicious; then to disappear on top of that. My only concern was what would she do with the product she took?

Dope has an expiration date. Cocaine she could sit on for years. I had become so curious to what the next step was. I had someone posted out-side of her momma's crib, Club BBW and her GED classes at C.C.P. No one had seen her but key people she reached out to, Momma M being one.

Removing the Dutch Master paper from my center console I needed my medicine. I did not smoke for recreation I smoked to obtain clarity. Relax and think outside of the box. Effectively playing my hand, meant anticipating what the other players on the board would do.

Money, baby, and life was gang-bangin' my mental. The air is on full blast in my CTS. It was barely 7am but the thermometer in my car read 87 degrees. Sunday morning I had pulled up to the back of the afterhour's spot where I met two of my team captains and Snipes for money drops.

From where I had parked I could not clearly see the back door. Which also meant no one could see me. I tucked my Beretta under my 5-X white tee and proceeded to get this money. Removed the key to the back door from a separate set of keys. When I went to insert the key the door was already unlocked. The weight of my hand made the door crack open.

I stepped away from the door and looked into the dumpster, empty. Down the alley to where my car was parked. Took a deep breath and kicked the door open with my size 13 white on white air force one. With my pistol in my right hand, the safety off I was prepared for trouble. The corridor to the back of the afterhours was five feet long. It took forever for me to get to the door where the office was. My heart raced, sweat dripped from underneath my red Phillies fitted. Never in four years of me collecting this money has that door been open. Nothing could have prepared me for what I saw when I entered Snipes's office.

Rell and Remmy was hog tied, blind folded and gagged. Stripped ass whole naked, with four car batteries surrounding their bodies. Blue latex gloves were all over the floor and two metal buckets. Between the blood and the stench I did not want to confirm what my mind already concluded. From the looks of the gruesome scene, it started off as a beating- robbery. Blood was splattered all over the walls and floor. As I walked slowly around their bodies I thought I kicked a rock only to see that it was a tooth. Looking down at the eroded flesh of two of my best workers I saw that no mercy was spared as someone took the time to pour Battery Acid (Sulphuric, hydrochloric, phosphoric--all of these are strong because they eat through flesh)... All over their pubic region. If they were not two different complexions I would not have known one from the other as their faces had been beaten beyond recognition. The door to the cabinet size safe was wide open and empty. Snipes was nowhere to be found.

After I walked through the entire building. I went to the computer where the surveillance digitally recorded from the front door- bar and register. I did not know the password so I disconnected the hard drive. Dialed 911 and fired two shot and left the building.

Falling
Lamar

Mo'Najah only stayed at the penthouse for three days. The first two nights were the longest slumber party I had ever had. I got her drunk, we talked and wrestled like teenagers on their first date. From Playstation 3 to Monopoly. She even tried to get me to play truth or dare.

The walls to her secret life were high but I could tell she wanted someone whom cared enough to climb them. The stories were random. From her childhood to her previous relationship but they all ended the same. With someone so lovely and loyal being hurt. Listening to her stories somehow pulled me in deeper than I was ready to accept. I did not want her to return to them. But I already knew she would never run from her situation. That is what made me want her more. Knowing that I had to play my position in her crazy, chaotic existence. I was serenity in her life and she was my adventure. Not the traditional combination. But somehow it was what I needed.

Between showering together and attempting to sleep next to her and not be intimate. Even thou my body did not cooperate my mind was determined not to allow sex to rule yet another relationship. I wanted to not just be her lover but acquire the title as a friend. Which would have merit and worth long after we stopped fuckin'. I knew she would never tell me everything. But she let me in, after two days of being locked in the penthouse with take out and Netflix. The gate opened just enough for me to crawl under and now that I am in I will not leave her.

Mo'Najah did not expect for me to save her. She simply wanted to know that I would pick her up when she fell. My heart would do anything to prevent such events. If it was important to her than it became relevant to me. However when she confided in me how much money she had on stash roughly. I accepted the fact that honesty, companionship and trust would be our bond. Not money or fame. My lips found hers under the sheets. "I love you Mo'Najah Harrison".

All bets were off at that point. Just as the words left my lips my penis extended to maximum capacity. The kiss started as slow and endearing. Then engulfed us both in a passion that we both needed the other to feel. My lips found their way to her left ear where I whispered how much she meant to me. Which caused her to shove my hand down the front of the boxers she had been wearing. Wetness greeted my fingers and demanded that I go deeper into the tight and warm depth of her essence. I could not restrain my needs to taste her. I had never lain beside a woman for more than a night unless their menstrual cycle was a factor. For her I would put my needs and desires to the side. Focused on the requirements of being what she needed first then what she wanted. At that moment she wanted me to taste her juiciness. Legs spread on my Italian sofa I kneeled before a true Queen. Prayed into her vagina that I would be the man she needed. Licked into the softness of her labia that love would return tenfold. Attached my lips to her clitoris and began to suck and slurp on her thick meaty pussy as if my life depended on it. Only her confession of loving me in return saved her from the pleasant-pain I had planned on dispensing.

"Lamar Justin James I am in love with you." Only this time it was said as she held a fist full my locks looking dead into my eyes. As her womanly fluids saturated my face and beard making them glisten and shine.

"Now please put that dick inside of me."

"Let me go get the condoms."

My dick was already standing at full attention but I swear it found another inch by listening to her talk.

"Are you sure, you had a really rough week. I don't want you to have any regrets."

"The only thing I would regret is leaving here and you never knowing how much I trust, admire and love you Mar."

Grabbing Mo'Najah by the waist I took her off the couch and laid her on the plush rug. I went to the wall size window and opened the electronic blinds, the city would bear witness to my confession of love tonight. I had never wanted to connect with another soul this deeply. When I lowered myself on top of her she seemed so peaceful. My locks caressed her first. Danced wildly on her pecan skin. Her hair sprawled out all over the cream carpet as she tucked her arms under her head. Firm, full breast and caramel colored nipples begging for attention. The piercing that lured me in my new favorite toys. Her legs not spread open but crossed angelically at the ankles. Her perfect ruby red toes. That night I found out that sex with a 100 women could not compare to making love to the 1 woman you never knew could capture your soul.

Ambition
Mo'Najah

Most of my life my ambition was to simply be loved, respected, and provided for by the one man who took me from one hell only to place me in another. As the time slipped past I became more detached from reality. Haneef's lies, became law; his stories my truth. Resentful, begrudging were the women that went out of their way to expose his actions. After all, who would not want to be where I was?

Cold, harsh reality shattered my little fairytale. These women were not fictitious. The affairs as real as the money that got stuffed in my G-string every night. Yes I was in love but with what? The facade of marrying the man you gave your virginity to and living happily ever after. If I could have gotten a dollar for every tear I cried alone. Fifty cents for the ones he decided to stand there and catch. I would not be dancin' or hustlin'.

After missing nine days at the club I really did not want to go back. The reasons and rational I had when I first started at Besta Both Worlds, no longer existed. I was not lost anymore. I had accepted the fact that I had been used by people my entire life from my mother to my lover. Abandoned by my father and tolerated by my brothers. This new consciousness however did not make it easier to decipher the two. With this awareness, accompanied the harsh reality; everyone has a purpose are you disposable or irreplaceable?

With my dreams being an arm's length away. Staying the course was necessary, but daunting as hell. Mrs. Davis had not only found me the perfect house in Washington Twp, New Jersey. Being as thou I could not have property in my name, I had to have a company created and allowed Major Moves Inc. to purchase the home. My legal team handled the closing and transfer of the documents, which after four or five layers of paper work connected to me. My only hope was that no one would dig that deep.

The house was on the foreclosure list which meant I saved thousands of dollars. But it also needed some major work. With that said I indirectly hired M&M Repairs (Mo' & Miguel) to get the house habitable.

"Miguel, how are things going in Jersey?" I asked my brother as I accidentally ran into him at the bank."

"Mo', everything is coming together nicely. The crew is supped up about the $1000 bonus. This may be the house I want to use for our website. I am glad your man is not sparing any expense. Everything is high-quality and classy. Shit, in a few weeks the house won't even look the same. We're working on the sheet rock in the basement. The painting and heat marble floor will be last. We only have maybe two weeks' worth of work."

"Good, I will tell him he can walk through and check out your progress.

You know once we start advertising, you guys are going to be busy."

"Not that we are hurting for work now Sis."

"But I want you to get official. Miguel, you have put in a lot of time and sweat into M & M repairs. I think we can grow in the general contracting field, but I want you fully licensed and insured. If we're going to do this, then it has to be done right."

"Mo', what's going on? You have never taken an interest in the business before."

"Honestly, I am very close to having my dream. Helping you to secure yours will make me happy."

"Mo', you're talking in riddles?"

"Let's just say I will be making a lot of changes - honest ones."

"You're Maria and Naji's daughter. You don't have an honest bone in your body."

We shared a brief smile. My father had left a long time ago. It almost made sense that I could endure Haneef's bullshit for so many years and never think about leaving. Maybe being a heartless bitch was inherited, some sort of fucked up genetic trait. I had no remorse for anything I had done. Maybe I got that from my father. After years of fighting and beating Maria, he left and never looked back. He never came back for me, leaving me with a desire to be loved by a man, even if it hurt.

"Miguel, you may be right, but I won't know 'til I try. If I should fail, I won't cuddle up with a bottle to comfort me. That shit, I will leave for you and Mario."

"Ouch, that hurt. It's true, but it hurt. Look, no one is saying you're destined to be like either one of them. But make your decision based on what you want, Mo'Najah. Don't spend your life sacrificing for everyone else. That is no life at all. I love you, Sis."

Miguel leaned in, kissed me on the cheek and made his way to his Ford F-250 that was loaded with the crew and materials.

Nothing about my situation was comfortable. Lamar, being the one exception, he had offered to let me move into pay for an apartment in NYC and help finance the daycare. The man was truly amazing. But not having to lie about the basics was a relief in itself. I spared Lamar any details simply to keep him safe, the less you know the best you know. He was my square and I had peace whenever I laid beside him. At this point I only trusted three people, Lamar, China and Neko.

In order to stay on track for my G.E.D classes I had to use the battered women card. Not to mention that would have been a sure way for anyone to track my movements. Luckily for me my teacher was the victim of an abusive spouse. We agreed to do video lessons for a small fee and she emailed all the work I needed and my practice test I took from the presidential suite of the Wydham hotel in Center City.

After I had secured my money and the product; I hid in plain view until I was ready to deal with the bullshit. Trust, Haneef had everyone thinking I went to the prison and slapped the dog piss out of him. My mother, his mother, Sheed and any other fuckin sucker that would listen. Oh well, she who speaks last is rarely believed. The old me would have had a need to clarify and set the story straight. Mo'Najah today did not give a fuck about what they said, thought or felt. Twenty-seven years of being the world's door mat had me defensive, abrasive, and volatile.

Man Down
Sheed

Snipes's car was still parked out front of the Afterhours spot. His lady friend had not heard from him since the night before. The barber shop was closed on Sunday. I had two dead bodies, and an empty safe. Not a clue to who or why this shit was suddenly happening. *Mo'Najah was my first thought. But I knew her thought pattern she was blunt force to the face, see me coming, know that I did it. Not the sneaky type. If she wanted the whole pie she would not have only taken half in the first place. Plus with the money she swiped from Haneef. She would wipe her ass with the few dollars that Snipes and Rell would drop off. If she wanted the crown she would have taken me out to get it. Snipes and Rell would only put me on the defense. Not her style. Joey Black, had been calm since before Haneef, got bagged. Was he lookin' to take over my zones? Who would benefit from Haneef's down fall? Was this even about Haneef, Snipes was an ole' player with older enemies maybe this was about him? I had too many questions and only one person I could trust to answer them.*

"Momma M, has your son called today?"

"No, not yet he doesn't usually call until four. Gives me time to get out of church and start my dinner, why Sheed what's wrong now?"

"Too much to discuss over the phone; I will be there before four. Mom has Mo'Najah been there recently?"

"Why is everyone looking for that poor child. The best thing you and Haneef can do for that girl is leave her be. If she is done with him and that life let that young woman have a future."

"Mom, I will see you in a few hours." Ending my call with her only generated more questions. *What if Mo'Najah was next? How can you warn someone who doesn't trust you? Anything I told her, she would automatically assume Haneef was behind it.*

Gunshot wounds, stabbed to death even an ole' fashion hangin' I can say never made me flinch. But a beating so badly that your teeth come out of your mouth and your dick melted off with acid. What sick bastard would take the time to do all of that?

I attempted for the fourth time today to reach Mo'. With the phone going to voicemail. This was definitely not message material.

As I turned my CTS onto Ruby street my head was pounding my heart heavy how was I gonna tell these dudes Mothers and girlfriends that not only are they dead but how I found them. Some shit is just too much for man to bear. When I walked through the door, all of that turmoil, ceased to exist.

"Fried catfish, collard greens with smoked turkey butts, four-cheese baked macaroni, and Momma Mason's don't-eat-the-last-piece of my thick-ass cornbread. Now sit down and let me fix you a plate to take home to that girlfriend of yours. I don't believe you're about to be a father. And, I have not even met this girl yet, that is not like you. Well, is she that ugly, son?"

"Momma M, you got jokes. I just can't afford for anything to fuck this up, my bad. If I bring her around y'all, she might run in the opposite direction."

"Oh, so she thinks you work for UPS or something? No, one better, you work for the sanitation department and you handle all of Haneef's dirty work?"

"No, she knows how I earn my money, she knows about Haneef. I actually met her at Allenwood, so who I am is no secret. But what I use to be is."

"Shawn, what do you want that you don't have, son?"

I stood up from her kitchen table, towering over her little frame.

"Paper and power, not fear. Right now the streets fear me, Mom. When I'm gone, I want the same respect that Haneef still gets and Mo'Money is earning every day…Respect."

"Boy, you dumber than I thought you was. Respect? These streets, jails and cemeteries done claimed better men and women than the two you, know of make that three. Ain't no future in your career path, Shawn. Get out while you have something to hold on to. Family…Buy you a piece of property and get a fucking job, boy. If Kalief was here, I swear before my GOD he would tell you the - "

The ringer on the phone interrupted her sermon; saved by the bell.

"You have a call from an inmate in the Virginia State Federal correctional institution. To proceed with the call, please do not use three way calling or your call will be terminated. To continue with this call please press one now." Instructed the automated system.

"Haneef, some sick shit is going down. Can you call me back from a safe line?"

"Yeah but it will cost me Benji for 30minutes."

"Money well spent trust me Brah."

It took five minutes for the house phone to ring again this time a 904 area code came up on the caller ID. It took exactly thirteen minutes for me to explain all of the details from Mo'Najah, Rell and Remmy concluded with Snipes. Haneef was speechless on the other end of the phone.

"Just tell me what the fuck to do man?"

"Sheed, on my son I don't have a fuckin' clue that could have been anyone of them nigga's beef and the others got caught in the crossfire. Switch up the routes on everything. If someone was meeting you at 2pm make them wait until 4. Shake dat' shit all the way up no more routines or patterns. Eyes and ears open. I will have Goldman cut a check for 12 grand; pay for the funeral."

"Tanya, Lil Neef and Taliah are fine. I saw them personally I talked to Kayla on the phone and Lu-Lu was her usual pissy self. Mo' won't answer my call. She has not even been to her GED classes."

"Have Maria flush her out. She will ignore God but not her mother."

Hopeless
Zylar

"Zylar, I really don't think you should be traveling. We can always send someone for your things. Your rent is paid for the next few months. There is no rush."

"Mother, I am fine. Like I said, I have a few loose ends I need to wrap up. When I return home, I am home for good."

"What could be that important for you to go all the way to NY in your condition?"

"Mother, I am pregnant, not paralyzed. For me to be close to three months, I am not showing at all."

"Are you going to tell Lamar about the baby, Zylar? Is that why you're being so secretive?"

"No, mother, I am not. Lamar has chosen a life that does not include me, and I am simply abiding by his wishes. Freedom comes with a price, and his will be not knowing my child."

"Zylar, dear, I think you're handling this all wrong. Lamar is a good upright man. I see him taking full responsibility for you and that baby."

"Do you think I want a husband out of guilt, Mother? Times and society have changed. Woman every day have children without a man around."

"Yes, I know, and in my day we called them tramps."

"Mother, are you calling me a tramp?"

"No, but you have some trampish ways. Zylar, this is not what your father and I wanted for you. There is still time to correct this problem."

"Mother, listen, I understand everything you and Dad have said. My child has given me a different perception of what is important. With or without a man, I will be is a good mother, just like you have been to me. No, I don't plan on doing it at your expense. Life is not meant to be easy. Working hard to be half as good a mother as you will be a challenge in itself, but I intend to do just that. I'm sorry if my decision embarrasses you and Daddy, if it contradicts the teachings and the practices of the church. God blessed me with this child. Altering that would be a sin also. Lamar offered me a lump sum of money. With that, I can rent a nice two-bedroom here and a small car. My degree is in education and communications, so I will send out my resume. Let's see what a Wingate Woman can do on her own. Mother, you have to let me make my own mistakes."

"Zylar, this pregnancy is making you delusional. You're definitely in no position to travel. You can't cook; you barely clean. And a job? Teaching who, what? The first and last job you had was at summer camp darn near ten years ago, and you quit that. So you think you're going to pop up out of nowhere, ask for a check, and disappear with his child? What episode of Baby Mama Drama are you reenacting?"

"Yes! To get rid of me he will. Lamar does not like public spectacles, so paying me to leave him alone will be his pleasure."

"You're not going to New York to beg that man for anything."

"Mom, please stop, let's agree to disagree. This back and forth is giving me a headache."

"Maybe your father can talk some sense into you. You're not following my orders, you're not following the doctor's orders, and all of this for a few damn dollars? Zylar Wingate, you're really pissing me the heck off!"

"Mother, I know what I am doing. My plane leaves in less than four hours.

I made a quick phone call. "Yes, Brianna Davis please. Hey Bri, I need a huge favor. Could you please pick me up from the airport around 8 p.m.? My plane lands at JFK at 7:30."

"Sure. I will have Ebony with me. Maybe we can grab something to eat?"

"Sounds wonderful! I would like to meet the little person that has my good friend bubbling."

"Zy, how about you just stay at the house with us? It will be a slumber party."

"No, I can't, I have to try and connect with Lamar in the a.m."

"Zylar, are you gonna tell him about the baby?"

"No, I am not. There is nothing to tell him. We have some unfinished business that I would like to settle. Then after Menace's album release party, I am moving back home."

"Sorry, Zy, I just thought that maybe this time away had given you a change of heart, some time to reconsider your options."

"During this entire time I have not gotten as much as a text message from Lamar. It's obvious that he has moved on with his life, and it's overdue that I begin to start mine. Will you pick me up at 8?"

"Yes, Zylar, I will be there with bells on."

Why did I agree to dinner with her? Miss-fucking-perfect was gonna pick up right where my mother left off - on my last nerve.

Brianna dropped me off at my condo. It must have been close to eleven. The security guard in my building was drooling, head leaned so far back you would have thought a dentist was about to do a full root canal. After enduring a long drawn-out dinner with Bri and Ebony, I was not in the mood for his excuses. I did capture the moment with my iPhone. Shit, my parents were paying for me to be safe, not for this bastard to sleep! Digging out my keys from my Birkin bag, I could not wait to lie down. This trip had been exhausting. Shower and bed were the only things my body craved.

When I walked into my apartment, the smells of jasmine and mango hit me. The 8x10 photo of Lamar and I at the BET awards ceremony...the vase that used to stay filled with fresh flowers... Suddenly I remembered why I left NY. Everything here reeked of Lamar - our love and my future. Uncontrollable tears streamed down my makeup-less face. For the first time since the breakup I could not ignore how much I missed him. My space was not mine after two plus years. It had become ours. Bottles of cologne, from Issey Miyake to Armani...body wash...deodorant...I even had his boxers in my drawer. His touch and the sound of his voice echoed through my small condo. I conjured up an image of him naked on my couch as I played Houdini with his dick. Quickly glancing at my left hand, I recalled the ring that used to symbolize our love. What once represented our future was now a memory.

Maybe he had called the house phone. Rushing over to the wireless phone, I scanned all the incoming calls, hoping just one of them were from his cell or office number. Two years and four months gone, just like that, not even a look back. Love meant allowing your heart to exist outside of your body, hoping that the person who held it handled that shit with care. Well, I have about 100 pieces that say otherwise.

My emotions switched faster than a gay man on the runway from pity to pain. Why should I feel sorry for myself? Making him sorry would feel so much better. Two weeks' worth of mischief and mayhem...the key was not to get caught. My father had to pull some major strings to get me out of the last jam, but there was no fury like a woman scorned. I rubbed my belly. Something beautiful would result from all this pain.

Hot shower, soft bed, and plenty of rest. Some of my most devious thoughts came to me in my slumber, plus I had to catch Lamar before he went to the office. On Saturdays, he was usually there by 9:00.

Wishing I was awakening to birds chirping or rain drops tapping on my windowpane, I was beckoned by my mother's relentless calls, from the house phone to the cellular, since 7 a.m. Finally, she just called the building security and had him knock on my damn door. I didn't even know there was a direct line there! After being chastised for about twenty minutes, my mind was in full swing: six grand from Lamar, the Benz, sublet the apartment, attend Menace's album release, and then I had to be back home before the dust settled on his raggedy ass. I was sure Brianna would tell me about the entire ordeal. No need to witness it personally - that looked a bit suspect.

I still had the spare keys to Lamar's office and his BMW. It might not be a bad morning after all. After two attempts to Lamar's cell phone, I was perplexed. The man never turned off those damn phones. He had even answered the Juicee line in the middle of sex. Now they went to the voicemail. I must have been tripping! There was no way. I attempted to call from my house phone with the number blocked, and each time it went right to voicemail. Well, at least he unblocked my number.

Warning
Haneef

"Haneef, she said she would be here in an hour. That was forty minutes ago. Just be patient. She will come to see me; even if it's to make sure I am not officially dead yet. If she comes you're going to' make sure I get that $100.00 bucks you promised me right?"

"Maria, for a change this ain't about you. There is some serious shit goin' on in my camp and I need to talk to my Wife."

"Ummm your wife? She is no more your wife, than she is my daughter. Face it we both fucked up with Mo'Najah. Difference is she wants me to change and get sober. You will be a cheatin', lying dawg forever. I will give you credit. You kept her longer than I ever thought you would."

There was a long pause on the phone. I was not sure if Maria had nodded out on the line or if phone had disconnected. Just as I was about to hang up on the nurses phone that I was using, I heard coughing in the background. Not a cold type of cough but a chest rattling, lung shifted type of cough. That was when I heard her voice.

"Maria, what's wrong?" Mo'Najah asked with so much concern in her voice I could feel it through the phone.

More coughing and heavy breathing as I was witness to an emmy award performance.

"Meha I need you to promise me five minutes?" She begged her daughter as she coughed and choked on the mucus in her lungs.

"Sure, Maria I will stay for five minutes do you need a doctor?"

From the hall closet emerged. Sheed blocking the one entrance and exit from Maria's apartment.

"Are you fuckin' serious? You set me up you greedy ole' witch. You don't even know what these motherfuckers have been keeping from me. Damn I wish you were fuckable back then. Maybe just maybe I could have found my own misery instead of ending up in yours."

"Okay I am here… I am not giving back the money and you can forget about me moving back into the house. Either kill me in this living room or as God is my witness I kill you."

With his hands raised in submission Sheed ordered Maria to put the cordless phone on speaker.

"Mo'Najah, this is not about the money, house, cars or where you been sleepin'. I know you heard about Rell and Remmy. I don't think that was random Mo' someone is gunnin' to get me through all of you!" Haneef's voice was stern and direct. "Snipes is still missing and I think they will use what he knows to get to the rest of you; that is why they have not killed him yet. Mo'Najah are you listening to me?"

"Sheed tell her exactly what happened and if she wants to leave let her."

I sat in silence on the other end of the receiver. A scenario that I know I created. Helpless to the people I hold dear. Once Sheed explained the situation to Mo'Najah the apartment was still.

"How much did he offer you to get me here? Mo'Najah screamed at Maria. "How much did it cost for you to once again turn on me for him? One bottle of Gin, oh no your price has gone up since then. A month's rent?"

Reaching into her small pocket book that was straddled around her shoulders Mo'Najah grabbed every dollar that was in there and tossed it at her mother's feet.

"Now I am paying you to leave me the fuck alone. Next time I see you one of us will be in a casket. It really does not matter which one of us it is."

"Mr. Mason you could have had Momma M, Goldman or the Easter fuckin Bunny deliver the same message with less dramatic effect. But as always to get what you want, you will use the one thing I long for, the love of my own Mother."

I did not need to be in the room to see her cry. My eyes watered just listening to the shit over the phone. I would die if something happened to her. All I wanted was for her to know that no matter what we were still on the same team. Money would never come between what she and I had. I'd love her until breath no longer filled my lungs. I just wanted to warn her.

"Sheed let her leave."

V.I.P
Moet

My phone has not stopped ringing since I left Maria's house. I don't know who I hate more, myself for wanting her to love me, or Haneef for constantly manipulating my life. Most of my life he has controlled everything around me; why did I expect anything to be different now.

It's 11pm on a Friday night the club is poppin'. There are silver buckets everywhere. D.J. Fah D is killin' it as I walk thru the club to get to the dressing area. As much as I look forward to getting out of this place, I know I got strong here. Encompassed by all of these scavengers, leaches and vultures made this young sheep sharp. I have witnessed dancers turn prostitute, junkie and more than I care to remember dead. Money was all I came here for and all I left here with.

Speaking of money I almost forgot, I needed to call China and Buddah. It was time for them boys to start mapping out they routes. Just to cover my own ass, I needed to holler at Detective Latham. Trust no one, especially with my money!

There was a private party booked at the club that night. Since my little hiatus, BBW had "Stripper Extraordinaire" on Deck. We're talking at least four outfit changes, the champagne room poppin'. If I was working, someone was paying.

"Moet, there is mad money up there in the VIP," Xtastee giggled as she sashayed past me. "You better go get your cut, ma."

"Soon as I make this call, I'm on that, girl, thanks."

When I walked out, I was dressed in one of my most provocative outfits, my hair and skin shining. My mind was a bit preoccupied with other matters. When I entered the VIP there were about six guys in the area, bottles and blunts in an abundance. Finding an empty lap was a challenge. A few girls had sandwiches going on. I wasn't mad. When the money was flowing, straddle one and tease the other. Either way, they both throwing bills your way.

Before I could figure out who was throwing the most money around, I felt a slight tug on my arm. When I looked down, dude was charcoal black wit' gold fronts and more dollars in his hand than he could hold. *Beats fighting for a lap*, I thought. Dude pulled me off to the far corner of the VIP, close to the speakers and away from the crowd. I stood about ten inches away from him, removing my top. My nipples were pierced, and the rings tonight were flashing, spotlighting my full, shapely breasts as I moved with the music. French Montana's 'Aint Worried Bout Nothin' was blasting through the speakers.

Dude was entertained, but not excited. I came closer and threw my leg up on the couch. My left hand was on my pussy while the right caressed my boob. Now the money couldn't leave his hand fast enough! After a few more minutes, I was facedown, ass up, poppin' my ass all in his lap. The floor was covered with ones. His dick was rock hard; I could feel it through his sweats as he retrieved another stack of bills from his pocket.

Some slow shit came on, so now I was slow-humping his lap, grinding and winding my hips to the beat of "Don't Think They Know" by Chris B. Between the music and the darkness, my head was tilted back and my tits grazed dude's face. There was no eye contact. When I actually looked down, dude had his dick out of his sweats, dry-rubbing his dick against my crotch.

When he realized he was busted, he grabbed my waist, forcing me back into his lap. "Bitch, keep bouncing that ass before I snap your fucking wrist," he whispered in my ear.

"How much for you to suck this dick?"

"Nah, boo, I don't get down like that!"

"Bitch, I'm payin' you, you get down how I say. You lucky I'm even offering you money, hoe. I could just take the shit. After all, your pussy for sale anyway."

Every time he spoke, his grip got tighter and tighter. Security was not even posted at the entrance to VIP. The lights were so dark that no one saw our interaction in the corner. The speakers were vibrating so hard and loud that no scream would be heard.

"Yo, it's mad girls in here that get down like that, let me hook it up for you."

"Oh, you a high-priced whore. What you want, a stack?" Just when I thought I could pull away from him, he grabbed my hair.

"Feisty…yeah I like that!"

Feeling trapped, I stopped resisting, but he did not let go of my hair. Not one fuckin' dancer or guard was in the area.

"Yo, just let me go now and you can walk out of here. Hurt me and hide the rest of your life."

"Yeah, I like when they talk shit. I nut that much harder." Dude's strength was overpowering. Every fucking follicle of hair was screaming. My eyes started to water, the pain was so extreme.

He forced me between his legs controlling me with my hair. His dick was thick and short. "Open up, bitch!" he said with a slap to the left side of my cheek. His ring must have been turned, because I felt something jagged scratch my face. Furious, I decided that this motherfucka' was not gonna leave this club with a dick at all. I always gave my customers what they asked for. I proceeded to give this trick the best blow job known to man. You might actually think I was doing it willingly. I closed my eyes to stop the tears and pretended he was Haneef. I grabbed the base of his penis, stroking it firmly with my left hand, leading it to my mouth. My tongue did a slow, hesitant guide across the head of his salty, sweaty dick. I gagged repeatedly.

"Bitch, you better not bite me!" he warned. "Suck it right, swallow it all, and I got a bonus for you."

Tears leaked slowly from the corner of my eye. After about six minutes of some bomb-ass head, dude was at his peak, pre-cum coated my tongue. His grip never loosened, just rose and fell with the motion of my head. The muscles in his thighs tightened up and his eyes were closed. Dis nigga' was in for the ride of his life. He was moaning and groaning like we were old cut buddies. My right hand was unbuckling the strap on my shoe. That high, sharp, heavy heel that looked so sexy. Just as he started to nut in my mouth, I bit the shit out of his fully-erect penis. His scream was heard by the entire room and was followed by my six-inch heel to his fucking eyeball.

His boy ran up swinging. Finally, security was there to catch his arm before the punch landed. Blood was all over my face; his semen was in my mouth. Security was going in on dude and his boys. That was when Big Rick stepped back and started to swing a black 26' iron baton, all you heard was screams of pain.

Xtastee, ran over to me and lifted me from the floor. Suddenly the flood gates opened. I was crying tears from years of anger, hurt, loneliness, disrespect, and disregard. Tears were a woman's way of letting go of all the pain.

Torment
Tanya

I greeted every day and bid farewell to each night with a similar distain. I awoke to a pill and I went to bed with a bottle of wine and pill. Summer was coming to an end. I can't say I was not ready to see it go. This was by far one of the hottest must depressing few months of my life. Not a trip to the shore or a barbeque. I did not even celebrate Taliah's Birthday which fell in July. One night changed my life.

Something has happened. Sheed has been past my house at least once every day in the past week consistently. There is always a different car parked on my block not right outside of my door but too close not to notice. Momma Mason does not drop the kids off at night after camp. Everyone is buzzin' about the Snipes disappearance and the robbery.

As I sat on my bed debating on if I was going to force myself to make it to the market today. A task I had been avoiding for days sending Lil Neef to the store with the Access card (food stamp) to order subs for him and his sister. I dreaded going out in public. Reaching for the bottle of Percocet's I take one dry. The knock on my front door disturbs me. We don't just swing the doors open anymore; thanks to Kadir.

"Tanya did you see the paper yesterday?" Keema from across the street asked in a frenzy.

"No. What did I miss a sell at Macy's Keema?" Cutting my eyes wondering why she is even at my door.

"There is a story in the paper about Terrell and Reginald's death. If you look at the picture it was taken right outside of the afterhours spot down town, bitch! Don't cha' baby dad own part of that?"

"Listen Keema I am on my way to the market I have not heard anything about those boys getting knocked off. I really just feel sorry for dey' families. Theses youngin's don't worry about life insurance. They make dat' money and blow it twice as fast. Leavin' their hard workin' parents to figure out how they gonna be sent to rest. Shits tragic."

"Damn I ain't even think of dat' shit… But what I do know is da' boi Rell got mad family that will ride for him so whoever did this shit better lay lower than them coffins."

"Keema, I gotta go before my kids get home. Stay outta this sun it's suppose to be a record high today." I warned really not caring but switching the subject as I slowly moved towards the door giving her the hint.

Rell and Remmy were Haneef's best workers. They were so on point, that they got consignment and extensions. If they wanted to travel Hanz would bump a flunky quick from the road crew. No time for remorse none of the bitches gave a fuck about me or my pain. Live by the sword, die by the blade. That bit of info meant I had money coming to me. But damn did Kadir have to "merk" them to get it shit?

My last meeting with Kadir was bizarre'… A car arrived at my house a little after 11:30pm mid-week. Bearing, greeting and salutations were the same Goons from before. One delivered the note and the other stood there silent. They definitely did not get paid for their people skills.

Time is of the essence my beautiful Queen. Destruction is moments away I need to see you for two hours. My knight will watch over your seeds while you are gone.

King

When the car pulled up to the hotel entrance, Kadir was seated in the lobby. Give the lady your credit card and I.D. he whispered into my ear. Following his orders was imperative at this point. With 5 grand already secured I strangely believed he would deliver on his word.

When the lady handed me the key, I assumed that it was to an empty room that was randomly selected. False, when I slid the key code in the door. To my surprise two muslimah women were seated side by side. Fully garbed up with the exception of the Nasiq (which cover from the eyes down). No introductions were made. Both of the women stood as we walked into the suite. My heart pounded. *What the fuck was I doing?*

"Relax Tanya. Search the room there are no guns, voice recorders and no cameras. This is all about trust."

Reluctantly I followed the leader. One of the women grabbed my left hand and led me to the bathroom. The other ran the tub full of water. Both in complete silence as they undressed themselves and me. Then lead me to the jasmine-vanilla scented bubble bath. One washed me from behind with a body scrub of mango and rose. While the other washed my front. The scene was too crazee to enjoy. There is nothing about another woman that turns me on. Sorry strictly dickly.

When we left the bathroom Kadir was laid out on the king size bed completely naked; with his penis pointing upward.

"See I don't cheat on my wives. I simply talk to them about what I want and they make sure that my needs are met. You want something from me, Tanya you also must make sure my needs are met. In return I will also make sure I meet and satisfy yours."

Kadir's honey brown body was eight shades lighter than myself. His tall and lean physique, bald head and full Sunnah made him an average looking man. But to hear him speak any women with ears would stop and pay attention.

Deep, baritone and distinct voice commanded your undivided attention with the vocabulary to match. Sapiosexual. At the right time his eyes dance to the sun or grow dark by the moon. With the index finger of his left hand he summoned me to the bed. Both of his wives are now seated in silence while wrapped in hotel towels.

"Show them how you use to make Daddy's dick disappear." He whispered.

The invitation made my vaginal muscles contract. That and the fact I had not had sex or the desire to fuck since Wise left only magnified the feeling. Nothing about Kadir's bedside manner lacked. If my memory served me correctly. There was nothing he would not do in order to dominate and conquer the arena now referred to as Suite 23.

An audience of freaks is a turn on, but this man's wives? I was nervous and aroused at the same time. His penis has gotten thicker since I had fucked him last or my memory did not do that master piece justice. I looked behind me curious to what they may be feeling.

I had fucked Kadir for spite, and revenge many years ago. If you thought I was not gonna suck the skin off his dick to repair my face all **YOU** readers are crazy. I had no morals when it came to getting my life back. I did not care who I had to cross, betray and now fuck. This shit was more than serious. You don't know your price; until your back is up against a wall I never knew my own. I would rather die than live the rest of my life behind a veil.

Always being told that I was attractive "to be a dark girl"; "pretty little black thang". That was my signature and I will be damned if would not live the rest of my life being known as the Mahogany Princess or Black Barbie. Fuck, suck or steal for my place at the table.

By the nights end I had told Kadir where the house was located at in Ardmore, the details and connection between Ole G, Snipes and Haneef. Everything and anything I knew about Mo'Najah and Sheed. So the fact that Rell and

Remmy had been murdered around the afterhours was not a coincidence.

Sheed however on constant watch was not what I needed right now. Kadir was a wild card. Nothing to be contained or controlled. Not that I gave a fuck if Sheed lived or not but I wanted the purse that came along with the prize. One without the other was pointless.

By the end of my session with Kadir I had a name written on a yellow sticky. The bitch was the prosecutor for the city of Philadelphia. Kadir's issue with her was over 9 years old, but the grudge had never settled. Forgiveness was not one of his strong points.

As I whipped my car into the parking spot at the Shop Rite on 63rd street I am thankful that there are not a million people here today. As I rushed into the market I forgot my access card in the center console. I ran back out to retrieve it unlocked the doors with the remote and dropped the key into the abyss of a bag I was sporting that day. In an out had the shopping cart filled with groceries. Totally oblivious I pulled the handle to the maxima and it opened. I'd forgotten to lock the door when I made the second trip to the car. Tossed my Michael Kors bag onto the driver's seat I press the button to release the trunk. Moving out of shear routine I loaded everything into the back with the exception of the bread and the eggs. The relief that I had not been recognized and the pill that I had taken earlier were in full effect. I walked the cart to the return and entered my car placing the items in my hand in the passenger seat.

Before I could begin searching my bag for the keys. I felt the energy in my car, smelled the musk cologne. Before I could react. A leather belt was swiftly placed around my neck.

"Tisk, tisk come on Ms. Tanya you have to be more careful. Anyone could be waiting to catch you slipping."

Kadir whispered into my right ear as he applied pressure to the tool of choice.

"Do you see something as simple as you turning your back to return the cart or not locking your doors after you leave your vehicle could be just what some sick bastard was waiting for."

As I struggled to get space between my neck and the belt. I found myself clawing at my own flesh. Kadir's strength and position made my attempts futile. Accepting defeat I ceased to resist and embraced the fact that my miserable existence would now finally be over. Kadir released his grip on one side of the belt. While falling back in hysterical laughter. None of which I found amusing.

"You have had a lot of visitors lately Ms. Thompson. You seem to be a very popular woman lately. Getting close to you was starting to become a challenge. So I know you have heard about the recent occurrences. There was a small issue at the afterhours. Your info was impeccable love. However Sheed was not there on time and Snipes was not cooperating with the program. Those three fatalities raised the cost of the job significantly. The 70 grand got split 5 ways. Here is your cut. Kadir dropped a bundle of money on my passenger seat."

Still very disturbed that he would strangle me with a fuckin belt. The knowledge that I was too vulnerable and exposed was priceless. Silently I waited for my guest to finish his report of events.

"The house in Ardmore is a wash. The only things of value there was the motorcycles and the Hummer3. Grand theft auto that is so not my forte'. I actually thought I could manipulate a scenario and force Mo'Najah into a well laid trap, either Momma M's house or to her friend in Camden. Too my surprise, she is much more clever than my people expected. They lost her in a secured parking lot. After I get Mo'Najah's money you will have more than enough money to live comfortably. From what I hear, her account is quite impressive."

"So how am I supose to help you with your dilemma? I asked as I stared at Kadir from the rearview mirror.

"Here is a detail folder of everything you need to know about little miss perfect. Where she plays the lottery to where she gets her coochie checked. Restaurants, hobbies, likes, dislikes who she is before-during- after business hours. I don't care how you do it I just want it done and not come back to me."

"Kadir that was ten years ago and you are still not over it? Why are you so determined to end this ladies life?"

"You are one of the smartest-dumbest women I have ever fucked. Smart enough to use your body to advance materialistically but too dumb to allow it to elevate your mind-set or your situation. Just as you sought me out to help you achieve this surgery. You could have used this knowledge to get you and your family a better life long ago. Stop looking from the outside in and look from the inside out. Your value was never in your appearance or between those chocolate thighs. The scars on your face on match the damage that I know is on your heart. So no, I won't let the cities mouth piece have the last laugh. I too have scars just as deep mines heal when I return the PAYNE!"

Rebound Chick
Lamar

I was seated in my office late one evening when the magnificent idea hit me for the music video. I only had less than two weeks to get it recorded and edited for the album release. Menace and Alashia had been out touring. Tatia P and Scott had been in the studio heavy. How can I put "Rebound Chick" on the map? I had the perfect location to shot the video. Right at the studio in Queens. There was a full size basketball court and Jacuzzi. The vibe would be a major basketball game between the men and the ladies. Very shapely and athletic women dressed in boy shorts and long socks. With wedge heeled sneakers challenging the men. Very attractive, sweaty and muscular men goin' hard against the ladies. Ending in the ladies winning and everyone in the steam room/Jacuzzi mixing. Yes that would be so hot.

Everything was coming together the album was scheduled to be released on time. Venue was locked in and the tickets were sold out standing room only. With Mo'Najah by my side there is nothing else a man could hope for.

Between meetings and Mo'Najah I had almost forgot about my best friend. Devin has been aloof and distant. As much as I wanted to reach out to Brianna I really did not feel as though it was my place. Devin's decision to move out, I was totally opposed to. I have never seen a couple more compatible than my own parents except Brianna and Devin.

Reaching into the pocket of my 'True Religion' jeans I reached for my I-5, I really needed to reach out to my best friend. I was at the peak of my career, falling in love with an amazing woman and I missed him being in my life. The phone rang six times before the voice mail chimed in. Oh well back to work.

$ Tested $
Mo'Najah

Fuck being nice! Haneef was calling my damn phone every day from random numbers every chance he got. Suddenly, Sheed needed to talk to me. My test was three damn days away. Between the realtor and loan officer, I felt like my entire life was under a microscope. I was surprise the motherfuckas didn't ask for a urine specimen or to cotton swab my mouth. Times like this you need your bestie.

"Mo' baby, calm down, you're on overload," China said calmly into the phone. "I know you did not think that the underwriter was just gonna approve you for a half a mil just because your ass is phat. This is all part of the process securing their investment, making sure you're not going to default on the loan. Just be glad you got knowledgeable people working for you, not against you. That shit at the club just pushed you to your limits. Mo'Najah, you're really slippin' if you thought Haneef was going to just let you go. He will be sitting still for what fifteen years. What else does he have to hold on to?"

"Where should I start the list?"

"Why don't you come over here and we can chill? Or better yet, why don't you call CEO-dreadlock and get your back broke?"

"We do more than just fuck, China!"

"Listen, Stella, after two years, I'm glad you're getting some. I was gonna start locking my bedroom door when you come ova."

"Ha fuckin' ha! You just don't know what kind of anger I have in me right now. I wish the shooting range was open. Letting off some rounds always makes me feel better."

"Even more of a reason for you to call ole boy. Let him take the pain away. Fuck him like he owes you somethin'."

"It's barely past midnight. He is working on the video, at the studio with Alashia and Menace."

"Girl, you lucky I can't go to the album release party with you! Menace…that nigga can get it! I would love him long time!"

"Bitch, you're crazy! Get off my damn phone."

"Mo', I'm here if you need me. SFL love you."

"Sista For Life, China. Kiss the girls for me."

I was wondering maybe if I make you my baby, could we do the unthinkable? If you're asking, I'm ready… My cell-phone rang with Lamar's personal ring tone.

"Hello, Mo'Najah."

"How hard would it be for me to lay beside you tonight?"

"Damn, I'm still in the studio."

"I'm in Philly."

"What? Get here! Wait, wait, why are you not at the club?"

"How about I tell you while you are performing your best cunnilingus?"

"Wow, did you really just invite me to a feast at my favorite buffet?"

"Um, favorite? How about only!"

"That to. It's almost 1 a.m.; what time are you leaving Philly?"

"I was waiting on your call. My bag's packed and ready to go."

Damn, I was lying, but fuck it.

"Let me know when you hit the bridge so I can drink a Red Bull and head home."

"No problem. Later, Lamar!" I yelled before he disconnected, breathing heavily into the phone. "Thanks for calling back."

The entire time we were talking I was throwing shit in my Dooney and Burke overnight bag, textin' Buddah, and getting ready for the fastest shower of my life. Parts of me wanted Lamar's penis inside me so deep that it would block out what happened tonight. Then there were the parts of me that wanted him to rescue and secure the vulnerable, fragile parts of my mind and spirit. Sometimes a woman just wanted to feel like she had a man. China could have never been more right. What I needed was to be treated like I was loved, or at least highly regarded. No drinks, no food, no music. 90% of our conversation would be non-verbal and the other 10% would be in tongues. Grabbing my robe and slippers, I proceeded to the bathroom. This shower would not just wash away dude's semen, but hopefully the dingy feeling that was stuck to my skin. Yeah, I really needed to get a full physical and a psych evaluation.

Buddah took a cab to the Hotel and we proceeded to N.Y.C. I dozed off during the ride. Some company I was! When I opened my eyes, we were on the damn turnpike about to get off. It was close to 3 a.m. "Buddah, what are you doing for money these days?"

"Huh?"

"You heard me, how are you getting by?"

"Mo', I just do me. I'm good."

"Did you ever get that weed connect you was hoping for?"

"Nah, that didn't pan out, but after I sold all the shit Wise had in the trunk of the Maxima, I took care of a lot of loose ends, gave my girl enough money to get ahead on the rent, and we good."

"Buddah, I didn't know you had a girlfriend."

"What, you think I run the streets out of boredom? I got a shorty. We been together for a clip."

"Okay, damn, I didn't mean to offend you."

"Well, since I couldn't pull you, I had to go for the next best thing."

"Oh, really? What makes you think I would even be in your league?" I said with a smile, remembering Asa.

"Oh trust, ma, you would have been a Michelle Obama in my camp. I would have made you the first lady. Philly would have never been the same."

"Damn, too bad I play for the other team."

"That's 'cause Asa didn't go hard."

"What did you just say?"

"Nuttin', Mo'."

"How do you know about what Asa did or did not do?"

"Mo', the lesbian community is small. Gay and 420 friendly is even smaller.

When she found out I was on the road crew, she indirectly let it be known that y'all had history."

"Damn, even the girls kiss and tell?"

"Only when you bag a winner, Mo'Money. Trust, if you was some curious brown bagger, Asa would have kept that shit a secret. Think of it as the almost-gay awards."

"Wow! So tell me about your girl?"

"Nope," Buddah replied. "My relationship with you is business. No one knows about my personal life. That way I never have to worry about the two getting crossed."

That lesson is a bit late for me, but I am still learning, I reflected. Never too late to change. Retrieving my cell, I texted Mar, letting him know I was twenty minutes away.

I dropped Buddah off at Port Authority. I gave her an extra hundred and told her, "The almost-gay award winner would like you to spend that on your lady friend."

"Sincere! Her name is Sincere."

"Thanks for the ride."

Buddah probably assumed I was coming here to shop, but far from it. I pulled the duffle bag out of the back. 5 ¾ inch black, sexy platform heels with the cuffs and chain around the heel…charcoal-grey three-quarter-length trench coat…black brimmed Stetson hat. Tonight there would be little to talk about. My hair was bone straight to cover the scratch from dude's slap, not to mention MAC foundation and concealer. The hat was tilted over my left eye. Tricky Secrets lip gloss was poppin', just sexy for no fucking reason.

When I got to the door, the doorman had already announced his visitor. The outfit had him mesmerized, but far from stuck. When I walked through the door, Mar lifted me from the floor. Flipping me upside down, he dove face first into his dinner. My hands only half-secured me. Orgasm was unavoidable as the blood rushed to my head. Mar licked, sucked, and snacked on my yoni 'til I was begging him to let me down. My face was beet red. The room was spinning.

"Damn, what did you do to me?"

"Nothing yet," he replied.

I removed the handcuffs from my trench coat pocket teasingly.

"Damn, you should miss me more often! How long do I have you for?"

"'Til the cops come knocking or Sunday at 8 p.m., whichever comes first."

"That statement and your cum on my tongue has my dick so hard!"

"Let's see if I can fix that."

Lamar quickly grabbed the cuffs from my hand. My attempts to regain control were futile. There was a metal bar between the guest bedroom and the bathroom that Mar did chin-ups on. With the height of my shoes, he did not have to lift me to imprison me. His strength did not amaze me, but the technique and speed fucked me up, like he had used this bar for many a thing. I was looking forward to finding out all his sex secrets. My body was fully exposed.

Mar was shirtless, on his knees, making my pussy erupt and relax just so it could explode again.

"Damn, I really missed you," I confessed. "Wanting you is so hard. Oh shit, Mar, I'm coming, baby."

He was not tasting me, but his thick fingers probed my pink flesh. He was sucking my nipples with the suction of a child nursing for the first time. "Mo'Najah, I am so glad you're here. Can I feel that tight pussy?"

"No, I came all the way to NY to make you masturbate. Where are the condoms?"

"In the drawer, Mo'Najah, but I want to feel all of you."

Every woman had been there at the threshold of intense passion and the interruption of protection. I had no intention of sleeping with anyone else, but I had no idea where this man had been. Sexually, all I wanted was for him to make me feel like no other moment mattered. Weak, defeated, and just wanting to be loved, I agreed.

"Remove the cuffs if tonight is the first time you make love to me. I don't want you to be ruff. I don't want to be bullied; you're too big to go Rambo in this pussy."

"Whatever you want."

"The key to the cuff is on my shoe."

Being freed from my erotic bondage episode almost disappointed me. My mind was flooded with questions, but only one truly mattered. "Lamar, you just got out of a serious relationship. Are you sure you're ready for this type of intimate commitment?"

"Let me show you. 'Cause words sometimes just don't translate what a man's heart is capable of feeling."

Mar took my hand, guiding me step by step to his bedroom. When the door opened, I saw that everything in the room was new. There was a platform elevated bed with black and white steps surrounding it standing at least four feet from the floor. Tiles were on the floor where it was carpet last time I was here. The walls were ivory white with black-and-white framed photos covering each wall. Both the dresser and the nightstands were black, modern, neat, so masculine.

"When did you have time to do all this?"

"Mo'Najah, a man's home is his castle, and when my queen expresses feelings of discomfort, what was I supposed to do? Moving is not an option."

"I would have been satisfied with a new mattress," I confessed. Tears flooded my eyelids. Turning away from him was not an option.

Mar never let my hand go. "What's wrong?"

"I have never had someone treat me this way. My emotions are so off the charts. You're fucking wonderful."

"Okay, these are tears of joy?"

"Yes, surprise, pleasure, happiness, and astonishment. You care about the bed we fuck in? Yes, tears of joy. Sometimes I have to wonder if you are real. This entire relationship is just too good to be true. If you were just another dude wit' a few dollars, I would not be impressed. But you have this kind, gentle heart,safe aura about you. You listen to me speak even when it's my body that is doing the talking. We still giggle on the phone. I think we talk more now that we have connected sexually than we did before. Honestly, I just don't know what to prepare my heart for when it comes to you. It's scary to feel these feelings. Some of them I never had before."

"Please know that you are not on this ride alone. Remember, I was months away from getting married to someone totally unlike you. Casual sex is not me. Pussy is a dime a dozen in the industry. I stack Benjamins. So please don't lessen my intention or your worth. Before I touched you, we had a connection that sex could only amplify. You made me realize I was settling, but with you in my life, I feel complete, whole, as if some divine spirit sent you to me. Mo'Najah, I am a God-fearing man. My interest in you is nothing less than as my wife when the time is right, and if you will have me? I'm well aware that we have not been tested together. However, I have my results from my last physical. So the answer is yes, I am very ready to make that commitment to you if you're ready?"

"I love you."

Mar did not speak. He bent down only to lift me up to eye level. Too many kisses to count dried my tears. His lips were soft and full. I was cradled in his massive arms as he walked me to the bed, laying me on top of the white satin comforter. Black and white pillows were all over the bed. He removed his jeans, watch, and chain. Lamar laid his body completely on top of mine.

"Mo'Najah, what happened to your face?"

I ran my hands over his shoulders, lifting my head to reunite our lips. I did not tell Lamar the entire story, but I told him enough to cease the interrogation. Within moments, my night of hell, humiliation and horror were replaced with something I wanted, but was not sure Lamar could deliver: serenity.

Early Morning
Lamar

When I awoke, I was in my black and white paradise. The bed was so soft I felt like I had sunk into it. Mo'Najah was right beside me snoring. As I pulled my sex-drained body from the bed, I climbed out, tip-toed slowly through the penthouse to the kitchen. I went into the empty refrigerator I had to make a pimp decision. I really wanted to impress her no, not impress her show her how much I fuckin' dig her. Yes I could have easily paid to have breakfast delivered. But what better way to awaken a beautiful woman than with breakfast in bed. Made by the man who worked her out the night before. Who cares that I had never made a woman breakfast before in my life. Shit I had google and the food network. I left a yellow sticky note on the bathroom mirror. Figuring if she woke up that would be her first stop.

I did not even go back into the bedroom I grabbed some basketball shorts from the hamper and my wallet and jogged to the grocery store. I started with the little red basket and ended up with a cart full of shit. Just as I was about to call her I realized I left my phones in the house. We had both decided to power off the phones for a night. The interruptions had become annoying. She makes me want to place the world on pause when I am with her. No money or decision is more important than listening to her talk. That is how I know that I love her.

The older lady in the produce department was very helpful in planning the menu, scrambled eggs, pancakes and Goddshall's turkey bacon. With 8 ripe oranges for fresh squeeze orange juice. Garnished with a bright, bold red rose which looks to be about a week old. But her smile would revive this tired thing.

You would have thought someone was taking a photo, her smile was so wide and bright. Ass-hole naked with my locks down and the rose between my teeth I delivered her food. I toyed with the idea of forming an erection, just to put the icing on the cake but I did want to at least have breakfast first.

"No I don't wanna mess up the comforter. Take it in the dining room for me please she begged."

Just as we started to clear the table from breakfast. The house phone started to ring. At first I wanted to ignore it. Me doing dishes had turned my guest on as she started to kiss my back and rub my nipples as I stood at the sink. After the fifth consecutive call I figured it had to be urgent. Only my Mom or Devin would even dare to call so many times.

"Mo'Najah, can you answer that for me? No one usually calls the house; it may be Devin."

"Are you sure you want me to answer this?"

"Yes, my hands are full and wet."

"Hello?" she sang into the receiver. "James residence."

"How professional," Mar said from the kitchen, where I think he just brought the entire breakfast section of Food Town and cooked it before I woke up.

Silence on the other end had me wondering if I pressed the talk button. "Yes, may I speak to Lamar please?" A female voice on the other end asked.

"Yes, please hold. It's for you," I said, waving the phone is his direction. "It's definitely not Devin!"

Our eyes found that awkward space. He knew that it was her before he lifted the phone to his ear. One hand grabbed the phone the other held a dish towel. Not wanting to intrude, I excused myself. "Time for a shower."

Confirmed
Zylar

My stomach was doing the Jamaican butterfly, left leg and hands were trembled with anger. Disdain and disgust dripped from every syllable in my vocabulary. My heart ached more by the second. This only confirmed my decision to destroy his ass. Lamar was not worthy of my tears or the success I helped him acquire.

"Lamar, this is Zylar. Did I catch you at a bad time?"

"No, not really, just finishing up breakfast, what's up? "

"After some time and consideration, I was hoping your offer still stood?"

"Oh, most definitely. How much do I owe your parents?"

"Make the check out to me for $8,600."

"Oh wow. You know anything over two grand has to go through Devin."

"That is why I was trying to catch you before you went to the studio. But I guess you're not working today. Did I hear you correctly, you're making breakfast? Nice, I can barely recall you offering to make me coffee."

"Zylar, you can pick up the check from Devin's office on Monday. Is there anything else?"

"Yes there is, I'm glad you asked. Can I also use the car until I get settled?"

"Zy, I offered you the car, you declined it."

"Please don't call me Zy. You're right, I did decline it. However, I was in a public place getting my heart and future disassembled while my lover, fiancé, and friend demanded that I take a pregnancy test before exiting the building. So given my mental and emotional state, Lamar, I said some pretty rash things. Now I am asking if I can use the car until I get my own? It's either yes or no, Lamar."

"Zylar, you can have the car. I will sign the title over to you. Will that conclude our lose ends?"

"You can't be this cold. What did I do for you to treat me like this, Lamar? Just tell me how to fix it. I will do whatever it takes, just don't walk away. We have something worth holding onto. My love for you is deep enough to forgive this little indiscretion. We can get past this, Lamar. Do you still love me?"

"Zylar, I am sorry. Maybe in time you can forgive me. Hopefully we can be friends. There is just no easy way to hurt someone you used to love. Pick up the keys from the doorman. The papers will be in the glove box. Return the tags to 3D when you pick up the check." Click.

Damn, the trick must suck a mean dick to get breakfast in the morning! Cell phones off and house phone privileges… My mind was racing; anger, rage, and revenge owned my thoughts. "Used to love" - past tense already. I wondered how hatred could rest on his callous-ass heart? Lamar thought some cash and a car would fix what he had broken? If I couldn't have him, I'd be damned if she would! All was fair in love and war. Miss Moet was dealing with a veteran!

Regrets
Lamar

Her family could afford to buy any car she wanted. Every fiber of my being was telling me this was not a done deal, but I had no regrets. Life was too short to settle for basic when you could have extraordinary. Never in my wildest fantasies did I think I would become captivated by Mo'Najah. I had never made breakfast for a woman before. Pancakes, bacon, cheese eggs, and fresh-squeezed OJ with a smile, and one long-stemmed red rose in a water glass. I was focused on the future, but I had learned from my past.

Soft kisses in the elevator as she prepared to depart. I really did not want her to leave me. Time sped by as we enjoyed one another's company, locked in my penthouse. I greedily consumed her body, soul and conversation. Eventually, she had to go, and I lugged her overnight bag to the trunk of her car. I was shocked as I approached the driver's door, only to find that it had been smashed, the glass shattered and the radio pulled out.

"Mo'Najah, you can take my BMW back to Philly."

"No, I will take the train!"

"Rental? Would you rather have a rental?"

"Lamar, just get the car fixed. I will take the train back to Philly."

"I know you're pissed, you called me Lamar. Babe, we had a great weekend. I'm so sorry your Acura got damaged. Next time we will make some arrangements to park in a secure garage."

"Mar, accidents happen. This is NYC, the home of the hit and run. Just get the car fixed. Here are the keys and all of the information on the vehicle. It's in my mother-in-law's name. What time does the train leave for Philly?"

"Can I at least take you to the train station?"

"No thanks, I need some time. I will just catch a cab, my brother will pick me up."

I had been in this building for years and never had I heard one tenant complain about vandalism or theft to their vehicles. With a 24 hour doorman and constant foot traffic. I called my local police station to see if anyone reported the accident. Then I had her car towed to the auto body shop that Devin used.

MONDAY...

$ Enemies $
Mo'Najah

My train ride back to Philly, gave me a lot of time to reflect on recent events in my circumference. Nothing was making since. Snipes, the dude from the club or my car suddenly being damaged. Even with today being one of the most important days of my future with the current situation I may not be around to enjoy it. When Detective Latham's Chevy Impala pulled up, I rose from the seat in the Starbucks. Dressed like a college kid, sporting a blue Polo hat pulled all the way to my eyebrows, Juicy Couture back pack, ripped blue Seven denim jeans and a four-dollar wife beater complemented by blue and silver Air Max's. I reached for the envelope that contained two grand. We both knew the current rate for info and I was behind on the payments.

The dude that assaulted me at the club that night mysteriously never made it to the precinct. I had to have Bella give me the surveillance tapes from the parking lot. Snipes, has yet to be heard from and Rell & Remmy's murder was still a 'cold case'. Not even I could ignore Haneef's warning. Something was goin' on and I was snack dab in the middle of the shit.

The damage to my vehicle came close to $8,000. There was no surveillance cameras pointed in the direction of where my Acura was parked, however, every bone in my body was telling me that the call that morning and my car getting hit were no accidents. Lamar could sleep on Miss Zylar, but I would put that ass to bed!

"Zylar Wingate, originally from Charleston, South Carolina. Lamar Justin James from New Jersey both of them are currently NYC residents. Yes, Detective, I need everything you can find as soon as possible. I don't have a name from the episode at the club I can only tell you the tag number from the car they got out of. I am still trying to understand how they were placed in a cop car and never arrested."

"Mo' do you even know which officers responded to the call?"

"Latham, I am gonna be honest I was so shaken up after the entire ordeal. Leaving was all I was concerned with. I even left 1500.00 behind that night. Bella gave me that when I came to get the surveillance video."

"Everyone is sayin' this Snipes, Rell & Remmy thing is an inside job. There is no way someone did not tell whoever did this exactly how the shit went down. Now you're telling me that you got assaulted and they were placed into a cop car and never made it to the station. Mo'Najah, you or Haneef have pissed someone off with a lot of power and a few dollars."

The vein in officers Latham's forehead read a bit more than concern. For the first time in my entire life I was worried about my safety, not just freedom. The shit at the club very well could have been Zylar sending me a message. But she would have no way in hell to connect Rell & Remmy to me. Curious to how she got my number in the first place was it the business card or out of Lamar's cell phone?

"Thanks again and I will see you on Friday before I leave town. Be safe out there."

"Mo'Najah, you need to do the same."

Today was test day. The most important part of my future started in less than an hour. My cellular was blowin' up. The ringtone told me who it was as Emimen featuring Rhianna sang "I love the way you lie". Against my better judgment I decided to answer it.

"Hello Haneef. I'm taking my GED test in less than an hour and I really need to be clearheaded and focused."

"Mo', I have one question, then you can go ace your test, babe."

"I think it was you who taught me not to ask a question you really don't want an answer to, Haneef."

"Are you seeing someone else?"

"Hanz, do you really want the answer to that question?"

"Yes, Mo', I do. I'm fuckin' trippin in this bitch. I can't sleep, I don't have an appetite. I'm stressing my Moms. I refuse to see anyone but you. This Snipes shit has me dumbfounded. I need to know if I have lost you forever?"

I paused before I replied to his question, knowing my truth could send him into a possible rage and depression, making his situation much worse than it already was. Love means you don't intentionally cause pain. But, being smart meant I knew when to inflict such emotions. I needed information. If I told him the truth how would I get to the bottom of all the shit that has happened?

"No, Haneef, I am not seeing anyone, including you."

"Hanz, since we are not together can you be honest with me for once?"

"What's this about Mo'?"

"Who from your past has the kind of time, money and connections to watch everyone you are connected to, male or female?"

"Mo' I have been runnin through the list with Sheed since dis' shit started. Every name I throw at him is coming up with short money."

"Would you tell me if it was one of your females?"

"A loss is a fuckin' loss and I would have you body a bird with the same quickness as any man that came at the fam' like this."

"We shall see, I gotta go."

Who's Watchin'
Sheed

I had 328,000 in my stash from this flip. A little over a half of brick left to work. Going back to NYC was not even an option. Since that shit at the afterhours I have rearranged everyone and everything. My team is on fire drill mode every six days. I even stopped getting my Caddie cleaned at the same spot. No more hair cuts at the shop, nothing routine. I even started parking my car in front of my old crib. Started taking a squatter out of the city. Fatima had found us a nice four bedroom split level in Bucks County; everything is in her name.

Things have been very calm. As if Rell & Remmy did not just get killed. Like Snipes is not missing. Folks just seem to go right along with their lives after the casket is dropped into the ground. They get to fight over your possessions or their status. Death, that is when someone's true colors come out. Grief is the ultimate truth serum. People can hold in their true feelings and pettiness for a lifetime. Death brings out all of the dirt, hatred, betrayal and greed. Family members that ain't even know you come out the wood work, just to see what you may have left behind.

Rell's mother was the only one who seemed appreciative that I handled the cost of his service. Remmy's Grand-mother cursed me out, called me everything but the son of God. But the ole' bat took the money. Both services were closed caskets. Very little details were exposed to the families; to assist in the investigation. But I will never forget how I found their bodies. Someone should pray that I never find the twisted fuckers who made it happen.

I had called Mo'Najah to try to apologize. But she would not answer my calls. Even at the funeral she passed by the casket so quickly, if I was not watching everyone who attended I would have missed her. She walked in the front and disappeared out of the back. A black breeze on a summer Saturday afternoon. It was hard being the one in the middle. I never could empathize with Mo's feelings because my main concern was always Haneef.

Just as I parked the CTS on Broad street, my pocket begins to vibrate. When I looked at the screen I was surprised to see Mo'Money's name pop up.

"What's good, Mo'Money?"

"Sheed, we need to talk it's serious."

"Time and location?"

"Meet me at tre'cee. You know the safest spot in the city."

Damn something serious has happen when Mo' starts talkin' in code. Tre'cee is 3:00 and the safest place is Momma Mason's. Cell towers are nothing but frequencies. Mo' has this theory that she convinced me of. That police can tap into the frequency of two cellular devices randomly. If the information is useless then it's disregarded but if it's not then your number gets flagged and you get monitored. That conspiracy shit is not all fictional; some of it is fact.

I arrived at the house at 2:40 no cars were out front so I assumed no one was home. Cutting thru the narrow alley, that led to the back door. That is the key I had always had to enter Momma Mason's crib. When I would get kicked out of my own crib. Kalief gave it to me and told me I always had somewhere to call home. As I climbed the basement steps I smelled her perfume. She was there already. Pacing the floor in the living room where all of the family pictures are plastered on the walls.

She did not turn around to speak to me. She faced the photos as if the faces on the walls would give her strength.

"I know I can never break the ties between you and Haneef. But I will tell you that if something happens to me out here. He will blame you just like he blamed you for Kalief. I was attacked at the club recently. Not your ordinary rude, touchy, feely, ass' dude. No this bastard went out of his way to get me into a corner at the club. Spent hundreds of dollars on buckets and VIP privileges. When he got me alone; he forced me to suck his dick. He damn near broke my wrist. But that is not the issue. My problem is after the club security beat the shit outta' him and his crew and called the cops. None of them ever made it to the station." There was a silence. The trust between she and I had been broken. Her posture and lack of eye contact told me we were not friends anymore.

"So I am only going to ask you this one time and it will always be between us. Who has enough money and power to hate him or me that much? To have watched us this long? I don't care if it's a female or male. I just need to know what I am up against. After all I am out here solo."

"Mo' I will keep it 1000 wit' you. I could give you every name of every bitch Haneef has fucked in the last five years. But none of those women have the money or the brains to orchestrate the devastation that we have been going through. The one problem we did have when Hanz' got knocked we settled it together. Joey Black, is barely moving ounces fuck keys. Tanya, is the only bitch that hates you past infinity but if she had a dollar to rub together it would be to get her face fixed. Not to have you raped. Or Snipes disappear and Rell & Remmy killed."

"What if all that other shit is just to take the attention off of me? Plus they were robbed and killed. So whoever did the job made at least 60 grand. Depending on what Snipes had in the safe. What would be there reason for taking him? Unless he is behind this whole thing?"

"Mo'Najah, we are all tryin' to figure this shit out. But why do you think it's all about you?" I asked shocked that she would think someone gave two fucks about her but Haneef.

"There are only three things Haneef would pay for Momma M, his son and me! Someone has been thru the house in Ardmore. I am talking three sets of foot prints on my hardwood floors. They knew the code to the gate and they disarmed the alarm system. So you tell me who they were looking for Haneef is in a federal prison and you don't live there? Not to mention the soda spilled on my desktop which caused the hard drive to seize and the wires clipped to every camera after they entered the house."

"Why the fuck you ain't call me when all of this shit happened? Are you lookin' to get murked?"

The room had a shortage of air. No, the shit had not been calm at all just the storm was in another area. Not many people knew where the house in Ardmore was let alone the gate code. This shit was snowballing. At that moment I knew there was no way I could keep everyone safe. Bad part of it all Mo' was right, if something were to happen to her Haneef would tell me I let the shit happen.

"Look Mo' I already know you ain't about to go into lock down or run from whatever is out there. But on all that I love I don't think Snipes is the money or the master mind behind this shit. If nuttin' he is a victim just like the rest of us. If he is still alive it's because he knows so much."

"I'm out!"

"Mo' before you leave, can I ask for a favor?" The look on her face even with the polo cap pulled low. Her body language is screaming. Why the fuck should I help you do anything? But one of her favorite lines from the movie Player Club is 'Closed legs, don't get fed.'

"What could I possibility do for you Sheed?"

"Can I get Benny D's info?"

"What makes you think I have access to him?"

"Haneef and I spoke indirectly about my situation and that came up as a possible solution."

"Well honestly, I do, but the offer was made to me personally, being Haneef's wife and all. But since the divorce...(sucking my teeth)! I guess you can have the number."

"Word, Mo'?"

"Sure, just don't expect anything else from me."

"Damn, you sound mad, Mo'."

"Who me, mad? Never! Money is like air to me; I'm surrounded by it while others are on respirators. Mo'Money breathes easy. I will text you Benny's number; just don't use my name when you call. We have gotten quite close over the past few years. I don't want him to think I am involved in anyway."

"That's cool. So do you still want the invite to the shower, Mo'?"

"Nah, I'm gonna pass on this one. But with the money you did not give me, pay for your kid's first year in college."

"Yo! Mo'Money, we need to talk. That shit ain't even fair. Haneef wanted you out, not me! Hanz came up with this big idea that I did all the work and split the pot 50/50. Mo', you know how long I paid my dues. How the fuck could I agree to that shit? My own son or daughter will be here in a few months. I still pay fuckin' rent where I lay my head.

Y'all own property and cars, mad money on stash, lawyers on retainer, cops in place. I don't have shit but a fucking gun collection and some paper. If anybody understood my point of view, I thought I would be you. I may have not been the brains that put the shit together but I'm mos' def' the brawn that has kept the shit rollin'. I deserve my forty acres and a mule too. So yeah, I told him I would pay you accordingly, but with you taking half of the product and the money. The profit margin got cut by more than half and product skyrocketing, there was no bread to break. But your brother is eating lovely. If you or Haneef expect me to risk my life and my future just so you can be comfortable, you and him got the wrong Shawn Anderson."

"Listen, every man has to choose sides. Your alliance is to Haneef and Kalief. I guess I would be a dumb bitch to think that a man's blood, kidnapping, or money could come between that. After I text you this number, I could care the fuck less if it's you, Haneef, or the coroner. Our affiliation is done. So let Haneef, know there is no need to send any more messages or messengers. I'm a big girl and I can handle my own. By the way, I did not take half of everything for no reason. I plan on getting my money!"

"Wow, you think you can out-hustle me?"

"Thinking comes from not knowing. You have already lost half of your loyal customers. You have cut the product so much, you're losing money like the Ford manufacturers. But I won't be giving you a bail-out like Obama did the car companies. When I get permission to give you that number just know that is your lifeline. I'm out!"

TUESDAY...

Deception
Devin

"Mr. and Mrs. Davis, I would like you to meet Mr. Preston. He will be handling your adoption and monitoring Ebony's transition into your home on a permanent basis." Stated the social worker from the group home where Ebony is living.

"Good afternoon, Mr. Davis. I already know your schedule is hectic. I will not take too much of your time. These meetings are mandatory and they require both parents for at least three sessions. Let me explain my function. You have decided to offer your home and hearts to special child. My job is to make sure that merger happens as smoothly and effortlessly as possible. Questions, concerns any and all episodes; call me personally. Even though I did not work with Ebony personally I have her case file and her social workers direct line. I would be better equipped to get to you in a timely fashion than the social worker. My main responsibility is making sure this transition is successful."

I stood to shake Mr. Preston's hand. As he briefly interviewed us about our background, education, occupation, hobbies, and things of that sort. Then he asked us individually why we wanted to be Ebony's adopted parents?

"I already have all of your required paperwork in order, Mr. & Mrs. Davis you should hear from me in a few business days."

After we pretended to be the happy couple, we left the facility.

"Brianna, I can't do this. If you want to take on the problems of someone's abandoned child, so be it, but I am filing for a legal separation. This is not going to change anything. You could adopt ten children. That does not make you a MOTHER, Brianna. This charade is ridiculous. I don't know why I agreed to help you."

"You can't be this ignorant. I may never be a mother in your cold ass eyes. But I have the ability to be a damn good parent. Devin, we have the opportunity to change someone's life. Stop thinking with your penis for ten minutes. God does not make mistakes. We do."

"Brianna, I think it is time for us both to accept the reality of the situation. Yes I love you, but not enough to waste a lifetime. I want the joys of fatherhood. If it comes with child support and drama? I may even deserve that for what I am doing to you. But don't be disappointed with me for wanting what I want."

"But while you stand on your pedestal, high and mighty, strong and fertile, your wife, your better half, the woman that has been loyal and faithful to you from the start, has had to relive her own personal hell. My demons lay beside me at night in the spot where you used to lay, my past playing over and over again like a scratch recorded on a stereo. Why does a woman have this need to be loved and accepted? What is so wrong with me that they would take something so special? Maybe I deserved to be violated, disrespected, and then forgotten, because here I am, years later, being given the exact same treatment from the man I choose to love. So, thank you Devin Dickerson Davis, I too have reached my limit, but it's not a bottom. It's a peak of admiration, acceptance, and joy. My God has seen me through some troubled times. So if this union cannot sustain this storm, my faith will guide me to a path of righteousness. These tears are of acceptance. I love the woman I am. I look forward to meeting the one I will become in spite of you. My success will not be measured by the lives I bring into this world, but by the ones I affect while I am here. Devin, answer this question for me. If you died today what impact have you had on the world? Put that in your calculator and tell me the sum total of your existence."

With that Brianna leaves the parking area from the adoption facility.

Sum total of my existence? What Oprah program did she get that shit from? I am an intelligent, educated, black man. As I reassured myself not 100% sure that was a sufficient answer...

But who would miss me {or you}?

Express Karma
Zylar

When I initially arrived to NYC, I was a bit over zealous as far as my career was concerned. Which is how Menace and I became so close. Kurtis "the connections" Darby, was a manager/promoter/thief. I was so excited and naïve that I over looked the fine print. You know the twelfth page of the twenty page contract that you barely read. Which placed Menace and I in a really horrible predicament. Menace's career was actually building momentum but he was barely getting paid from the shows he was doing. After I faxed my Father's lawyer the contracts we signed. I was told in plain English, I had given this man more than I could make.

That was how Menace and I met Seven. Seven had the reputation of handling things for people who could not fix their own issues. Menace, explained to him the problem and I paid the money. Seven managed to get us both out of your contracts for seven thousand dollars. I don't know how or what method he used but I got legal papers ending my contract with Kurtis Darby management. My lawyer looked them over and I never heard from him again. I had not used this email address in years. You did not call Seven, Seven called you. Since I was the one that paid him I was the one with the connection.

"Twenty-eight, grand total, $7,000 due up front, wired into a personal account, and the other fourteen held in a verified escrow account, released upon completion of each project.

Once job one is done, I get paid for job two, and so on and so forth. The first job is the Ruby Street project?"

"That is a lot of money for me not to have any guarantees. The issue you resolved with my wanna-be management was much cheaper." I said into the phone that had been delivered to me via overnight mail.

"You're paying for my reputation, referral, and my risk. You sought out my services, not the other way around. Based on the information you have given me, I think price is more than fair. If you would like to shop around, be my guest. But you seem like you're working with a time constraint. I would hate for my price to go up because I had to rush. Ms. Z"

"Fine, here is all the information you need on the first and second jobs. I would like the Ruby Street thing to look as accidental as possible. Friday evening or Saturday morning would be perfect."

"Leave the details up to me, Ms. Z. Tell me when you will have the money secure, and we have a deal."

"The funds can be in place in as soon you give me the account number. Please know that I am not just some little rich girl on a tirade. If you fuck this up, I will spare no expense in correcting your errors."

"This is the number you can reach me at. After part two is complete and the final payment is made, the number will no longer be active. Ms. Z if you could have handled this you would have not contacted me. I know you're a woman about your money. As I am a man, about my business."

Twisted
Tanya

Kadir had every move District Attorney Kathy Petrini made down to a science. From the time she woke up, until she went to bed at exactly 10:15pm every night. This lady had O.C.D about everything. Her meticulousness made her anal about her files, desk and work space. Very detail oriented, she ran a fine tooth comb over every case she worked. Which assisted her in having the highest conviction rate. Watching her was like watching the same movie over and over again.

Every morning she would enter planet fitness at 6:30 am wipe down the treadmill twice before running a total of thirty-five minutes. Then wiping it down a last time after she used it. Returning to her home she showered and arrived at the WaWa for her 20 ounces of French vanilla cappuccino. Then she drove three blocks to her office where she never left for lunch. Court sessions were the only time she left the building. Her Friday evening trips to Canal's in Jersey was a surprise. As she had them order an expensive Tuscany Italian wine Sassicaia 2007. They did not even keep it on the shelves. As the attendant had to go in the back and retrieve this special ordered item.

I had watched her for days. Kadir had someone watching my every move. The plan was simple, yet effective. I gave my watchman a note that told him what I needed. Digitoxin (tastless – ordorless toxin that attacked the heart.) If the person was in good health it may take up to two hours to kick in which would be perfect. She would be at her office when the chemical took effect.

Her liquid addiction (coffee) had been embedded into her daily routine. Even if I had to dilute the cream with the toxin I was sure she would use it. Kadir was not at all delighted with my plan to deliver D.A. Petrini's death. He wanted a painful, volient suffering. I was having no parts of that. No face to face confrontation at all and definitely no contact. Google was more useful in my plan than I had ever imagined (internet is a gift and a curse).

Since she was a time freak I had a complete advantage. I had the stage set with two people in the store previous to her arrival and me entering behind her. Kadir's people followed orders. However I went an extra mile to ensure that Ms. Petrini drank her special coffee. I even had her lipstick on under my nasqid.

As she pulled into the parking lot I had Kadir's dude insert 15 CC's of the toxin into the creamer as she always used the coffee station closer to the food (the workers wiped that area more). As she entered with her normal good mornings. I entered behind her making a cup exactly the same size and content but adding an additional dose of Digitoxin.

Just as she arrived at the counter. I had orchestrated an older white man falling to the floor clutching his chest. Instinctively the public servant went to his rescue. Which allowed me to switch her cup that was now on the counter. I stayed in the store during the commotion. Person two announced they are a R.N. at Temple hospital clearing the space around the man, telling the clerk to dial 911 and unbuttoning the shirt of the alleged vicitim. As the situation seemed to be under control and the workers from the store assisted the man to a seat, Petrini, gathered her pocketbook and coffee offering once more to help she sipped her cup on her way out of the door. I walked back to the coffee station and disposed of the creamer that had been contaminated.

Not wanting to leave anything to chance. By the end of business I would have someone come into the store and erase the video footage or just send a virus to the computer. Either way I would not leave any loose ends. That is if my planned worked.

Taunted
Haneef

Shocked that Mo'Najah even took my call. It had been weeks since I heard her voice. With that being said I heard the distress in her voice. The weight on her shoulders, I wished I could carry. The drama in the streets, her G.E.D testing and not having me home; my lady is more than stressed. My mind can't help replay the question Mo' threw at me. "Who has the money and the man power to attack your team?"

I had to sit back and ask myself not just the money but the motive?

I took out a pen and paper something I rarely did. Sat back and composed a list all of the jokers I had beef's with since I got locked up, corrections officers that I had disrespected, nigga's who bitch I fucked, bitches who bitch I fucked. Just about anybody I ever had a confrontation with. The list had 53 names of men and women. Ex-lovers to business deals gone bad. If I ever had to lay hands and feet on you your name was on this paper. Mo'Najah was at the top of the list, but dude from Florida Caesar the Cuban cat that jammed me up, stood out in my mind. *But why would he wait two years to get his revenge. This shit ain't adding up at all.* Racking my brain wasn't getting me anywhere. But now that I had the questions I needed to bounce them off the only other person linked to me that is not blood. Sheed.

I made a $100 trip to the infirmary to use the phone.

"Yo! Can you talk?" I asked Sheed never knowing where or what he is into.

"Call this number back 1-267-555-1111."

"I got a chance to talk to Mo' this morning and she hit me with some real gangster shit. So I am gonna lay the same trip on you. She asked me who had the money, power and connections to do all the stuff that has happen? Then she hit me with who would benefit from my team falling apart? I been sitting here writing out this list. Man its damn near fifty names on here."

"Is that all you and Mo'Najah spoke about?"

"That and her test."

"Haneef, what names are on this list you got?" Sheed asked, sounding impatient.

"Nah, man back that up, what else was Mo' and I suppose to talk about?"

"I told her it was between us man. I really hoped that she had talked to you."

"Sheed I only got this phone for twenty six minutes. What the fuck is going on with my Wife?"

"Mo'Najah said she was attacked at the club a few days ago. Plus someone broke into the house in Ardmore and clipped the wires to the surveillance cameras." The silence on the other end of the receiver has me making sure the call was still connected.

"Hanz' she thinks all of this is coming from some bitch you dealt with or a dude you & Snipes could have done dirty? But whatever is coming she told me she was going to handle alone. She said to pray for whoever is lookin' for her. Because now she is lookin' for them."

"Haneef are you there?"

"Yeah, I'm here. When I spoke to her I could hear the anxiety in her voice. She ain't answer my call because she missed me. She answered my call to get the info she needed. When I could not give her any names she was done."

"She did the same shit to me Haneef. I can't keep everyone safe."

"Sheed what time did you make it to the afterhours that morning?"

"A little before 7am, why Haneef?"

"Don't you usually go right after Snipes closes 4-4:30am?"

"Yeah I do but Fatima had started spotting that morning. We were in the emergency room until six and you know I was not taking her to handle the business. So I was running late. Why?"

"Sheed what if the trap was really meant for you and not Snipes? By them not killing Snipes they got information on all of us, Mo'Najah, Goldman, you and me!"

"Plus the cash." Sheed finished my sentence.

WEDNESDAY...

Paper Cha$in'
Sheed

With all of the crap that was goin' on in the family, I had to stay focused. Being distracted would only mess up my paper. Sitting at the head of the table with a 80/20 split with Haneef is a come up I never imagined. Parts of me was glad that Mo'Najah made her position clear. Haneef on the other hand was not letting her go so easily. Conversations like this had me ready to say fuck it.

"Sheed, I wanted to call you and apologize for how I been trippin' lately. I know I ain't making this shit no easier on you. But I finally got to talk Mo'Najah. There is still a chance I can fix this shit, but I'm really gonna need your help."

"Look, Haneef, I really don't want to get involved with all of that bullshit. This paper is all that moves me right now. You and Mo's personal shit...I'm out of it from here on out."

"What? Nigga, I'm telling you I need your fuckin' help to get my wife back and you turning your back on me? Dawg, if it was not for me, there would be no money for you to focus on. I built the shit you maintaining and you flippin' on me?"

"Haneef, I don't owe you shit man, but my loyalty as a brother and friend. I'm not getting involved with your personal bullshit with these females, Mo'Najah, Tanya, Lu-Lu, Tena, Ada, Chocolate and C.O. chick the list can go on forever. I got enough shit on my plate. I can't delegate mines, so you're gonna have to deal with yours. When was the last time you asked about me, my girl and my kid that's on the way? Since you have been locked up bro, I have been able to manufacture a life other than drugs, drama, and dollars."

I guess you can imagine how the rest of that conversation went. But one thing about Haneef when he wants something done one monkey don't stop no fuckin' show. Haneef will have a broad he fuckin' bake another bitch a birthday cake. You may call it 'GrimmiE' I call it 'Pimp Shit'.

After I touched base with Benny D, my trip to Miami was a go. My money was right my team had fallen off a bit, but I was good, "less is more", ain't that what Jigga sayin' these days. Mario was holdin' down the fort and picking up the slack from Rell and Remmy.

"Mario, I really need you to be on point for this Miami trip. This shit is too big for us to fuck up."

"Sheed, trust, I got you. Everything will go just as planned. Stop stressing so much, man. How many times did you and Haneef make this exact same trip?"

"That's not the point. You can never be too safe. That was something your sister used to drill into my head."

"Sheed, you really need to settle the beef between you and Mo' Najah."

"Mario, even if I wanted to, I think it's too far gone. Don't get it twisted, I got mad love for your sister. At times I wished I had a woman like Mo'Money to hold me down. But I would never cross Hanz like that. Nothing and nobody comes between the brothers. Kalief was my dude, and I promised him I would look out. A man in today's society already ain't got shit. My word, pistol, and my paper, are all I got left."

"You know she is getting into the game full time?"

"Yeah, she told me that night when I got the number for the connect that she was gonna out-hustle me."

"Wow, really, she told you up front?"

"Mo'Money is a lot of things, but sneaky ain't one of them. If she wants to hurt you, you will know it's her that is hurting you."

"Do you think that's gonna be a problem Sheed?"

"Listen, I was hustlin' while Mo' was in diapers. It's free enterprise out here. I don't own the streets. I'm gonna get my money regardless. Mo' can make moves, but she knows the code. We have dealt with enough disrespectful-ass niggas out here for her to know how to conduct her shit."

If Philly in August was hot Miami was the pit fires of hell. Fuck a palm tree and blue water. My ass was baking, big boy hot, thighs moist and the sweat dripped from under my man boobs. Shit if I could sit in the airport and handle this transaction I would. Walking to the rental was a fuckin heat stroke waiting to happen.

Benny still had the bakery. But things had changed a lot in the past few years. When we arrived at the bakery we were given directions to a shipping and receiving warehouse, an hour away. We did not meet with the Benny's, Haneef's attorney George Irvington III greeted us as we got into the lot.

"Benny sends his regards. He has missed conducting business with Hanz' and has a gift for Mo'Najah, successfully completing her test as he knows she will. Mario you are her blood brother is that correct? Irvington asked from the driver's seat of the 2013 Aston Martin V8 Vantage Roadster convertible that he was driving with the speed and precision of a Nascar driver.

"Yes that is my baby sister, is it cool if I call you Irv?"

"No, my name is Irvington, address me as such. I do not normally handle Diaz 'family business'. This is an exception because of the problems Ms. Mo'Najah is having. Benny has sent his personal bodyguard to Philadelphia to ensure that not one hair on her head gets touched again! Also to display to Haneef that his loyalty was not in vain.

When we pulled up to law firm you will both have to walk through medal detectors. Just bring your money."

As we walked behind Irvington I don't know if I should be impressed with the power Benny has or scared that he knows so much. Mo' did tell me that they had gotten close. Damn, with friends like him I too would feel sorry for my enemies.

Irvington reached into his desk and pulled out a thin, black velour box and handed it to Mario. He then reached into his sport jacket and handed me a room key.

"300 thousand I said looking this I.V. league educated mouth piece in the eye."

"More than Haneef spent I like that." Irvington replied with a chuckle.

I took it as sarcasm knowing this faggot would never get his hands dirty doing anything other than counting the money I would die for.

"Price for you Mr. Anderson is 23 and 27 a key which is significantly less. But I am sure you're aware of that, if not you boys would not have come all this way."

"Eight and four should put me close."

"Eight is 184 and four is 108, 292 to be exact. Irvington says while removing this Oakly shades from his forehead."

The money is wrapped in increments of five thousand. Which was stacked inside of empty text books. To clear airport security (still fiction). Pulling out three books I removed eight stacks and gave him the rest.

"Your rental car will be at that hotel, parked on the 4th floor. Your order will be in that room when you arrive. Gentlemen I think our business is done. If you have any problems please call me. Safe travels Shawn, Mario."

Extending a soft, small well-manicured hand. We bid farewell to the mouth piece.

Money
Moet

My life was hurricane Katrina, dead bodies, and botched investigations. No one had any answers, only more questions. One thing I had learned was that hate was a powerful and timeless emotion. If you hated someone ten years ago and the opportunity to display that hate came around. Many of us would take it, even me.

Sheed was in no position to handle all that was happening. Haneef was trying so hard to conceal his own bullshit that he would only tell me half the truth. So that meant I needed someone who would look out for me; right, wrong or indifferent. I made a call to Latham and sent a message to Benny.

"Rocc will remove everything and anything that has the potential to be harmful. Even if it's family Mo'Najah." Was the warning that came with the number Latham had given me.

"Right now I don't have a choice. I can't second guess what direction the next wave of shit is coming from. Thanks Detective."

My next call was about money. I had not made a dollar since the incident at the jail. Sitting on so much product I needed a new team. Who better to get this money with but my Bestie and my down as bitch Buddah.

"China, are you sure this dude can be trusted?"

"Mo', you told me to hire a team. I may not have your knowledge of the game, but I have fucked enough hustlers and killers to know who is certified and who is bitch approved. Trust, these cats will ride hard for this paper and they will keep their mouths closed. As long as they are compensated for their work, you have their loyalty."

"I can respect that China, I just have never run shit from the sidelines. I'm used to everyone knowing where the orders and the bullets are coming from."

"Mo'Najah, we both know you got too much to lose. So let's keep the plan the same. You're the silent partner of the operation. I will run the day to day. All of your old people will deal with me directly, with the exception of Buddah."

"Cool. Buddah has already set up in three key areas around the southeast and the Germantown areas. She deals with only you, China, in my absence, not Ibn or Black. I need the government names of the other five workers. Your dude Black, has to be on point at all times. If my dudes think he slow or can't keep up with their flow, they will attempt to run game. My crew can smell weakness and will take advantage of any sign that your boi' ain't official."

"Glad to hear dat, Black is a beast in the streets. He has been home for eighteen months and just took his last piss test. Starting at the top is just where Black is supposed to be."

"If he was in Rahway for five years, how do you know so much about him China?"

"Black is Ibn's older brother, so he comes highly recommended."

"When my money comes back, I will be the judge of that. If shit don't come back right, be prepared to buy him and his brother matching coffins. If I can't find these criminals on paper, they already fired."

"Mo', handle your end and I will handle mines."

"Buddah and my road crew will be back by dinnertime. Let your boys know it's time to clock in."

Black, Hawgie, Ross, Storm, and Pretty Boy…those were the five ruthless ride or die motherfuckers China had put together. They had street knowledge, muscle, and pure fuckin' recklessness, not to mention Storm, was a computer geek.

Part two to covering my ass was to have all team members in a car that I could locate and on a phone that I had cleared through a new cellular company call Touch Me. Touch Me gave you original numbers and put you on government signals. Not your standard frequencies and satellites transmited from companies such as AT&T and Sprint used. Trust your congressman and senator don't worry about what they say over the phone. Neither should I. (This is fiction lol.)

There were eight cars at Mike "The Magician" shop. Mike did everything, from hidden cameras to bulletproofing. There were even explosives with detonators in four of the vehicles. Each car had live streaming video with sensors in the seats to my personal i-Pad. When you made love to the game, getting fucked by the players went without sayin'. Details about the cars only China and I knew.

One of the key elements to being a silent partner was watching everyone. With my recent issues I did not tell China or Buddah that I was a moving target. I had one more part to my test to take. I needed another 2.5 mil in that account in Cuba and they could have this shit.

Next was Buddah who had started to work the stash I already had. I had her meet me in the parking lot of the police station downtown.

"Mo'Money, shit is poppin' already ma. I know you want to set up new areas, but when the money is willing to come to us, I gotta grab it."

"I trust your judgment Buddah, that is why you're running things on this end. Do your thang, let's get this paper. I will be leaving on Friday. My phone will be on 'til about 6 p.m. After that, I won't be available 'til I get back Sunday morning to take inventory."

"Mo', real talk, this shit here is gonna sell itself. Now the streets know you back. I can put our team in position and just serve on some burger and fries type shit."

"Here is your phone, the keys to a squatter."

"Mo', I have a whip and phone."

"Learn to follow directions Buddah. Everything is done with a purpose and a plan. What kind of protection you got?"

"It ain't latex, Mo'! Trust, I don't do naked in the streets. Ya' girl is always strapped, locked, and ready to rock."

"If you need something clean or concealed, call China, she can set you up. Buddah, this ain't *The Wire*, this shit here is reality TV. Follow the directions and I can cover your ass all the way around the board. Do you own thing and I might not be able to save you."

"Chief, Indian, I get it, Mo'."

My phone rang. "Mario, I'm very busy today."

"Mo', I really need to holla at you."

"Talk then, you got my ear."

"Nah, not over the phone, I need to speak to you in person. Can I stop past?"

"No, Mario, I will meet you at the house at two Thursday, but I'm in a rush, so don't be on CP time. I have to pick up China's girls and Lil Neef to run some errands and I have to be at the club early (I lied), so I have a full day. Can it wait 'til Monday, Mario?"

"No! Mo'Najah, it's really important. I will see you asap."

Everything in my body was telling me that this was about business. Sheed and his package arrived back from Miami safely. He was still using one of the same stash spots. Enemy or ally, I had to know where all the players in the game were. Knowing Sheed's movements was money well-spent, especially since I had taken 25% of his customer base, not to mention sixteen soldiers. This was about money, not friendship or loyalties. Money was thicker than blood. I learned that shit from the woman that birthed me.

Thursday...

Play Your Position
Lamar

"Mar, I will be there on time. Just relax babe, I know how important this weekend is for you. I would not miss it for the world. You're nervous; I think it's cute."

"Mo'Najah, I just want to hold you. Life is so serene when you are here with me."

"I take the last part of my test tomorrow. I have some papers I need to get in order for the loan officer. I promised Lil Neef that I would take him shopping, so I figured I might as well take my goddaughters also. By Friday, I will be with you in Atlantic City. As a matter of fact, how about I call and reserve two spots at the Red Door spa? Will my car be ready by then?"

"Yes, actually, you can see the repairs online. I will send you the link. I also took the liberty of adding a few small enhancements to your already-plush ride to express how truly sorry I am that your whip got trashed while you were here."

"No problem babe, accidents happen."

"Thank you Mo'Najah."

"For what Mar?"

"For creating this feeling that is so deep and so indescribable that I wonder sometimes if you are real."

"Not only am I real, but tangible, edible, and so horny."

"Babe, that is Menace on my other line, I have to take this."

"L, what's good, I just got your message."

"Listen, I canceled all appearances for you for the next two days. I don't want anything to go wrong between now and Saturday. In fact, I want your name on everybody's lips. So lay low: no parties, no strip clubs, just be real still for the next forty-eight hours. Alashia will be out doing some cameo appearances promoting the single. People will be looking for you to show up. Your presence will be felt through her. Everything looks good. I don't need to remind you to be razor-sharp: nails, beard done, everything. The spotlight is yours baby boi."

"Yo! L, there is something I needed to holla at you about."

"What's good Menace?"

There was a silence on the phone. "Not that it's any of my business, but I want to know what's up with you and Zylar? I asked her to be my guest for my big night."

"Look, it's your night, do you man. I know you and Zylar go way back. She loves you like a brother. No heads up needed. I am moving on and I want her to find the same happiness."

"L, are you sure?"

"Menace, Zylar is a non-factor. We are not beefin'. There is no malice or animosity; we are adults."

"Cool. Saturday is gonna be 'TURNT UP'. None of this would be possible if it were not for you."

"Menace, you made your success possible with your talent, tenacity, and perseverance. This is your spotlight, not mines."

Friend
Zylar

I listened to the message on my voicemail, contemplating my choices. I had hoped that one of them was from Lamar, most of them were about the wedding getting canceled. Deposits that would not be refunded and things of that nature. The last one was from Menace aka Maurice Talson.

"Zylar Taylor Wingate, if you make me come personally escort you to the 40/40, I will. Woman, you pushed, screamed, and motivated me when I had given up on myself. You would scoop-up a nigga' in a cab to take me to open mics and showcases. Your friendship means the world to me. Please, promise you will be there to support me? Zylar, I can tell you're hurting right now, but healing takes time. None of this would have happen if it were not for you. I understand you and Lamar are going through some things, but your personal life has nothing to do with our friendship. Zylar, I have two suites reserved at the Golden Nugget Hotel & Casino. Lamar, is not even staying in the same hotel. Bring your girl Brianna. I got some of my fellas coming through. I get to finally enjoy my hard work, and we are going to celebrate our album release. Everything is on me. I will have my limo driver pick you and your guest up Saturday around noon. Be ready, woman!"

To delete this message press 7 now. I looked at the screen on my HTC phone. I had two days to decide if I was indeed going to attend the album release party. I loved Menace and we had indeed come a long way. I did not have many people I considered friends between him and Brianna the list was rather short. I dialed Brianna's number to beg for her to attend the party with me. Menace would be busy entertaining his guest. Lamar, would be busy networking. I needed someone to chill with that I could laugh at the 'ratched' dressed women with. After the third ring my friend picks up.

"Hey Zy, what's good?"

"Brianna I need a huge favor?"

"What can be bigger than the secret I am already keeping for you Zylar?"

"I need you to be my guest Saturday night at Menace's album release party?"

"Zylar you do know that I am in the middle of an adoption process. Running the streets with you is not conducive to that process love!"

"How about I fly your mother up from Atlanta to get to know her new granddaughter and I will have you back home by 2pm Sunday."

"Let me call my Mom and see if she is available? Zylar you know I love the bad boy, hip hop scene but this is more important."

"Brianna you are still allowed to have a life. I am not telling you to duck your obligations I am only suggesting you get a sitter for one night of fun. Compliments of Juciee Inc."

C.Y.A.
Tanya {Cover Yo Ass}

After the episode at the WaWa, I needed to ensure that my part was done in its entirety. I did not want to find out second hand that she had gone to the hospital and made a miraculous recovery. Thus far my alliance with Kadir had generated twenty four thousand of which I spent two to keep my hands as clean as possible.

It was of no surprise that the top story on the NBC 11 news at 5pm, was the sudden respiratory failure of District Attorney Kathy Petrini. I had patiently sat outside of her office building for hours. With the hopes that an ambulance would be called as she started to experience effects of the drug. After four hours I had started to doubt the results. Wondering had she actually consumed the toxic drink with so many unknowns. I began to doubt my plans success. Plotting my next move I knew Kadir would not rest until his dirty deed had been done.

Satisfied with the broadcast that confirmed the death of the cities D.A., I plotted my plan to retrieve the surveillance tape from the WaWa. Not wanting anything to link me to being one of the last people to make contact with D.A. Petrini.

Everyone was always looking to save a dollar on their internet provider. So I came up with the idea of offering them a higher speed and better service for less money than they were currently paying. However the clerk at the store was in no position to make those decisions, as he furnished me with the owners name and contact info. Blowing the dust off of my MacBook Pro and Brothers printer, I found a program on my laptop that would aide me in fabricating an invoice. Figuring if the owner was not there to dispute the service the clerk would graciously allow me access.

Next stop was to Wal-Mart where I purchased a blue Dickie two piece work uniform. As I found patches that would look almost identical to the ones the Comcast workers wore. With that my plan was set for the following morning. I would simply accidentally erase the tape or I would down load a virus to cause the entire system to crash. Either way there would be no data of me ever entering the store.

Imagine my surprise as I arrived at the store a little after 9am the following morning to see the entire front of the store being board up. The large window pane was missing.

"What happened?" I asked the clerk genuinely interested.

"I guess you can say we had a robbery sometime last night."

"What do you mean you guess?"

"Two men entered the store last night, sprayed mace at the night time clerk and pistol whipped the security guard. The only thing they took was the computer system from the office and a 1999 VHS recorder."

As I slowly walked from the store, my mind already knew who and why the store had been vandalize.

Kadir!

Friday...

Last Lap
Mo'Najah

After completing the final part of my GED test, I felt as if a weight had been lifted. My head was pounding, but I knew that I did my best as I left the classroom. The woman that administered the test handed me a note to report to the main office. When I arrived, there were two dozen long-stemmed red and white roses sitting on the desk. The room was dreary, to say the least, but the floral arrangement commanded your attention.

"Nice flowers. I was asked to stop here?"

"Ms. Harrison, there are 2600 students and 300 faculty members here, but someone sent you these," she stated, holding the flowers in my direction.

My smile was bright and broad; every tooth in my mouth had to be showing.

"Girl, take these, I am already jealous," the secretary said. "Mo'Najah, does he have a brother? My husband ain't sent me nothin' in over a year, good for nothing-ass nappy-headed man!"

Looking at the clock on the wall, I saw that I had less than an hour to meet Mario at the house. "Thank you!" I said as I rushed out of the office and across the campus, grinning from ear to ear. Not one person that passed me could help but compliment me on my flowers. I couldn't wait to read the card Lamar had sent.

With my Alexander Wang backpack over the left shoulder and flowers in my right hand, I clicked the unlock button twice to open all the doors to the Land Rover. After throwing my belonging into the backseat, I grabbed the seatbelt from the passenger side, attempting to secure the black and white vase. I quickly pulled the card from the flowers.

CONGRATULATIONS I'M SO PROUD OF YOU, THE BEST IS YET TO COME!

No signature, no name, not one clue to tell me who possibly sent me these. If they were addressed to Moet, I would know they were from Haneef or Neko. Mo'Najah it would have to be Lamar. I would hate to thank the wrong person. China had agreed to meet me at the mall with the girls. I could grab Lil Neef on the way. I had no time for secret admirers, not today. Fuck it; I would just wait 'til someone asked me about the damn flowers.

When I arrived at Haneef's house, there were balloons and a box sitting outside the gate. Looking around, the block seemed to be filled with the usual cars and traffic, with the exception of a vanilla-almond-colored car with tinted windows about twenty feet away, which caused no alarm at this time of day. I pressed the key code to the gate from within the car, exiting the vehicle so I could retrieve the balloons and the box. To my surprise, it was rather light. Haneef was known to be elaborate and gaudy with gifts. *Maybe he is getting the message after all*, I thought.

Just as I lifted the box to return to the truck, the vanilla car was driving in reverse with the windows down, blasting Tanks "Please Don't Go". Once the car was in front of the house, Mario exited the vehicle smiling like he just won the Mega Millions or some shit.

"Who's car do you have? Why are you blasting that music so loud? You know my fuckin' neighbors don't play that hood shit."

"Mo', the car is yours!"

"That's a coffin or an FBI investigation, take your pick. Who in their right mind would drive around with a price tag on their forehead?"

"Don't shoot the messenger. I was told to deliver the car and this," my older brother said while holding out a black velvet box.

"This is from Mr. Benny D. Can you open it I have been dying to see what a motherfucker wit' dat much money would buy as a present?"

"Why would Benny send me a car and jewelry?"

"No, no, no the car, balloons and this ring are from Haneef. The little black box is from Benny, he gave it to me when Sheed and I went to Miami."

I was speechless and motionless. All these fucking years and he was still Haneef's flunky. I should shoot his ass and save my mother the shame of having a bitch for a son.

"Either you're trying to get me wet up or you trying to get me set up. Either way, I'm not beat. Tell your boy - "

Before I could finish the statement, Mario's cellular phone rang. He handed me the phone.

"Mo' babe, can you hear me?"

"Yes, Hanz, you're on speaker."

"Will you marry me? Mario, give her the ring please."

"What?"

"Mo'Najah, I need you in my life, by my side. I promise I will change. Like the song says, 'Please don't go'. I know I fucked up. I will be honest about everything and anything."

"Do you hear yourself, Haneef? You're a federally mandated fuckin' prisoner for another fifteen years. Do I look slow, stupid, or just desperate? Maybe you have me confused with Maria!"

"Mo', what the hell are you talking about?"

"I'm not a little fuckin' girl anymore. I can't be brought, bullied or passed around like a toy. In my heart, I thought I was sparing your feelings. But it just came to me the only things you understand are PAPER, PUSSY, and POWER, followed by PAYNE. Love is not supposed to devastate or destroy. Love leaves you with dignity and respect. I guess you have not learned how to love yet. I don't want shit to do with you! I moved out of this fucking house. You don't own me, you own my mother, and by the looks of it, my brother also. By the way, I am in a relationship with real man, so the answer to your proposal, just so we're clear, is NO. I don't want your car, ring, or apologies, because they are not sincere or genuine. You need someone to control or manipulate. Start with Tanya, then bounce to the CO bitch, then trickle down to the mother of your daughter that lives less than thirty minutes away. I would go get the folder of all the other random one night stands you have had from Club Onyx to Night On Broad, but it really does not matter. All of those things you did then and now, Haneef, I allowed them to happen. You have succeeded in teaching me one very valuable lesson. Because of you, I know a man when I see one and can recognize a fraud from a mile away. All of my numbers will be changed within the hour". Call terminated.

"Mario, why are you doin all of this?"

"Because I am your brother, I don't want anything to happen to you and I want you to be happy."

"Better late than never I guess, but being Haneef's fuckin' puppet is not going to make me happy."

"Damn, that was a lifetime ago, Mo', and you're still rubbing that shit in my face. How come, you can forgive the man that gave you the STD. But you hold malice towards me just because I was holding the camera?"

"Mario, I can forgive anything. My faith has taught me that I have to in order to grow. But forgetting is just not something I have learned how to do."

"Mo'Najah, you really don't understand what it's like to be man. There are things men expect from one another. There are unspoken rules just because you're born with a dick, and just like they say, there is honor amongst thieves. There is one amongst hustlers, killers, and bitch-ass niggers also. Haneef and Sheed, they were the nigga's to fuck wit'. They kept the baddest bitches around and the best product. Back then, being in the circle meant more to me than air. So yes, I kept a lot of their secrets from you. Damn, I was a kid! It took for Hanz to get locked up for me to realize how independent and strong you have become. Fuck being like them! The last few years, I have gained so much respect and admiration for my little sister that I have a new respect for women. Mo', I'm sorry for not telling you what Haneef was about back then, but he was paying all of our bills. I honestly thought you would still be with him either way, so why jeopardize my chance at getting the brass ring? As your brother, I had an obligation back then. I failed, I'm sorry, but I won't betray you again Mo'. We have all grown up. I can tell you now, family is more important than money. I'm asking for your forgiveness?"

"Mario, you hurt me. When I found out about all those girls, when I saw the video, it amazed me that my brother, my blood, the same brother that taught me how to tie my shoes, would let me be so stupid. Even the dumbest female deserves a warning. Haneef could have given me anything. You just sat by and kept quiet. I had to learn about the tape from Tanya."

"You're right, Mo'Najah, but you forgave him. It took some time, but you forgave him. Why can't you forgive me?"

"Mario, I forgave you a very long time ago. That is why there is so much space between us all. My entire family from my mother to my brother chose money over blood. Time has healed the hurt, but it has not done shit to my memory. I will always love you. But if you really want me to trust you again, your actions speak louder than your words."

Right then we both stood watery-eyed. Parts of me wanted my brother back. It was so hard being in this game and not being able to trust a soul. But I would test him. That was just to be on the safe side. How much thicker was blood than money?

"Mario, I don't care what Haneef tells people. Sometimes it is better to leave on bad terms. That way, you don't have to worry about trying to stay friends, holding on to something you were meant to be let go of. Haneef will always be my first love, but I have to learn how to live for me. Living without him has been difficult, but everything in the past twenty-eight months has been hard. Sheed and I got close, but if his loyalty interferes with our friendship, so be it. I don't need to worry about who will tell Haneef what. I just want to live my life. Matter of fact, here are the spare keys to the barbershop and the after-hours. I will have to get the ones to the detail shop; they are in the safe. You can have the ring the car and the balloons. I am done."

"If you need me, I will be here. Mo', I love you. Your dad would be so proud of how you turned out to be such a classy woman."

"Okay, now that we are done with the Lifetime moment, I have to go. I promised my son a shopping trip."

When I arrived at Momma M's crib to scoop-up Lil Neef, there were more balloons and flowers even a congratulations cake with a diploma on it. I plastered the smile on my face and accepted the dysfunctional family I had grown to love. Before we could cut the cake someone knocked on the door. Lil Neef rushed to open it.

"Grandmom it's the man from the gas company."

"Hello my mother is busy how can I help you?" I said standing behind Haneef Jr.

"Good afternoon ma'am there has been a gas leak reported in the area. I am here to do a basic check on the furnace and the connectors that run from the street to the house."

"May I see your work order?" I asked not knowing what PGW work order form actually looked like but the van was definitely official. Before I could move out of the way of the front door Sheed walks up behind me.

"Hey Mo' what's going on?"

"Something with the gas lines can you take him down stairs?"

"Neef, grab some cake for Milan and Najah and let's go I will be in the car."

Momma M was two steps ahead of us as Lil Neef, walked out the front door with a plate that was securely wrapped in aluminum foil. Once Haneef junior got into the rental car he secured his seat belt. Looked around the car crossed his retro 3 Jordan sneakers. Looked me dead in my eye and said.

"Mo' I need a loan!"

"What?"

"I need a loan to help my mom get her surgery."

"I wrote my Dad this letter, but I already know the money comes through you. But I promise to pay it back when I turn 21, Mo'. Don't think of it as you helping my Mom. It's really for me, I feel guilty because I know all of that happened because of the Wise situation."

"Here is your father's new address. You send him this letter he should know what a great son he has raised. When I get back from my trip I will bring you the money you need."

Evolution
Lamar

Business before pleasure. Mo'Najah had given me a phenomenal idea about hosting a pool party. As we sat and discussed, talented artist that would perform for her charity event. She reminded me of all the people that I knew that would work or perform for pennies just to be on the stage with one head liner either Tatia P or Menace. My projections for the "Juicee and Wet swimsuit party" were mind blowing. Devin, created a mockup of the income potential all based off the numbers from previous events. Charts, power point slide show I was beyond prepared. I had gotten some celebrities to volunteer for a small yet intimate fashion show. Local but popular DJ Fah D to keep the crowd hyped. Up and coming designers to donate their talent and time. One Pure Blend being the main attraction. Just to have the opportunity to get notoriety and exposure of a star studded audience most people would donate not just time but their talent. My confidence was on high right now. I was rushing through the NJ turnpike traffic headed to the shore for my 1 p.m. meeting with the food and beverage director at Harrah's Entertainment.

Mo'Najah's Acura was a smooth ride, the repairs were so meticulous. If I did not have photos of before and after I would not believe the damage was ever done they were even able to match her custom metallic blue paint. I made it to Atlantic City in one hour and forty minutes.

I valet-parked the car and had my luggage sent to the room while the bellman pointed me in the direction of

Conference Hall B, which was where my meeting was being held. Laptop, projection equipment, and papers were all in tow. I arrived about a half hour early, which gave me time to order some refreshments and set the stage for my presentation. The meeting lasted forty-five minutes.

"We will have the contracts ready for you to sign before you check out Sunday, Mr. James."

Now I could spend the rest of the night pampering my princess. So what do you buy a woman who can afford anything she wants? You flood her with romance. Exotic flowers that you can never pronounce the name of, without the florist being right beside you. You do the running man in a G-string and timberland boots just so she knows how crazy you are about her. You find a way to make every moment you are in her presence priceless.

I never knew my heart could feel this way. When she told me "Mar, I feel safe when I am with you." That is the most sincere compliment a woman as ever given me. Not is she only physically secure, but emotionally at peace. When you have a woman's trust you have the keys to her heart. Nothing is more valuable than that.

Just that quickly my mind drifts to Brianna and Devin, my ideal couple. Secretly I had always admired their kindred connection. A love so deep it had evolved from college sweethearts to a lifelong commitment. My Mom would tell me I would need nothing else when the right one came along. I guess she knew what she was saying. I hope that my best friend figures out his mistake before someone else finds his precious partner. Snapped back to reality as her text message made my hip tingle.

My train arrives in Atlantic City@4:52pm

I had two and a half hours to get my night of seduction together. Tonight I needed, wanted, and would be engulfed within this woman. Mo'Najah had complemented, elevated, and consumed my spirit and imagination. Work did not seem to leave me stressed and fatigued. Even my artists had noticed a change in my mood and my attitude.

I had made plans to take her and my parents on a little trip to the Dominican Republic. My mother would love her, fatten her up a bit, but adore her nonetheless. Thoughts of Zylar were oddly nonexistent until she called or emailed. Lately I had come to the realization that I was going to marry Zy because I was supposed to. But Ms. Harrison would make a brother throw his player card into the pits of hell, never looking back with no remorse on the hearts or toes crushed in the process.

Mo'Najah's thought process is nothing short of a CEO, she analyzed everything. If I had something troubling me at work. I used her as a sounding board. She made the solution seem like basic addition. As she processed the situation her insight was totally neutral and unbiased. She looked at everything as if it were a hustle. Price, product, profitability and potential market if you could make people buy it, at the price that made you money then it was worth doing. If not leave it alone.

Nothing in my life had felt this real or so dreamlike, my life was a constant contradiction. I couldn't fathom anything making her less perfect. It was bizarre as hell. Wrong or right, good or bad, I chose Mo'Najah. Every day was a better day because I had her to talk to. There was no fear in loving her; my heart had no restrictions. Flaws and all, she was all that I needed and more than I could have prayed for.

Blood $
Tanya

The annoying sound of my alarm shattered what sleep I was able to find. The time read 7:45am. I had to drop the kids off at camp and make my 10am appointment on time. As I swung my perfectly pedicure toes to the floor. The bottle of Percocet's sat center stage on my dresser. As much as I wanted to believe I did not need to take them I could not resist the urge. I took a pill from the bottle and swallowed it dry. Grabbed my robe from out of the closet, I proceeded to get the kids ready. Lil Neef was already awoke with the X-Box controller in his hand and the head set attached to his face. Half eaten bowl of captian crunch on the floor. Taliah the Princess was still sleep. Half way off her full size canopy bed. Drooling and snoring like she had a fuckin' job.

Today was my consultation for my surgery. I had more than 25 thousand stashed in that safe in my basement. Today I would leave a cash deposit with the physician handling my surgery. When I entered the office on Chestnut I was depressed, but excited. What if the surgery was not a success? What if something went wrong and I never woke up after the anesthesiologist put me under? What if my life never would go back to the way it was before? I had question after question attacking my mental.

"Doctor Shakim, will see you now." Stated the Barbie doll look alike receptionist. Her blonde hair dangling down the small of her back, bright blue eyes and perfectly straight white teeth. If Barbie had a voice it very well could match hers.

"September the 11th at 9:30 am I will meet you in general admission at Hannahman Hospital. I will set it up with the hospital that I get billed personally. Go to this address for your pre-admission testing and follow the orders to the letter before the procedure. See you in two weeks Ms. Thompson."

Too Bad to be Good
Devin

Six of the eight boys that were mentored in Juicee in the Hood attended the trip. Bryon and I were the only counselors on this mission. Byron Brandon was a bachelor doing an internship at Juicee. His role here was out of obligation, not dedication. The boys looked up to Byron, strangely enough. He was young, successful, had a nice car and a lot of females. The brother could ball a bit too. Each young man was required to bring basic camping needs: sleeping bag, flashlight, and hygiene products.

The trip's mission was to remove the boys from their natural habitat, make them rely on one another as a unit to build awareness and strength as a team. It was also to make them more appreciative of the luxuries their mothers were working so hard to provide. For me, this trip was an escape: no wife, no business, no drama, just fresh air and simplicity.

Byron was assigned three boys: Mikal (age 15), R.J (age 14), and Daniel (age 13). My group was composed of Kaliem (age 14), Jovon (age 15) and Asmar (age 16). Once we arrived at Hunter Mountain, each group had a task. My group was to set up sleeping quarters, store water, and chop firewood. Byron and his crew were going to fish for dinner. My squad was weak. They were already wandering off, bickering and bullshitting.

"Asmar, I'm gonna need you to unpack the three tents from the van. Jovon and Kaliem, unload the cooler and get the water jugs. The quicker we set up the tents and get the fire started, the quicker you guys can have some freedom. But right now we need to get started on sleeping quarters."

Asmar was 5'10", big for no damn reason. He was not interested in sports, music, or girls, but he was very technical and loved computers and games. Jovon was the lil' pimp of the group. If I left them alone, he would somehow manage to convince the other boys to do his portion of the work. Kaliem...he was the one who tried to make everyone happy, my peacemaker, the problem solver. But he was solid, strong as a horse. I had yet to see him snap out, but I was sure there was a beast inside of that small giant.

"Counselor D, why don't we put the tents together and the other boys can get started on the other stuff?"

"Sounds good Asmar, but I don't want us to separate. Plus I want all of you guys to experience putting together a tent. So we will put together two of them then show the other team when they return. Let's do the big one first."

It was a 10x18 Field and Stream estate dome tent. I already read the directions before we got here. It took all four of us about twenty-five minutes to set it up. The boys were very proud of their work. The second tent was child's play compared to the first. The other two tents were North Face four-person dock tents. Lamar spared no expense when it came to organizing and financing this trip. Everything was top of the line and organized. I knew he wished he could be here with the kids this weekend. Lamar, lived for stuff like this.

"Kaliem, I need a huge favor. I need a cameraman for this trip. This is a $500 Nikon camera. Can you handle that?"

"Nah, Counselor D, I think Asmar would make a better camera guy. I don't like taking pictures, or maybe Jovon. He got mad girls' pictures on his Facebook page."

"Counselor D, if I take the flicks for the group, can I avoid all of this manual labor? I just got my nails done before I left," Jovon said from five feet away while admiring his fingertips.

"Boy, you keep it up and you will do double work and take the pictures."

"You got played!" Asmar screamed in Jovon's face as all of us started to laugh.

Retrieving both of the axes from the van, the boys and I walked over to where the logs had been left for us to split. Bryon and his group were walking back to camp with ten fish on a hook. Asmar and Kaliem showed Bryon and the other boys how to set up the last tent. We all learned how to clean and cook fish, compliments of Counselor Bryon.

Missing Him
Mo'Najah

As I stepped foot outside of the Atlantic City rail station, I saw that there were several cabs waiting, but there was one private car with a driver holding a sign with my name on it. Damn, this man thought of everything! I handed the driver my two-piece Versace luggage and climbed into the rear of the Lincoln Town Car.

"Mr. James arranged your pickup, Ms. Harrison."

There was something different about this entire trip. My stomach had been doing flips since I boarded the Aces express train to AC. I had checked in with everyone from Buddah to Maria. After forty-five minutes on the train, I called and got my phone number changed. For once, I wanted to know what it felt like to be free. That wouldn't happen on this trip. Haneef made it his business to call me from a secure line to have the final say in our discussion. I couldn't afford to take his threats lightly.

"Bitch, I've buried men and their families for betraying me. I'll spend the rest of my life in jail before I let another nigga have you. Talk that slick shit, Moet, but laugh now, cry later. I'm locked up, not boxed up. Your little man friend is in the fuckin' way, know dat. 'Til death do us part."

One thing for sure, two things for certain…Hanz's money, power, and connections reached far and deep. The wrong word in the right ear could easily have me wearing black tomorrow. But he couldn't hurt who he did not know. I didn't fear Hanz. Death would only end the misery, sorrow, and disrespect that I had endured my entire adult life. Between him and my mother, death might actually be a come up.

The driver opened my door and the bellman took my luggage. "Your room key, Ms. Harrison. You're in the water tower – the first left then the second right."

I handed the driver a $20 bill, that he respectfully declined. "My services have been taken care of already, thank you."

To hell with Haneef, the game, and all this drama. There was a gorgeous, intelligent, and caring man upstairs waiting on me, and I was stressing over shit I couldn't control. Mar and I could talk about my issues on Sunday morning over mimosas by the pool.

The hallway to the room was like two miles long. When I put the electronic key into the door, my senses were met with the pleasant smell of hazelnut. As I entered the room, there was a note on the bar to my right with a candle burning beside it, making it rather hard to walk past. My smile and my spirits had gone from misery to amazed.

The room was phenomenal. As I peeked into the living room area, I saw that there were two massage tables set up with little waterfalls and candles. The note read:

I have finally met a woman that makes me want to love and feel from my soul, not just my pocket. Tonight I do things I have never before thought I would do. This is how I know that I love you. Please use the bathroom behind you to change in.

Love,
Mar

Ms. Boss
China

"China, where the fuck are you?"

"Ibn, stop screaming in my damn ear. I'm headed to Camden to meet Black. I should be arriving at my pick up in less than fifteen minutes."

"What the fuck are you doing that you have not answered either line in more than three hours?"

"Handling this business! I don't work for Sprint, I can't make no money answering no fucking phones."

"Look babe, I know you're a grown-ass woman, but trust and believe, it don't take long for shit to pop off. I would lose my mind if something happened to my China doll."

"Bad thing is, if something did happen, I still would not be able to get to a damn phone, so bitchin' and whining is not gonna make me answer. But I will try to check in more often. I gotta go, I love you. Later."

I tossed the phone back into my Versace Ltd purse. Damn, I forgot to tell him about Storm and Mike. Hitting exit 5B from the bridge, I was less than five minutes away. When I turned the '09 Altima into the parking lot of McDonald's, there was heavy traffic on Haddon and Federal. Note to self: find another spot to meet.

Digging my phone out of the handbag, I called Ibn back. I was so off-focus when he called bitching and biting that I had left out some important details. "Babe, Storm should be calling you within an hour doing a drive by. Mike called and said he was knee-deep in some pussy, but he is sending the Camry with the tall Russian bunny. Her name is Sasha. By the way the, Camry is fully-loaded, I just need you to deliver it."

"Who gets the car, Storm?"

"No, after I meet Black for his drive by, he gets the newer whip. When I meet you at the check cashing, I should have 175 stacks and you should have 50.

Babe, I need to call Black, I have been sitting here for ten minutes."

Before I could press the end button on the phone, the driver's side of the Altima was rammed by a black Ford F-150 with a chrome crash bar, sending the car sideways into the parked car next to me. Sittin' fuckin' duck...are you serious? My nose was bloody from impact. My face hit the steering wheel.

The passenger and the driver of the truck got out, both holding Berettas, wearing army fatigues and black shirts with ski masks covering their faces. The tall one began to shoot at the windows of the Altima. Realizing the glass was bulletproof, they then began to fire at the doors of the car.

Inside this car was about $50,000 in drugs and pills. Moet getting our primary cars presidential style was money well spent. However it did not stop me from flinching every time they aimed at my head. I retrieved the 9mm from the compartment inside of the steering wheel and grabbed the stuffed animals that held the drugs, pushing everything into a backpack. My heart was pounding so fast. I didn't how the fuck I was gonna get outta this damn car. The doors were reinforced but damaged so badly that neither of them would open. I couldn't sit and wait for the cops to come rescue my ass.

"Yo! Ram this piggy bank again, make this pussy pop open!" the stocky one yelled to the taller guy, who ran and jumped behind the wheel of the truck.

Once he backed away from the car, the Altima dropped about four inches back to the concrete. I threw the car in reverse and mashed the gas. The wheel was cut from when I pulled into the parking spot, sending the ass end into a concrete divider but making the dude with the gun dive out of the way, losing his weapon in the process.

Reverse was no longer an option. I shifted the car to drive, mowing over the man that had just tried to kill my ass for fifty grand. The front of the car tapped the crash bar of the F-150, barely moving it but trapping his partner under my car. After unloading about five bullets into the floor of the car, I heard screams of agony. My only exit was the sunroof, which made me an easy fucking target. All of these people out here…someone had to have called the police. Music to my ears…police sirens. The dude heard the same shit I did, because he backed that truck up quick as hell. I climbed out of the sunroof just in enough time to get a glance at the plate number. I had to detonate the car. I found the black box that was placed right above the rear wheel well and close to the gas tank. I pressed the button; tossing my gun underneath the vehicle. I turned to run to leave the parking lot, guess who the fuck showed up?

"Black, where the fuck have you been!"

"My bad ma, I was tied up waiting on a few soldiers to come drop off that money."

"Who the fuck are you beefin' with?"

"Even though a nigga late, seems like I got here right on time." Black said with a smirk as if I should be thanking him for showing up.

"We got two good minutes to get away from here; where is your phone?"

"You would not believe the last fifteen minutes Ibn."

"China, where are you? What the fuck was all that chaos in the background?"

"If you stop talking, I can answer your damn questions. These two cats in a black Ford F-150 just tried to rob me. The license plate is MHT13B out of Jersey. I need everything and anything you can find ASAP."

"You need to call Mo'. That shit needs to be handled!"

"I'm not calling that bitch. I will handle this shit myself!"

"China, you don't even know who the fuck tried to rob you. What if they are looking for her also? Don't you think you should at least call her so she knows what's going on?"

"What I need you to do, is get over here. They will be dispatching a coroner and a shit load of police to the scene. Once you find out who the fuck I shot, that could make it a lot easier to find the fucker that got away. I need to get to Mike's for some transportation. Bring me a phone. I will meet you at the safe spot. Love you. Later."

Scorned
Zylar

"Here is the key and the alarm code for the main entrance to Juicee Inc. I am positive that no one will be there tonight."

"Good, all I need is about an hour with his computer. Your boy will not be able to deny any of the allegations that are made against him."

"You do great work. Your confirmation for the money transfer is P5R637v. As long as your girl backs up the emails and sticks to the story, the sexual harassment suit should be simple. The kiddie porn and prostitution will make him look horrible in the public eye. This info leaked to my reporter friend will have Lamar James registering as a sex offender within the week."

"Scandal like this makes men into mice."

"Good, because that is just what Lamar has become, a mouse, running from responsibilities and commitment, playing in trash. The relationship may be over, but revenge lasts a long, long time. Parking is horrible in that area, so you may need to make some arrangements for a quick exit."

Now all I had to do was get back to Charleston before this belly got any bigger. Fighting with my mother daily about my health, not to mention my return, was becoming exhausting. However, this pain, disappointment, and hollowness, won't allow me to just leave. Every night I tried to pray for the strength to let this go, be a better woman, accept that things have changed and walk away without destroying what he worked so hard for. I had not had the urge to sing in months. You know your spirit is crushed when you can't even find harmony within your heart. Hatred ruled my emotions. It was amazing how you could love something so deeply that you could hurt it intentionally without remorse. With the help of the man I only knew as 'Seven' hurting Lamar only scratched the surface of the pain I was feeling every day.

Bonding
Devin

"Counselor Bryon, can I ask you a question?" Kaliem asked from a small pallet on the ground.

"Sure, what's up?" Bryon replied.

"Can a girl get pregnant if you fuck them on their period?"

Bryon almost choked on the Gatorade he was drinking while I thanked God they did not ask me the question. "Yes, Kaliem, it is very possible for a female to get pregnant during her menstrual cycle. Would you like to know why?"

"Nah, I'm good."

"B, I have a question."

"Why is no one asking Counselor D any questions?" Bryon protested.

"Because he is married and corny," Asmar interjected from the other side of the fire.

"Okay, Mikal, what is your question, then I am going to bed?"

"Can a female burn you from sucking your dick?"

"OMG, who are these girls? I never had my dick sucked at thirteen."

The group exploded with laughter.

"Yes, man, the mouth holds the same bacteria and germs as the coochie I mean vagina. Wear a condom at all times, man, or better yet, beat your dick."

"I got a question for Counselor D. What is going to happen to Jared and Jason?"

"Jovon, what are you talking about? The trip was not mandatory. They are still a part of the program."

"Nah, man, they ain't come 'cause they got placed in protective care by the Department of Youth & Family Services. From what I heard, they mom's boyfriend was beating the brakes off them niggas."

"Oh, well I heard dude was on some homo shit, making them jerk his dick and shit," JR added to the conversation.

Blank stares, eight speechless men, all thinking the same thing: what would I do if I were in that position? Personally, I was wondering if any of these young men had been there already. The sound of the fire was the only sound that was heard as we all wondered what Jason and Jared had gone through.

"Let's get the facts first boys, and then we can figure out a solution. But whatever the situation is, know that Jared and Jason are the victims, and as their friends, we need to support them. Before you guys take it down, let me tell you one thing: you can never fix a problem without all the details. Knowing only one side of the story means you only have resolved half the issue. Good night."

"3D, I have a friend that works in the investigations division with youth and family services. Should I make a phone call?"

"Byron, let's get all the ducks in a row before we start aiming at targets."

Saturday...

Light It Up
Sheed

"Don't trip, she is gonna' love you Fatima. She will make you feel bad for waiting so long to come and meet her. But trust, Momma M is the nicest lady you will ever meet, as close to a saint as us sinners get around here."

"Sheed, I have not even met your real mom. What makes Haneef's mother so special? How is Momma Mason so close to you and you rarely talk about your own Mom & Dad? You stuff money in mail boxes and send gift cards for birthdays for your own family. But for Haneef's, the world stops. We are three months away from having our own family. Who will our baby know as Grandma?"

"I don't think you will ever understand but I will try to explain. My Mom's was not an addict, she did not beat us. My mother was a love chaser. Every man that she fell in love with she changed to be everything that man needed. If he did not like kids, she made us disappear. If he only liked me; I got to tag along on an outing. We were always optional in my mother's life. When she found herself alone that was the worse. We were neglected even more as she would lock herself in her room. Men would move in and out of your home at such a rate. We did not bothering remembering their names. My sister and brother raised themselves. But Momma Mason was not having that shit.

~ 183 ~

One time Kalief and I got suspended from school and my mother refused to take me back. Drilling into my head that I was a big, worthless nigga' just like my father. I don't know what Henrietta Mason said to Charlene Anderson. But I was in school the following day. My clothes were clean and I had permission to chill at Kalief's whenever I wanted. I guess I love her so much because she decided to stand-up for me when I could not stand-up for myself."

"That is so sad Sheed, baby I am sorry."

"Sorry for what? I ask grabbing Fatima's hand kissing it. I know what a mother's love is and is not. It ain't got shit to do with the DNA. But don't expect the little grandmother type. She a pistol. We will be on Ruby Street in a second."

"Babe, that is Ruby Street up there and it's blocked off."

"That's strange. I wonder what happened? Let me pull up and we can walk over."

As I approached the two-story row home, nothing in life could have prepared my mind for what I saw. There was yellow caution tape and blue barriers preventing anyone from getting close to the house. Leaving the mother of my child, I ran full speed, praying to the only God I know to not let it be 239. *Please tell me she is okay. I was just here! No, God, please!* Pulling out my ID, I told the cop that this was my mother's house. We all used this address – hustler's code, send everything important to ya mom's crib.

The officer told me that the fire started around 5 a.m. It started at the house next door and spread rather quickly. Right now there were four people in ICU.

"Can you release the names of the injured? My nephew usually stays with my mom on the weekends."

"No, sir, I don't have the names. I was not the officer on call. I am just here 'til the city can send someone to clear up the debris."

"If I go to the station, can they tell me where they were sent to?"

"Let me make a call to the firehouse. After all, you are next of kin, they may be looking for you."

"Do you have any idea of what caused the fire?"

"Sir, I am just here making sure no one gets hurt and sues the city. This is a hazardous area. Let me find out what hospital they were dispatched to." After a minute, he gave me the information. "Temple and Jefferson, but the report does not say who went where sorry that's all I can find out."

180
Menace

Yo, this was gonna be the best night of my fuckin' life! My video was so sick right now. My single was playin' so much that I was sick of hearing my own damn voice. Zylar would be by my side. I would finally get a chance to tell her how much I loved her. If that nigga' Lamar couldn't keep a queen like her, trust, I would be the king she needed. I had been big on this woman for years, but I knew I was not ready to play my position. But now with this recording contract, my album was obnoxious. I had someone wanting to create a clothing line around me. Now was the time to let her see I was the man she needed.

Zylar's voice played in my head. Shorty is BAD! Top of the world, everythings falling into place. From ashy to classy...I know what B.I.G. was feeling. From starving to feeding families...it makes a man humble and appreciative.

Messenger
Haneef

"Mason, when you're done eating, you need to report to the Warden's office!" yelled a rookie CO into the crowded mess hall.

"For what?" I replied.

"Don't know, don't care. Pass is here on the desk when you're done."

Before I entered the warden's office, I got patted down by another Uncle Tom-ass CO. "Someone sent for me. What the fuck are you searching me for?"

Walking into the huge office, I saw the Warden sitting behind his desk, the Chaplain of the jail, and Mrs. Adams, the social services worker.

"Mason, I need you to sit down, son."

Usually I would have blacked all the way out by this cracker calling me son. However, the grim look on everyone's face told me that being called son was the least of my problems. This couldn't be about the phone call yesterday. They would have just sent my black-ass to lock up, hitting me with some new charges. With the recent developments on the home front, I was not prepared for more bullshit, whatever it was.

"Why am I here?" I asked Mrs. Adams.

"Haneef, your legal advisor is on the phone. Goldman are you there?"

"Yes, Mrs. Adams. Is Hanz in the room?"

"Yeah, G, I'm here what's this all about?"

"Hanz, there is no simple way to put this, so I am going to be swift and direct. There was a fire last night at your mother's home on Ruby. She and your son are being treated for smoke inhalation and burns. I have no idea how serious or simple this situation is. I am getting all of the information second hand from Shawn."

"Call the medic!" Mrs. Adams yelled to the officer outside of the room.

Tragedy
Tanya

Thunderous banging on my front door broke my sleep. Followed by the vibration of my cell phone; then more incessant banging. The time on my cell phone read 8:52am. I had to be dreaming. Neither of my children where at home; to answer the door. Groggy from my pills and the Ciroc I had consumed the night before. *What could be so damn urgent?* I thought to myself as I swiped the phone finally aware and awake.

"Tanya, where is Haneef Jr.? Keema asked out of breath and still pounding on my door.

"Keema are you crazy do you see what time it is?"

"Tanya just open the damn door. Did your son stay home this weekend, yes or no?"

"No! He is with his grandmother where he is every weekend Keema from Friday at 7pm until Sunday at 5pm. So why are you bangin on my damn door like a lunatic?"

Keema pushed past me forcing her way into the house. Walking over to the 60in LED television in my living room she grabs the remote turning on the news. Still very confused to why Keema, was in my damn house I began to get impatient. Her silence as she operated the wifi on the television began to make me anxious. Her left leg shock as she pulled up the 8am Fox 4 news on my television. As she scrolled to the previous story that had her, now beating my door of the hinges.

Just as I was about to lose all patience and go completely ballistic on my neighbor. The news caster was standing on the corner of Vine and Ruby street. This was the report.

"Good morning ladies and gentleman, this is Tynetta McCray, reporting live on the scene where a three house fire has claimed the lives of two people and sent four others to local hospital. Authorities have yet to release the names of the victims or the cause of the tragic summer blaze. This close knit neighborhood helped save lives this morning. As they started the rescue before the fire trucks arrived on the scene. Fire Chief Greene is heading a full investigation into the incident. Back to you Jack."

The room started to move sluggardly. My chest started to echo in my ears as the palpitations started. Panic began to consume my consciousness. Reaching for the house phone I call Momma M. Once, twice by the third attempt I hurl the receiver into the adjacent wall screaming aloud. Shattered glass and plastic fragments from the phone scatter around the now silence living room.

"My son is fine, my son is fine. Keema, tell me my son is fine!"

As I found comfort in the wall the tears took over. My body surrendered to the likely hood that my son may not be fine.

"Get my purse and my keys Keema. I gotta see for myself. Hurry up I pleaded with my neighbor for dear life. Please God you can't do this to me. Not my innocent son. God no."

As Keema backed out of the drive way, I find my phone in the bottom of my purse and I send a text message to Kadir's contact person.

   HAVE HIM CALL ME ASAP!!!!

When Keema and I arrived on the scene the police and the Chief of the fire department where on the block. The entire back half of the house where the kitchen and bedrooms are had been completely burned and water logged.

"I am ruling this fire arson" announced the Chief. "The electrical panel has been tampered with. It may have not spread so quickly if Mr. Randolph did not have all of these gas cans and lawn mower equipment. The accelerant only helped the fires momentum."

Replaying this message to Kadir word for word.

"Okay Tanya what would you want me to do?"

"I want you to explain how torching the house of a 58 year old woman is going to be beneficial to our plans?"

"Huh… Torching what and where? I am a business man and I do not work for Allstate. Fire is volatile and unpredictable it has the potential to hurt innocent people. Not my style unless I am clearing a crime scene. At that point nothing there is of value to me dear. Fire is effective but very, very sloppy Tanya. You know King is not sloppy."

"I don't believe you. Momma M has lived on this block for the better part of thirty years. Never an issue with her furnance or plumbing since I have been around. Maybe you don't realize that this is one of the safest blocks around here. Has not been a shot fired in over ten years. Now houses are suddenly burning down and people are dying. I make a deal with you and the one place that we all have called home at one point catches fire. Ain't that ironic? My son is laying in a hospital bed breathing out of a fuckin tube. Fire is someone's forte' and you are the only person capable of such a heartless act. Our deal is done!"

"Tisk, tisk Tanya don't be so hasty to hang up on me love."

Kadir paused for about 10 seconds to ensure he still had Tanya's attention.

"Ms. Thompson, you have not controlled this plan since you gave me all of the information about your ex-lovers connections; Goldman, Snipes, Mo'Najah and Sheed. I am not one to leave things undone. As I have already started this mission so you benefiting from my work is of no consequence to me. I still have the desire for revenge running through these cold veins. Thanks to you Black Barbie I can enjoy the view from my I-Pad or up close and personal. I would hate to see you make yet another foul decision. But you answered your own the question. There is no benefit in burning down that ladies house. I actually am very, very fond of Momma M. Quite as it's kept Haneef and I were raised as brothers."

Pleasant Surprise
Mo'Najah

Just when I thought nothing could top last night, Mar arranged a brunch on the beach in Brigantine. It was almost as if he had someone find this small piece of paradise, secluding it just for us. Every time I looked into his sexy eyes, I could see flashbacks of last night's performance. If I did not know better, I would have thought someone made a few dollars on the side during their college days. Between the hour long, deep-tissue massage, the bath for two, the lingerie, and the strip tease…I could not spoil our night with talks of Haneef.

"Lamar, I have something I really need to talk to you about."

"If this is when you tell me you are leaving me for another guy, can it wait until Monday?"

"Now you know if there was another guy, I would have not tied you up last night and made you into my personal sundae with whipped cream and cherries on top."

"Good, because that would have made this gift seem like a waste of emotion."

With a slight motion of his hand, Mar signaled the waiter, who was carrying a small dessert tray with a lid. Placing it down in front of me, he then disappeared.

"Lamar, wait. Before I open this, I have to tell you something."

"Mo'Najah, do you love me?"

"Yes, but love has nothing to do with what I need to tell you."

"Open the tray Mo'Najah. This is my great grandmother's wedding band from my mother's side of the family. It's been in a safe for over sixty-five years. It's not an engagement ring, but a promise ring."

"A promise to what, Mar? I don't understand."

"A promise to handle any and all obstacles life may throw our way together."

"Well, I am relieved that you said that. Obstacle one: Haneef may try to kill you if he finds out who you are. Can you please pass the jelly?"

"You're kidding, right?"

"No. Yesterday before I left, Haneef had my brother present me with a Maybach and engagement ring. He was not happy with my response, making it a point to call me and remind me how many bodies he has buried."

The silence was loud. The water rolling up on the shore was drowned out by his thoughts.

"Haneef is not one for idle threats; however, the only person that knows I am here with you is China."

"So you're telling me you're hiding this relationship?"

"No, not at all. However, in my business, you have to keep personal things private. It's safer that way."

"Mo'Najah, I don't know your ex, but I also have connections to a not-so-sophisticated lifestyle. These young gunners in the street would do a lot just to walk into a building with me. I too am well-connected, just not heartless."

M.I.A.
Sheed

"You have a call from an inmate in the Virginia State federal correctional facility. To accept this call, please do not..." I pressed the #1 incessantly. The sound of the automated voice had me annoyed.

"Haneef, Mo's phone number is disconnected. I have had someone posted outside of the house for hours at a time. The staff at the hospital have instructions to call me if she arrives. I have been to the club, I even knocked on that chick's door over in Camden. Where else could she be?"

This is not like Mo'Money. She always checked in, even if she was going out of town. Nobody, from Mario to her mom, has heard from her since Friday. Someone had to know how to reach her. All of this shit happening at once had me vexed to say the least.

"Haneef, do you think something could have happened to Mo'? Why the fuck would she just disappear, disconnecting her numbers? I'm starting to think that something shady is going on. The fire chief has yet to tell me the cause of the fire. All they know for sure is that it started next door and spread to mom's house. They believe there was some kind of gas leak, but the investigation is still not concluded. Mr. Lawrence from next door was dead on arrival. Now Mo' is missing. This shit is not adding up!"

"Look, Sheed, Moet and I had a huge argument. Some shit was said to her that may have been taken the wrong way. She may be hiding from me, you, and anyone connected to me."

"What the fuck could you say to her that would make her leave Philly, Hanz?"

"It don't matter what I said to her. She will surface in a few days maybe a week. Sheed, on everything I love, I can't lose my Mother. Every time I get called to the social worker's office, I swear its bad news. Thoughts of Kalief keep poppin' up in my head. Yo, I can't lose her while I'm in here helpless."

"Just stay positive, Hanz, your son is going to be fine. Momma Mason is a fuckin' G. She not going nowhere 'til she knows her boys are straight."

"Man, I am taking pills to sleep and function. I straight passed out when Goldman told me."

"Hanz, remember when we stole the keys to the station wagon? Momma M beat the brakes off of all three of our dumb asses. Then she took us to the empty lot and taught us how to drive. She is blessed, Haneef, you have to know that, and even if God does see fit to call her home, that means he needed her there more than we do."

"Shawn, I just can't let her go like that. Don't lose no sleep or money over this Moet shit. Dat bitch is laying low, hopin' I don't pull an AT&T, reach out and touch her ass."

"Sounds like some shit I don't want to know about."

Scanning through the numbers in my phone I had Buddah's number. She was definitely one of the people Mo' utilized during problematic situations.

"Is this Buddah?"

"Yeah, who dis?"

"Sheed."

"Oh, what's up, my Nig'?"

"Have you been in touch wit' Mo'Money lately?"

"Nah, not really, it's been a clip since we kicked it. Why, what's up?"

"Some shit has popped off with Haneef's son and his mom and I really need to touch base with her. It's serious. If you should see her, please tell her to call me."

"Damn, okay, let me get in the streets and see what I can make happen."

With that I ended my call with the last person I could think of. Not even her mother could reach her.

Peak
Mo'Najah

We arrived at the 40/40 around 11p.m., getting dropped off by Atlantic Limousine Service. The line to get into the club was wrapped around the side of the building, and the music was vibrating the concrete. Cameras were flashing, there were film crews outside. Security escorted us into the building then right up to the manager's office so Lamar could handle some finishing touches.

"Atlantic City is on fire tonight!" screamed DJ. Fah D to a capacity crowd.

The waitresses were running the bottles back and forth to the VIP, food in one hand, chrome buckets in the other. The turnout was better than expected.

"Mo'Najah, I would like to introduce you to Scott. This is my writer, producer, and studio engineer. Scott, this is Mo'Najah."

"Pleasure to meet you. Are you in the music industry, or are you a model?"

"No, heavens no, neither. I am about to start my own business actually."

"Scott, Mo'Najah, can you excuse me? I need to talk to the DJ before Menace arrives." Leaning in, Lamar gave me a gentle kiss on the cheek. "You look too good to be out in public. Don't be in a rush to take those shoes off tonight, I love you. Glad you're wearing your new ring."As he rushed off to attend whatever was next of this epic roller coaster ride.

"Let's get a drink, Monet."

"It's Mo'Najah, but you can call me Moet," I replied to Scott as I followed him to the bar in the VIP.

Everyone was enjoying the music, food, and the sights. Money was synonymous with music, the jewelry, the clothes, the bottles. My Philly crew would have a ball in this camp. The females would be lining up victims for the dudes to squat on when the club closed. This was some fairytale shit: black cards and gold bottles. If I was not standing in the middle of the it, I would swear someone was shooting a video, and at any time Hype Williams was gonna yell "Cut!"

But this was Lamar's life, every day, all day, without a scale or a pistol, just a dream and a lot of hard work.

"Can I have a glass of Moet please?" I screamed to the bartender.

My thoughts were everywhere. *This man was wonderful, but my life was dangerous. With all these people around, why would he choose me?*

ShowTime
Lamar

The lights went completely black in the club. There was the sound of a chopper landing and sirens coming through the speakers. "This is an emergency, please don't panic."

Red and blue lights were flashing, giving the crowd some reassurance that everything was under control. Then it went dark again, followed by a thunderous explosion. Menace appeared in the center of the crowd holding an iced-out microphone while singing the verse to his last single. His swag was so hood: white wife beater, $7,000 Breitling watch...the platinum chain was bananas with a huge J hanging to his belly. His jeans were half off his ass, showing off the Polo draws with some Gucci shoes and visor tilted to the side. My designer did not intend for this to be worn like that but that was Menace. As soon as the hook stopped, Alashia appeared at the top of the steps, also wearing a half-cut wife beater and some skinny jeans with her Gucci hat and belt cocked to the left, ripping her verse over the beat. While the attention was split between the two, they were slowly moving towards one another. The crowd parted as they moved in. The performance was Juicee, to say the least.

It took me about a half hour to make it from the DJ booth back to where I had left Mo'Najah and Scott. Mad love was pouring in from family, friends, and other artists. Photos were flashing. I had collected about eight business cards as I walked up the stairs to the VIP. As I reached the top of the steps, my business partner was signaling for me to come have a drink. I had to hear what Mo'Najah thought about the performance.

Insider
Mo'Najah

The crowd was in a full uproar after Menace and Alashia's performance. Scott pulled me off to a section of the room before everything happened so I could see the entire show unfold. Mar was so creative and talented. I couldn't wait to congratulate him. They definitely ripped the crowd. A sense of pride and admiration overwhelmed me. I had a man that was capable of doing great things.

"Scott, where is the ladies room? I need to freshen up."

As I turned to go in the direction of the restroom. Halfway across the room, the hairs on the back of my neck stood up. I felt a sudden surge of energy that was not present before the show. I felt like I was being watched. Quickly, I turned to scan the room. All the faces were unfamiliar and no one seemed to be looking directly at me. My stomach was suddenly in knots and a layer of sweat was forming across my forehead. My glass was not even half-empty.

I had retrieved my phone from my clutch. To send Rocc a message.

 Stay close by!

As I proceeded to the ladies room, Mar wrapped his hands around my waist from behind, making me spin and fall into his arms.

"Oh my gosh, babe, that was unbelievable! Why didn't you tell me that was your plan? I'm so glad you asked me to be here, this is amazing."

"I wanted you to see why your man works so hard and so long. Mo'Najah, I have someone I have to introduce you to. Come with me."

We left one VIP area and entered another one. It was nowhere near as congested. There were about thirty people in here instead of 100 on the other side. The security guard removed the velvet barrier that divided the room into two sections. Every step we took, Mar was introducing me to someone from the music business, holding my hand the entire time or resting his long arms around my neck.

I smelled his cologne before my eyes made contact with his face. "Nickolas, I'd like to introduce you to my very special lady friend. Mo'Najah, this is my business partner. Without him, none of this would be possible."

Neko - I mean Nickolas – stood up to shake my hand. His jet-black ponytail was free tonight. The suit and tie I usually saw were replaced with a pair of Naked and Famous denim jeans, a chocolate V-neck shirt and loafers by Salvatore Ferragamo Python. His wrist was so exotic I couldn't even tell you what he was wearing. From pharmaceuticals to music...I couldn't help but wonder how deep Mar was into the life I was so worried about him being a victim of.

"This is my sister's only son. Manny, meet Ms. Mo'Najah," Neko said with his eyes on everything but my face. Manny jumped up, looked at Lamar and then his uncle, and said, "I don't shake women's hands." He opened both arms to hug me. During the embrace, he whispered "Haneef" into my ear. I nodded slightly, confirming who I was to Manny.

"Mr. James, Menace needs you on level one." One of the security guards tapped Lamar on the shoulder.

"Mo'Najah, please excuse me."

"No problem. I have to use the ladies room anyway."

I grabbed Mar's right hand and we left the VIP section. A photographer somehow got Lamar to stop for a photo while I was in full stride to the ladies room. Neko, Manny…how much closer to Haneef could I fucking be? If Sheed showed up, I might as well send the Hanz' a 5x7 photo of Lamar and I together with me perched perfectly on his lap.

Coincidence
Brianna

"Zylar, I have to go to the bathroom. The one down here is despicable. I am going upstairs to VIP."

"Bri, give me a few minutes. I need to talk to Alashia."

"Girl, I will see you when I get back."

We had been drinking the entire limo ride down from NYC. We barely had time to see what the suite at the Golden Nugget, looked like before we had to meet Menace. Bollinger 1996, champagne had me doing the pee-pee dance all the way up the stairs. When I left the stall, I headed straight to the sink to wash my hands and touch up my make-up. I saw a head full of spiral curls, sporting the hottest shoes I had seen in months. "Girl, your shoes are fierce!"

She looked up and replied, "Mrs. Davis?"

"Mo'Najah?"

"I would have never figured you for a Menace fan?"

"Don't get me wrong, I don't know Menace, but my best friend Zylar and Menace are very close, so you can say I am a friend of a friend."

"You are wearing those jeans! Let me know you do more than sell real estate!"

"Your hair looks amazing curly. How long did it take?"

"Let's not even go there."

We shared a laugh.

"Mo'Najah, we are in V.I.P. who are you here with would you like to join us?" I asked.

"Nekotas and company, also in VIP," she replied.

The door to the ladies room swung open. We both stopped talking.

"Girl, I have been looking all over for you! Did you see Lamar?"

"Zylar, this is one of my clients. Mo'Najah, I would like you to meet Zylar."

Zylar flashed a quick "bitch, please!" smile and continued with her line of questioning. "Bri, did you see him? He is looking so good, girl!"

"Zylar, can I have that MAC lip gloss you have?" attempting to silence my friend.

"Do you think I should wait until later to say something to him?"

"It was nice seeing you, Mrs. Davis, enjoy your night," Mo'Najah said as she departed the ladies room with a calm peculiar look on her face.

I stood there frozen in time. The connection between Mo'Najah, Lamar and Zylar just clicked. Zylar, is my best friend not telling her was not an option but to tell her here?

"Zylar, I that is the woman Lamar is with."

"What, who?"

"You said the name on the business card you saw said Moet, right? She is an exotic dancer from Philadelphia, right? Well, both of those things fit the woman that just walked out of the bathroom. But I also need to add Queen Pin to the list of titles she holds."

With a perfectly arched eye brow and her jaw damn near on the floor.

"Brianna Davis, are you telling me you have known who Lamar was seeing all this time and you're just now telling me?"

"No, I am telling you that just now after seeing her here and factoring in all the details you have told me about the woman Lamar has left you for. That maybe her, Zy." Grabbing Zylar's arm, I looked her deep into her green contacts. "This is not the time or the place. Please don't make a scene here."

"Scene? Lamar did this when he brought his whore to the premier of one of his artists, not me!" She stormed out of the ladies room in full dramatic diva mode.

Bombshell
Mo'Najah

When I returned to the VIP section, Lamar and Nickolas were toasting to the success of Juicee Inc. 'Neko' spotted me entering the section and delayed the toast for Lamar.

"Es su novia?" he asked.

"No, mi mujer." Mar turned around and welcomed me back with a soft kiss on the lips. Neko and Manny were both trying to avoid eye contact. Lamar poured another glass of Ace of Spades into a champagne flute and handed it to me, holding my hand as if this was what was missing.

"To the future," said Lamar.

All six glasses clanked in agreement.

"Tatia, did you meet Mo'Najah?" Lamar asked holding my hand tightly.

"No, I am sorry, she rushed off before we could be introduced."

"I love your entire CD, I am truly a fan. I can go home now that I have met you."

"Lamar, you need to bring her to more events," Tatia stated with a smile. "She is way nicer than the other one."

The entire group laughed at that joke.

"Speaking of your ex, I just had the pleasure of meeting her in the ladies room," I whispered into Lamar's ear.

"Lamar, is she cool?" the bouncer asked, indicating the woman beside him.

"Let her in, good lookin' out, man. Brianna, this is my business partner Nickolas, his nephew Manny, Mo'Najah, and you already know Tatia and Scott.

"Lamar, can I please have a word with you in private?"

"No, you can say anything you need to say right here."

I stepped to the side, but stayed within earshot so I could hear the conversation.

"Lamar, Zylar is here!"

"Yes, Bri, I know, Menace gave me a heads up a few days ago."

"Lamar, is Mo'Najah Harrison the woman you have chosen over Zylar?"

"I don't see how any of that is relevant to why we are here tonight, Brianna."

"Look, Zylar is my best friend and you are my husband's best friend. That woman is obsessed with you, and your little album release is about to turn into Jerry Springer and a fucked up episode of *Cheaters* all in a blink of an eye."

"Zylar knows I have moved on, I suggest she does the same."

"Lamar, Zylar is -"

Menace approached Lamar from behind. "How we do, baby?"

"You did your fuckin' numbers, son, you and Alashia. Where is she?"

"I think she is talkin' to some people downstairs."

"Mar, I will be right back," I announced as I walked past.

"Yo! L, who is that? She fine as fuck!"

"Oh shit! Mo' babe, let me introduce you to the star of the night. Menace, this is my lady Mo'Najah."

"Damn, ma, tell me you got a gang of girlfriends that all look like you!"

"Pleasure to meet you; your show was amazing." extending my hand to the new star.

"I will be right back Lamar," I said, leaning in to give him a quick kiss, confirming for Menace and Mrs. Davis that we were indeed together. I made a right out of the VIP section, walking down the stairs. I noticed, Zylar and Alashia in deep conversation in the far left hand corner of the room. Knowing where my enemy was seemed very relevant. I continued my path to retrieve the watch I had delivered to the club. After being given such a precious gift this afternoon, I had to make a gesture of my own: Joe Rodeo's hip hop watch, 26.7 carats, black diamond bezel with a black stainless steel wristband. I tipped the manager of the club $100.

"This is the first time I have had such a strange request. Can I at least see this watch?"

"Sure, I guess I should see it before I give it to him also." I said with a giggle and so much pride for the man I was falling in love with.

"Wow, that shit is hot! Ms. Harrison, if he don't love that shit, you can definitely bring it back to me. I would floss the shit outta that piece."

"Thanks again," I said. As I left his office, closing the door behind me.

"You're worse than a roach; you just won't die," came a voice from behind me.

"Excuse me?"

"Stay out of my way, strip bitch, or next time you will be in your little blue Acura when it gets hit!" Zylar hissed in a tone that set me off.

I cocked back my right arm and my elbow hit the wall before my fist barreled straight into her face. The thump of her body against the wall made the manager appear out of his office - God, Allah, and Jehovah work in mysterious ways - just as she recovered from my blow and lunged at me, grabbing a head full of hair. Rocc had just entered into the hallway. My clutch and $8,000 watch were on the floor. My right hand was intertwined in the bitches weave and my left was trying to throw punches to her face and ribs from around the massive chest of my guard.

We must have been gone for way too long. Suddenly Brianna and Lamar were running towards us also. It took all three of them to get the situation under control.

"She had my fuckin' car hit!" I yelled.

"Mo' Najah, are you sure?" Lamar asked, skeptical of my allegation.

"The little bitch just said to stay out of her way or next time I will be in that little blue Acura. When I get done wit yo ass you gonna wish I was in that car too, trust me. You wanna see me, step the fuck outside!"

"Brianna, I really think you need to talk to your friend, I think she may be drunk." Zylar spoke calmly to her friend as if I was the one out of control.

"Lamar, you should be a bit more selective of the trash you surround yourself with. Come on Bri let's get this party started right..."

Brianna pulled Zylar to the top of the stairs, far away from me.

"Lamar, I need you to think about this. My car was fine sitting outside until I answered your phone that morning. She called my business line weeks before we even had sex. When you dial 215 on most phones it tells you the area your dialing, so let's deduce the obvious. When she came to pick up the car, the only vehicle that had Pennsylvania tags on it was mines. She already had suspicions that you were fucking someone out of state. That night, my car gets randomly hit. How would she know what color my car is, or even the make?"

"Mo'Najah, I can't explain her behavior. Maybe I need to talk to her. The woman I was engaged to has suicidal tendencies, not homicidal ones."

"Well, little miss fragile just confirmed to me that she is capable of fucking some shit up when it comes to you. So I see Haneef is not the only cannon in this equation." During the entire conversation, I was rolling his grandma's ring around my finger, hoping like hell this dead woman could give me some guidance. One hour and ten minutes away from my team... this album release could be a goddamn crime scene with one call!

Drama Queen
Zylar

"Zylar, what the hell are you doing?"

"Bri, I am sorry, I did not mean to get you involved in this. I just could not let her walk past me and not say anything. Lamar is supposed to marry me. I am carrying his child."

"Are you trying to lose this baby? I thought tonight was about Menace, Zylar?"

"Ho'Najah just changed all of that. Bri, what am I supposed to do when I see the love of my life with some random, undeniably gorgeous bitch? I hope like hell her hair was fake. All I have left is fight, because accepting that I lost him is just too much to right now."

Walking into the VIP section of the room, I found Menace talking to some people and instantly joined the conversation as if nothing ever happened. With a few glasses of wine and no more Moet sightings, I began to relax and enjoy our night with the star of the show. Menace took my hand while he introduced the world premier of his first video. The remained of night was about Brianna and I. Bri was more than drunk as she walked barefoot to the limo. Escorted by one of Menace's friends.

"Zylar, I really need to talk to you once you get ya girl situated," Menace said.

"Let me put the drunk one to bed and I will be down the hall in about a half hour. Menace, you have come a long way and tonight is just the start!" Hugging and kissing Menace on the lips gently I went to tend to Brianna.

Blind Eye
Moet

"Mo', he does not know," Neko said in Spanish as Lamar left to oversee Menace's final performance of the night. "I am a silent partner because his background is so clean. No one would look to investigate him if something goes wrong. All of the funds are filtered through an account set up through an investment firm."

"Nickolas?" I asked with an arched eyebrow. "Why are you telling me all of this?"

"The same reason you met me in that hotel room. You needed to know if I was an ally or the enemy. Te necesito para mantener mi secreto."

"You're asking me to keep a secret from the man I love and that knows everything about me and my business?"

"A continuación, hacer lo que una buena mujer que hace y lo proteja y le dejó la vida el sueño como un productor de Mega."

"So that is what good women do these days; lie, deceive, turn a blind eye to events because it suits the needs of the family?"

"You need to give Lamar a choice. Let him know that he is risking more than his job. I'm catching a cab back to the hotel. This is too much shit for me to be without protection. Please let him know."

Scheme
Zylar

"Alashia, my peoples over at LYL production loved your performance. Your style and voice are just what they have been looking for. Juicee is not going to sign you. They just wanted to use you, honey. That five grand is not shit compared to what you should have been paid. Just do this favor for me and I will not only pay you, but make sure you get the spotlight you deserve.

"These are some really serious allegations you want me to accuse him of."

"You don't owe Lamar shit, girl, he used you. How long were you in the studio? How many hours did it take to produce that video? You made the song hot. He robbed you without a gun. We all know the stories on how these record labels use people's talent then cast them aside. Listen, you're a big girl, make your own decisions. Just let me know by tomorrow if I need to make that call to my boy at Live Ya Life."

I hoped she was as money-hungry and grimy as I heard. I showered and then made my way to Menace's room.

SUNDAY...

Recovery
Sheed

"Tanya, Shawn...Mrs. Mason's condition does not seem to be improving," said the small Indian doctor. "Her burns are severe and she inhaled a lot of smoke. Luckily, your son was there to tell the firemen what room she was in. Right now, all we can do is wait. She is in and out of consciousness. You can go see her, but please, only one at a time. I do not want her excited or angered in anyway. Even if you have to lie to her to keep her tranquil."

"Sheed, you can go first," Tanya rather graciously offered.

Entering the room, the smell of the hospital curled the lining of my stomach. How could someone so strong be hurt this bad? My feet were moving towards the bed, but my body did not seem to be getting closer to her side. The lump had already formed in my throat. Seeing someone I respected, admired, and loved hooked up to all these monitors and machines was tough. The bandages and gauze just on her face and hands alone had me scared to touch her.

"This is not the kind of vacation I was trying to send you on, Momma M. If you wanted a new house, all you had to do was tell me. You can't leave me yet. My son or daughter will need to know who you are. There will be a million questions, from formula to diaper rash. You need to fight, Mom."

The tears were inevitable. My head was low and my heart was heavy. I was losing my best friend all over again. "Haneef wants you to know that he is sorry. Sorry for not protecting you, sorry he could not save you from the fire. Okay, I'm about to go Mom. Tanya is waiting to see you next."

"Mo'Najah…"

"Mom, you're weak, you need to save your strength. Mo'Najah is on her way. Shhh, just rest. Your boys love you."

Finding a spot on her forehead that was not bandaged, I kissed her. I never knew my heart had this many fucking pieces. I wanted to fight, I wanted to fuck ten different females and produce more children just so that the love I had for this woman would not go to waste. I'd die right now just so she could live. *Why take someone who was constantly making those around them better? Karma was a motherfucker.*

Tanya patted my arm. "Sheed, I'm going to stay, you can go get some rest."

Rewind
Mo'Najah

"Mo'Najah, I understand that you are angry and upset, but leaving won't resolve anything."

"Lamar, I just need to be around people I know and trust right now."

"What the fuck does that mean? You know and trust me."

"Yes, I know you, but trust is suspect right now. For the past hour, you have been defending your ex-fiancée to me. The broad intentionally provoked me tonight and had my car vandalized. Then the crazy bitch tells me to my face that she is gunning for me. Neither you nor she knows me that well. It took every ounce of love and respect that I have for you not to set your party all the way off. Philly is a phone call and sixty five minutes away. Just give me the valet ticket to the car. Let me go home and calm down."

"Mo'Najah, why can't you stay with me? Let me fix this. I can handle Zylar."

"So the fuck can I, but I don't think we are talking about the same kind of problem resolution. I'm thinking yellow tape and body bag. You're thinking communication and mediation. I believe in this ring you gave me. But I really need to leave."

"The valet ticket is in my wallet on the night stand."

The humidity that night was thick. A heavy fog had settled in and you could barely see six feet in front of you. Unmoved by the conditions I was leaving Harrah's, Zylar and all of the drama right here. I did not know how New

Jersey laws worked but there was a jail cell with my name on it if I stayed. After thirty minutes on the expressway I decided to give Buddah a call figuring she was up all hours of the night anyway.

"Buddah, slow down. A fire where?"

"Mo', you need to get home, shit is crazy! They saying Haneef is looking for you. He has a reward out for anybody that can tell him where you are."

"Buddah, rewind that, who was hurt in the fire?"

"Lil Neef and his G-mom and two people next door. It was in the paper and everything."

"Call Sheed on a three-way."

Click. "Mo', you there?"

The phone rang six times and went to voicemail. "Hang up and dial this number," I told her. "1-267-555-5819."

"Hello, who dis?"

"Sheed, it's Mo'. I have Buddah on the line. What is going on?"

"Mo', are you sitting down?"

"I'm driving back to Philly now. Tell me what is going on."

"You may need to pull ova Mo'."

"Just tell me what the hell has happened to Lil Neef and Mommy. Sheed, tell me the fuck now!"

"Stop yelling! It was 5:00 in the morning. A fire broke out in the row home next door to Momma Mason. It spread immediately to mom's house. Lil Neef heard the smoke detectors but was trapped upstairs."

"What about Mom? Stop stalling and tell me, damn it!"

"She is at Jefferson. Go see for yourself."

I made a quick phone call. "China, wake up! I need you to meet me at Jefferson Hospital. I should be there in twenty minutes."

"Mo', we really need to talk. So much shit has happened since Friday."

"What the fuck else? I leave town for two damn days and the bottom falls out?"

"I got attacked Friday evening. The Altima is a wrap, but the cheese and the trap are still in place. I think Black set me up. I don't have any proof. I won't know until we run the tapes back from the car or the phone to be certain."

"Just meet me at the damn hospital."

Rachetness
Alashia

In my Givenchy bag was three stacks, compliments of Ms. Zylar. My future was dangling by a thread. Even I knew what the right connections could do for my career. However, was making a deal with a jealous ex' going to make that happen, or was it just another empty promise? I did not know shit about Zylar, and honestly, her presence was quite annoying the few times that I had been in the same room with her. The way Menace went on and on about her…just maybe she could be the connection between my dreams becoming, reality.

When I got out of the taxi cab on Fulton Street, I was standing directly in front of the police department.

"I would like to make a formal complaint against a Mr. Lamar James."

"What is the nature of your complaint?" asked the officer on duty.

"He assaulted me and has been stalking and sexually harassing me for weeks now," I said to the officer behind the thick glass with tears streaming down my face.

"Young lady, these are some rather serious allegations. If you and your boyfriend had a fight, this is not the way to get back at him."

"I came to report an assault and you're telling me that I am lying?"

"Keep calm, ma'am. No, I am not saying that you are not telling the truth. What I am saying is that I get a lot of young women who come in here and make complaints against the men they are involved with only to drop them later. Are you sure that this is how you want to proceed?"

Even with the dramatic performance, I felt like the officer knew I was lying. Becoming irate would have not made my story any more believable, so I went with what I knew best: Guilt.

"You must don't have any daughters, do you, officer? Because if you did and one of them was violated in any way, the last thing you would want was some insensitive police person not taking them seriously. So how about you get your sergeant out here!"

"You're going to have to talk to one of our detectives. Please be seated, she will be right out." The older white man disappeared from the window and never returned.

After giving a detailed report and some pretty personal information about the incident, I was taken to Orange Regional Medical Center for an examination. There were no bodily fluids, but they found a lot of bruises and evidence of swelling. After being released from the hospital, I was taken home by a patrol car. As promised Zylar, had the printed-out pages of Lamar's alleged advances towards me in a yellow envelope under my door.

When I checked out of the hotel that morning, the limo took me back to Brooklyn. After my brief conversation with Zylar, I was $3,000 richer with a meeting set up with the CEO of Live Ya Life promotions. It was a rough road to the top. I guess Lamar and Juicee were speed bumps.

In The Way
Moet

"Only one person is allowed to see Mrs. Mason at a time. Let me call and tell the other visitor that you're here and then you can go back," stated the young lady at the desk.

After several attempts the clerk informed us that no one was answering the line. She would get someone to cover the desk and walk back there personally. When I arrived, Buddah was already in the waiting room.

"Moet, just calm down, everything is going to be fine. This hospital specializes in this type of care," China said while holding my hand.

"If something happens to her and I don't get a chance to say goodbye, I will hate myself forever, China. She taught me everything from how to cook, sort clothes, and to love myself first. This can't be happening. I feel like I am having the night from hell with short furloughs to heaven just so I know how the other half lives."

"Listen, Mo', you're exhausted. Maybe we should come back later after you get some rest and a shower."

The look on my face made it clear to China, Buddah, and the nurse that I was not leaving without her knowing I was here.

China and Buddah walked outside to smoke a boggie while I waited for my chance to see Momma M. During my ride up the expressway I had Buddah pick up some personal things from the house in Ardmore. With the night that I was having, being without my gun was no longer an option.

"Damn, what is taking them so long?" Buddah said.

"You're right. I almost forgot I am waiting for someone to come out so I can go in."

"How you holding up, Mo'Money?"

"Girl, my head is banging, my stomach is tied up in so many knots, I'm scared to fart, the palms of my hands are sweaty as hell. I just need to see her and Lil Neef. Once I see their faces, my fears can stop taunting me. It's so quiet in here, as if death needs silence to be dispensed."

Losing what was left of my sanity, I walked back to the nurse's desk. "Can you please ask whoever is back there to just give me five minutes?"

"Glad you could bless us with your presence. Oh hail your Majesty, Moet is finally here. Did you bring your magic wand, or better yet, your black card? Whatever pole you just climbed off of...please go the hell back."

"Tanya, nice to see you also. What hospital is Lil Neef at?"

"Don't worry about my damn son!"

"Not now Tanya, this is not the place nor the time. They really need all the love and support we all have in order for them to make it through this. Let's put our differences to the side for the good of the family."

"Do you not speak English?" Tanya screamed. "They are not your fucking family, they are mines! If you gave two shits about anyone but yourself, you would have been here yesterday."

"What difference does it make when I got here? I'm fucking here, so please move so I can go see my damn mother."

"Ladies, I am really going to need you to calm down. This is the intensive care unit, not the corner of 22nd and Allegheny," the nurse warned.

"I'm really starting to lose what little patience I have left with you, Tanya. Your mouth is about to get you rocked. At least you're already in the hospital."

Walking past her was not an option, since the hallway was rather narrow. The scar on her face fit her attitude to a T. The day from hell was about to go from hot to explosive. I took a step back, semi-turning my back to throw up my hands as if I was about to leave. Then I charged at Tanya with all the energy, rage, and frustration my night held. She lost her balance and fell to the floor. Tanya grabbed my neck with one hand, my hair with the other, and flung me to the right side.

But she was slow rising to her feet. She was barely halfway standing when I grabbed a fist full of weave and started swinging. Tanya caught my arm after the sixth punch and bit the shit outta me. Then she came at my face like a wild woman. I was in full fight mode, on the balls of my feet, hands up, ready to just knock the bitch out.

Trying to stay away from her wild-ass blows, waiting for the right moment to crack her nose wide open. I fell over a fucking potted plant, landed on my ass - game over. Tanya landed about three good punches, all to my face, before China came and puts my 9mm to Tanya's head. Fight over!

Buddah helped me up off the floor. "I think we need to leave," she said. "I'm sure the nurse called the cops once y'all started rockin'."

"You and China go 'head. I am going to see my mother. Give me the gun and take out the clip."

"Here, I never loaded it," China said, handing me the empty gun from the trunk.

"Ladies, don't move."

"She has a gun!" screamed the nurse from behind the desk.

The officers pulled out their service revolvers and called for backup.

We were in a holding cell for damn near three hours before they would even let us make a phone call. Because it was a Sunday, they wanted to send us to county until Monday.

"None of us would be here if you would have just let me pass, Tanya. You don't think about the consequences of your actions. What woman is just gonna let you go in and not say or do shit? We have been fighting for fucking years over nothing. Haneef has been gone for more than two years. What has this fighting gotten us?"

"Yo, go 'head with that Oprah shit! I'm being dead ass right now."

"Tell me why you hate me so much? Tell me why every chance you get to provoke me, you take it. What did I do to you, Tanya?" Silence.

"Moet, just leave her alone. How long can they keep us without a phone call? This shit is in the way, for real," China said.

"Buddah, I am sorry. You're the only person that did not do anything and they still took you with us."

"Do you really want to know why I despise you, Mo'? You have everybody fooled, thinking you're some angel amongst a world of devils. From the day you stepped foot on the block, you were crowned Queen. Haneef, would leave our bed to go home to you. You were his project, his new pet, and he would fuck me up for even saying your damn name. My son thinks you invented water and air. Everyone I love for some reason loves you more. You're no better than anyone else. You're a killer, a dope-dealer and high school drop-out! But it doesn't matter how many lives you take or destroy. You throw some money around, smile and everybody forgets the havoc you caused. I lost my man, my son, and even my sisters don't fuck with me because you had a miscarriage. Momma Mason is slipping in and out of consciousness calling your fucking name, not her sons' names - dead or living - and not her grandson's.

No, she is calling for her 'Mojah'. When we get out of here, I will still hate you. But at least now you know why."

"Are you fa real? I'm sitting in a fucking holding cell because you're jealous? Reality check, sweetie. You have two God-given healthy babies. Your crib is paid for. You have a damn associate's degree in business management. You come from a middle-class family that you alienated yourself from for whatever reasons. But you have woke-up every morning all these years despising me? Newsflash, Tanya: you could have kept his trifling whore ass! You could have the gonorrhea, the lies, the bastard children that I am not supposed to know about - not including your daughter - on the presumed list of heirs to the throne. You definitely could have had him once I saw the sex tape of three different bitches sucking his dick without a condom while he popped off in their faces. No, you want the suicidal thoughts, the feelings of worthlessness while I attempted to understand how someone can give you everything and break your heart every fucking chance they get. You should have spared me that and kept your fucking baby father.

At that age, I had no idea of the woman he would make me. None of it - the pain, paper or the penis - was worth the price I paid every day. So while you loath, envy, and continuously wish for my downfall, know that I would take the two kids and the child support check over the hell I have gone through to be the woman you see now. I just learned how to live, laugh and love. It feels good after all these years of tears, hurt and loss. All this time you lost sleep over what you thought I had, but guess what, Tanya? One million times zero is still zero. So if you choose to hate me, fine, there is nothing I can do about that. But know I am not fighting over Haneef, these streets, or my respect. If you approach me in an aggressive nature from here on out, I will have no problem making your bastard kids orphans, bitch. No, that's not a threat, it's a fuckin' promise! This

10th grade bullshit you're holding on to is in the way of my progress. I resolve problems; I don't avoid or ignore them. So if you hated me at my lowest, you're about to die slow, bitch. It only gets worse!"

"Harrison, make your call!" screamed the guard from down the hall as the cell door clicked.

"You're fucking kidding me, you're where? Why won't they give you a bail? Mo', that shit don't sound right."

"Sheed, it's me, China, Buddah and Tanya. Look, just call Goldman please. I need to see Momma M."

Road Trip
Devin

Two fights, one allergic reaction, and more memorable moments than I could count later... These young men bonded, worked together, argued but succeeded as a team this weekend. I was actually looking forward to next year's trip, strangely enough.

"Bryon, thanks for coming along this weekend. I know there are a hundred other places you would have liked to be, but you were needed here and I appreciate your dedication."

"Devin, the bad part is they know more about sex at fifteen than I know at twenty-five. If I wanted to cop a gun an ounce of cocaine or some pussy, any one of these boys could get the shit quicker than I could. That is scary to think about, that the streets are rushing our boys to be men just so they can become a damn statistic."

"Bryon, if we just make a difference in one young man, then my life has been defined."

"Devin, you really believe that?"

"Bryon, just this very moment I realized why God has not blessed me with a child of my own. My purpose is not to birth a child, but to guide the ones that I come in contact with every day. Learning how to become a man is hard when you're surrounded by pussy, and I don't mean that literally. There are a lot of pussy-ass men around these kids."

"Juicee in the Hood is doing something better than making a donation. Lamar is making a difference, and I am glad I got to be a small part of that," Bryon said while extending his hand to Devin. If I get the job at Juicee, you can count me in for next year's trip also."

When I entered the driver's seat of the van, Daniel the youngest of the bunch asked, "You want me to drive?"

"Hell no!" the kids screamed.

The entire ride back, I was on the phone with Ms. Boone and Mr. Stewart, the social worker over Ebony's case and my attorney. Jason and Jared were in a group facility for boys. I was seeking temporary protective custody until their case was heard. From no children to three kids…I'd better call my wife!

Leap First
Zylar

"Zylar, where did you end up this morning?"

"Bri, if I told you, you would not believe me."

"Try me, because when I woke up tossing my cookies all over the marble bathroom, you were nowhere to be found."

"Menace and I took a cab to the boardwalk. We walked and talked until the sun came up. Brianna, Menace has been in love with me for more than three years, but my happiness was always what he wanted. That is why he never said anything. He did not think he was good enough to be with me, but that's changed now that he has his recording deal and endorsement with the urban clothing line. Lamar and I are no longer involved. He is single and wants to have a committed relationship."

"Zylar, how is that gonna work when you're almost three months pregnant with someone else's baby? Are you even attracted to Menace? I remember you saying he was cute, but a couple?"

"Bri, puppies are cute, babies and handbags are cute. I like my men to scream sexy, handsome, and secure from every pore. Lamar did that plus. But maybe it's time I start thinking about life after Lamar. He has moved on, and so should I. Menace – or should I say Maurice - is talented and driven and moldable. Every reason I gave him on why we would not work, he had a response for. He even said that we could get married just to prove his commitment."

Scandal
Lamar

I should have known that Mo'Najah and Zylar could not function in the same space. Everything was too perfect, the performance and the interview was flawless. I had a capacity crowd with my lover and my ex being the only altercation of the evening. Well almost. I called a limo to take me back to Manhattan; nothing was available until 7am.

When I arrived home it was just enough time for me to shower and make it to the 11am service at Mount Pleasant. After the night I had I definitely needed God's guidance. Taking a quick shower and rushing back out of the penthouse. I sat behind the wheel of my BMW I had not talked to Mo'Najah since she left. I wanted to give her time to cool off. Avoidance was not how I chose to handle my issues. Imagine my surprise when I called her phone only to find that it had been voluntarily disconnected.

As I maneuvered one of Britain's finest automobiles thru city traffic, I was relieved to be home so much had happened in a 48 hour period that I was exhausted. Just before I hit the Nj turnpike a cop car pulls behind me and turns on his lights. From where I was in traffic I had to maneuver to get over to the shoulder. Reaching inside of armrest for my insurance and registration information. I place my hand on what appeared to be a sizeable amount of cocaine. Looking around my car I noticed a half full bottle of Armor All on the back seat. I slowed the vehicle down and signaled to the cop that I was moving out of the flow of traffic. Paranoid when he approached the vehicle I could not stop wondering what else was in my car?

"Do you know that your passenger side tail light is busted? That is why I stopped you." Stated the young Hispanic officer as he walked back to the patrol car. Giving the officer my information only brought me enough time to successfully empty the drugs into the bottle. However when he returned to my car his weapon was removed from the holster and pointed at me.

"Mr. James there is a warrant for your arrest in connection with an assault. I am going to need you to remove the key from the ignition and place it slowly on the dash. Then I will ask you to open the door from the outside with you other hand out of the window."

The polite civil servant was now transferred into Robo Cop. As I stepped out of the car I allowed him to handcuff me without any resistance. Two other cars arrive on the scene and began to search my vehicle. That was when I knew shit was real.

"Mr. James do you have a license to carry a concealed weapon in the state of New York?"

As I am being pushed into the back of the second squad car. The arresting officer reads me my Miranda rights.

"You have the right to remain silent. Anything you say can and will be used against you in a court of law. You have the right to have an attorney present now and during any further questioning."

"I do have a question, who did I allegedly assault?

"Name on the complaint is Ms. Allison Brooks."

"I don't even know an Allison Brooks you have the wrong man officer."

"Let me guess you don't know how that gun got into your car either. At least be original says the cop to his partner."

As I sat in the holding cell for hours before I was allowed to make a call, I just knew today could not get any worse.

"Mr. James the judge has signed off on a warrant to search your office and your home. Would you like us to use the key or should we gain access any way possible?"

"The keys are in my property that you took from me when I was booked."

"Thank you for cooperating with the investigation I will make sure they do not destroy anything in their search."

"What are you looking for if I may ask?"

"Emails and or phone records that indicate you have been sexually harassing and threatening Ms. Brooks. With guns you said you had at your office she alleges."

"All of this because some woman I do not even know has come in and made a complaint. What about my rights?"

"That gun in your vehicle made your rights disappear son."

Mom
Mo'Najah

By the time Goldman had arrived at the jail, posted bail and made arrangements at the hospital most of the day had slipped by. If something happened to Momma M or Lil Neef, while I was idle in a holding cell because of Tanya. I vowed to live everyday to make her life equally as miserable.

"Just drop me off at the hospital, please Goldman."

"What about the count, Mo'? You got money sitting in three different places," China, reminded me.

"You and Buddah handle that. I will come through to verify and do payroll. Work flow don't stop just because I am going through it. But trust, none of that money means shit if I don't get to tell that lady how much I love and appreciate her. We make the money bitches, da money don't make us." With that I hopped out of the passenger seat of the X-5 BMW truck at the main entrance to the emergency room.

Goldman had to smooth out a lot of ruffled feathers to get my visitation reinstated. The chief of staff was at the door when I arrived, briefing me on my mother's condition. None of these crackers needed to know I was not her biological daughter. Shit, with the money I was donating, I should have shot Tanya in the fucking lobby. $20,000! I called Mercy, Hanneman and Cooper. I was just gonna have her transported to another facility, but Goldman advised against it, reassuring me that the hospital would drop its charges against Tanya and I.

As I acquired my visiting pass from the nurse at the desk, I became tense all over again. My rage had allowed me to forget that the two people I love most in the world had been hurt. On top of the fact that I was not there when they needed me most. How often was I going to allow Tanya to take precious time and people away from me? No matter how much I matured, she was one that could push my button.

I had clearly made a wrong turn somewhere as my thoughts preoccupied my senses. Stopping a security guard I was pointed in the right direction. As I walked down the narrow corridor I realized that most of the rooms on this wing were empty as I searched for the room Momma M occupied. Out of nowhere he appeared tall, tanned light brown skin with a full sunnah. Dressed in all white from head to toe. Deep brown eyes, smooth skin, and thick lips. With a white kuffi adorning his head and the distinct scent of Sandalwood. As he passed me in the hall he spoke softly and graciously. "Sista." Never making eye contact but acknowledging my presence.

When I entered room 322, Henrietta Mason was bandaged from the waist up, with the exception of the left side of her face and barely the length of her left forearm and hand. I was literally scared to move, as if my shifting positions could cause her more pain or discomfort. She laid there lifeless while all the machines and monitors beeped, chirped and clicked.

The room all of sudden became short of air. My head started to spin, and the knots had balled up so tight in my stomach I felt like I could throw up and shit at the same time.

I blinked at least a thousand times trying to hold the tears back and held on the side rails of the bed for sheer support. I had no strength left. The tears fell like rain on a hot August's day. The cry turned into a full-blown sob while I begged God to make her better. Out loud, I could not beg for his mercy in silence. I know I did not deserve her. But what else did I have?

Her left hand moved. I jumped so far back you would have thought I was in the summer Olympics. "Mo'jah, how is Lil Neef?" she said in a voice so low I could barely hear her.

"Mom, he is okay. I lied, we are all worried to death about you though." Her breathing was ragged with heavy, violent coughs in between.

"Mom, I need you to rest, save your energy."

"Mojah."

"Yes, Mom, I am here, I am right here, shhh!"

"Mo'Najah, I need you to get free of this life you're living. The devil got his fork in you something deep. Ain't no winners in the game you playin'."

"Okay, Mom, I hear you, Please stop talking. I need you to save your energy so you can get out of here. Your coughing and breathing are taxing you, so please just rest." The more I asked her to settle down the more she coughed and defied me. My heart ached with each strained cough. I knew she had to be in pain.

"Mo', I raised you, I fought tooth and nail over you when that son of mines took you through hell. You're my Mojah."

"Mom, I hate that name. For the first three years that I lived with you, you refuse to call me Mo'Najah. 'Who the heavens would name they child that?' you would say."

"It was then that I knew Haneef would break you. You were too innocent, fragile, damaged. Had to call you Mojah to make you mad, angry, tough. If I babied you, then you would be just like Tanya is now: weak, bitter, thinks the world owes her something."

"Mom, you did a great job. I love you. Please stop talking, you need your rest."

"Girl, shut the heck up and listen! Haneef, made you sparkle, he made you grow up way too quick. But it was me that showed you how to burn him with the same fire he gave you. I might have raised five children, but you needed me more than the two I birthed."

"Mom, please don't leave me, I still need you. I have so much to tell you." Just that quickly she had drifted back off to sleep. As I stared ignorantly at the monitors. Not truly knowing what they meant but I could see the heart beat thing pop up constantly.

With all of the chaos and confusion, it dawned on me that I had never called Mar with my new numbers. My leaving so abruptly…he must be worried to death. "Mom, I need to make a quick call. I am going to step out into the hall. Let me turn on your TV for you." Both of Lamar's lines went unanswered. I left a voicemail. "Babe, I'm so, so sorry for not calling you when I got into Philly. I changed my numbers because the ex was blowing my phone up with the bullshit. I spent the better part of the day in a holding cell. Long story, but right now I am in the hospital with Momma Mason, Haneef's mother. Please call me when you get this message."

When I stood in the hall I could still smell the aroma of the man that walked passed me in the hall as I entered. Curious I peeked into the rooms opposite Momma M, both were empty. When I walked to the left side of her bed and closed my eyes. He had been there with her, his scent lingered.

Just as I was about to sit down and get comfortable in came the nurse to take her vitals. As they requested I step out into the hall so they could check her bandages the less germs the better. I took that time to make my way back to the desk. To inquire about the man that just left room 322. "No one has been to see Mrs. Mason since Tanya Thompson, Ms. Harrison." The nurse stared at me with a bewildered expression.

"Okay I know I am not trippin'. I am going to need you to call the Chief Administrator dude that walked in with me. Call him now please."

What seemed like eternity passed before dude was able to meet me. I waited patiently, with all of the drama going on, I could not take any chances that Momma M could end up dead or missing. Which was reason enough to have Rocc, outside of her door from this point on. Without disclosing too many details I was able to convince him to look at the surveillance tape from the time I arrived. Telling him that if I was wrong I would gladly donate five grand to research for Autism. Within minutes I stood in front of the administrator and the head of security as they humbly apologized.

Aggravated and exhausted, I walked back down the corridor that led to room 322. Without taking the scenic route, when I walked in she was alone and coughing violently.

"Mom, I love you." She attempted to make the un-bandaged side of her face respond. I stood again on the left side of her bed, rubbing her hand gently.

"Mom, who was that handsome man that was here before I came in?"

"Dat's just another one of my special boys, they have all been here expect for Haneef, but he's always late. I use to tell him you gonna be late for your own funeral. I even got to see Kalief, for a few moments, Mo'. That's when the fireman came and got me out. My three angel's Kalief, Kadir and Mo'Jah. God has been so good to me."

With the lump in my throat the size of a lemon I had not heard his name years...

Kadir

Walking the Walk
Devin

"Ms. Boone, are you serious? I can take them tonight?" I asked the social worker with surprise.

"Yes, Mr. Davis. I spoke to the family court judge personally. You must know some pretty powerful people. The judge faxed over a temporary order of protective custody for Jared and Jason about an hour ago. The social worker over at the group home spoke to the boys. They are excited about being in your care. I am inclined to tell you this, Mr. Davis. Jared, the younger one, has not spoken since they were removed from the home. Somehow there was a mix-up and they don't have any of their personal belongings. Allegedly, there mother Jada took the stuff to the wrong facility."

"So you're telling me they have had the same clothes on since Friday, Ms. Boone?"

"No, not the same clothes, just clothes that may or may not fit them. We get a lot of donations for the kids."

"I should be there within the hour. Don't worry about clothes or hygiene products. I will make sure they are provided for while in my care."

"Mr. Davis, you and your wife are a blessing. I wish there were more people in the world like you two."

"Thank you, I will see you soon."

Reasons
Lamar

"Mom, I did not touch that woman in any sexual or inappropriate way. I need you to call a lawyer on my behalf. Devin is still on the camping trip with the boys from Juicee, and he is not due back for another few hours. Mom, I know how the media is making this look. I am innocent. The most they can get out of me is maybe assault."

"Lamar Justin James, I did not raise you to hit women."

"Mom, I did not hit her, I kept her from hitting me."

"What about the harassment and sexual misconduct, child pornography?"

"I have no idea how that stuff got on my computer and I did not pay for sex with my credit card. Mom, I think I am being set up?"

"Lamar, you're telling me the music business is that dirty they would do all of this?"

"Mom, I hope this is related to business somehow, I just don't think it is. How would all of that stuff leak to a reporter, at the same time Alashia aka Allison decides to file these charges? None of this makes sense."

"Let me and your father make some calls. We will be over the bridge to get you. Lamar?"

"Yes, mom?"

"I love you son."

"I know. Please tell Dad what is going on. I don't want to have the same conversation twice."

Instant Replay
Zylar

"Girl, you were in rare form last night!"

"Zylar, I had a few drinks more than normal. So what?"

"Brianna, exactly what do you remember from last night?"

"Us in the VIP poppin' bottles after your stunt down stairs by the manager's office. Which by the way was reckless, irresponsible and dangerous."

"Bri, a lot of things happened after we got upstairs. You were so agitated that you wanted to calm down and you popped an E pill."

"Girl, I would never take a fucking drug, are you retarded?"

"No, I am not retarded or blind. Menace's friend Yasir gave you a pill last night. You were complaining about your head hurting and being ready to go. Do you remember that?"

"No, Zylar, the very last things I remember was Lamar and I breaking up the fight between you and Mo'Najah, you buying everyone a round of shots, then spilling yours accidentally. Then I woke up praying to the porcelain god and you were not here."

"Brianna, you and Yasir dipped off for about an hour last night."

"What? Are you telling me you let some guy take advantage of me while I was drunk and high?"

"No, I am telling you that you walked out of the VIP with Yasir and came back with Yasir."

"Zylar, what the fuck is a YASIR?"

"A five year younger version of Devin with cornrows and a six figure income…"

Professing
Mo'Najah

Momma M was sleeping peacefully, no coughing or jumping. The monitors all seemed calm. "Now that you are resting, maybe I get a chance to talk? Mom, I have met the most amazing man," I confessed while rubbing her left hand gently. "I have never felt anything like this before, thank God. I am scared and excited simultaneously. My heart races when I know I am going to see him and beats faster once he is near me. He is a kind, compassionate, gentle, and intelligent black man. You will like him, I already know. His charm melts women, his smile is intoxicating. He has a good job and a degree, no criminal background - you already know I checked. Did I tell you he manufactured the F they use in the word FINE. Mom, I am happier than I could have imagined ever being, and I want – no need - you here to enjoy my life after Haneef. This news is depressing. Let me try and find some Law and Order for you. Even while you sleep, you still like the TV on."

Before I could figure out how to work the remote control that was strapped to the side of the hospital bed, Lamar's face was on the screen. Walking over to the television to raise the volume, I heard: "Juicee's CEO, Mr. Lamar James, has just been released on a $100,000 cash bail. Let's see what Mr. James has to say about the allegations? Mr. James, are you guilty of the crimes you are being accused of?" inquired the reporter while holding a microphone in Lamar's direction.

"No comment," he responded.

"Mr. James, is this a publicity stunt to push your new artist?" fired another pushy reporter.

"Why don't you leave my son alone? He is a good, God-fearing man and you devils just need another sacrifice."

"Stay tuned as we keep you up to date with the latest in the James/Brooks scandal."

Confusion and concern consumed my thoughts. What could have possibly happened? Then I had to think about all that I had endured since I left Atlantic City. Only Lamar could answer the questions that ran through my mind.

"Mom, I have to go. I will be back in the morning." I grabbed my pocketbook and cell phone and proceeded to the parking area.

As I stepped into the main entrance of the ICU, I heard, "Code Blue, all available attendants please report to surgical room three stat!"

Dismissing the idea that Momma M, was the cause of the alert I continued to the parking lot. Where my car had sat in plain view for hours. My vehicles had always been my signature; from the Land Rover to Haneef's Hummer. I walked around the entire car. It appeared showroom perfect as clean as it was the day I drove off the lot at Sussman Honda in Jersey. I opened all the doors and the trunk. When I sat inside something told me to leave my car there. *Was I being completely paranoid? Go with your instincts second guessing at this game will get you killed for sure.* I removed my bag from the trunk grabbed two clips to the gun that I had in my purse. Walked into the main entrance of the ICU and out of the emergency exit. Catching a taxi on a parallel street.

Steppin' Up
Devin

Once I had Jared and Jason in my care, the looks on their faces crippled me. They did not have to say thank you, I knew it when they walked out and seen me. Joy danced in their eyes. Jason the older brother extended his right and shuck my hand like the little man he was. His pride would not let him hug me, but I knew he wanted to. Without even knowing all of the details I wanted to hug them. A warm deep since of obligation and responsibility to them showered down on me. These were not some random kids lost in a system; these were young men I had made a conscience decision to enhance their lives with my knowledge and success as a man. Anyone can give money, but who can make the time? For them I would.

When we pulled up into the parking lot of Wal-Mart, I instructed the boys to get everything they needed for the night. Assuring them that we would go to the mall in the morning for clothes. Both armed with a blue cart they were happier than I had ever seen two kids be. When I looked into the cart neither of them thought of tooth brushes or lotion. Just chips and underwear I guess at 14 & 12 that was all you really needed for a night.

Just as I approached the register, with everything from slippers to dental floss. Everything my wife had been expressing landed on my shoulders like a cement brick. Just at that moment, I knew I needed her in my selfish life. As I searched for my cell phone which I thought I had in one of the many pockets of these cargo pants. I needed to call her.

At that moment nothing but admitting how much of an ass I had been was relevant. I was taking Jared and Jason home so that I could apologize and beg for forgiveness.

Once we loaded everything into the van. I had six missed calls on my phone all of them were from Lamar. Without even listening to the messages. I called my brother back.

"LJ I just got back from the camping trip what is wrong you never call back to back?"

"Devin, I have just had the last eight hours from hell. I am going to need a lawyer."

"A lawyer for what Lamar, did something happen at the album release party?"

"I am gonna give you the quick rundown. Alashia shows up to my hotel room at 4am, wanted to talk about her career. Things get out of hand, I had put her out."

"Lamar, if you and she were just talking I am not understanding why you put her out?"

"I mean way out of hand brah. She goes into the bathroom comes out naked and flips when I decline to hit the pussy."

"Woo, woo, wooo wait I thought your girl was there the one from Philly?"

"Another long ass story… Short version she left, after her and Zylar got into a fist fight at the 40/40. I get back to the penthouse I am so aggravated, I decide to drive to Jersey and attend church with my mom. When the cop get's behind me. I got drugs in my arm rest, a gun in my glove box and a warrant for my arrest. Icing on the cake, Alashia, has pressed charges on me for assault and sexual harassment. Oh they get a warrant for my office and home where they find kiddie porn on my computer."

"Ohhh damn you need Johnnie Cochran."

"Lamar, I am pulling up at the house. Let me get settled and I will call you back."

I was very surprised to arrive at the house and no one was there. Brianna was a very habitual person, by 7pm she was usually sitting in front of the television. Watching old Law & Order re-runs. When we entered the house I told the boys to go take showers in the guest room while I ordered them a pizza.

Even if this was a temporary situation for the first time in my thirty plus years I felt alive and in God's favor. I was not beaten down by all of my own emotional baggage. To help a boy in his transition to become a man was what real men are born to do.

Backup
Moet

"Hello."

"May I please speak to Detective Latham?" I said nervously as I look at the phone to confirm that I connected to the right person when a female answers the line.

"Latham, has lost his phone while out of town, can I take a message? He has been calling in to get them frequently." The voice on the other end, attempts to reassure me.

"Yes can you tell him to call Mo' it's an urgent matter. My number has changed."

"Oh, he has been waiting on your call. Hold on let me three way him. He said for me to give you the number where he is, are you ready? 1-843-555-1212."

Dialing the numbers the woman just gave me a peculiar sense of uneasiness swept over me.

"Mo'Najah can you talk freely? Latham asked in a serious but protective tone.

"Yes." I replied growing more and more anxious.

"Mo' I am in a hospital in Charleston S.C. My rental car got accidentally and I use the term very loosely run off the road by two eighteen wheelers. After I left the police station inquiring about your girl. From my computer I could not even find a parking ticket on Zylar Wingate. So I figured I would take a 90 minute flight down south and get a few answers personally. Told the good ole boys down here that I was a private investigator and I needed some information on a local resident. They did have a file on her but the shit was empty. She had been arrested for something but I could not find it. So I decided to look into her parents and their background. Something is not right about this chick's entire family. You know too perfect. Not even a drunken uncle or a cousin that beats his wife or kicks his dog. When I reached out to some of her former classmates. The body language along with the stares I received told me that Ms. Zylar was not a woman of many friends. With foes that chose to remain unseen and unheard. I am guessing somewhere along my travels someone alerted someone else about my inquires. Just when I got the name of a young woman that Zylar had "crossed paths"with. That was when my car was run off the road. The young woman is in a facility for the mentally unstable. Where she has been since her junior year of college. When I get released from here I plan on getting another rental and going to visit this woman."

"Latham, come home I already got confirmation. This bitch is not just crazy but dangerous with enough money to compliment the combination. Since Friday I have been arrested, assaulted and Momma M's house has been set on fire and not in that order. How about I add another gallon of kerosene to your fire. Kadir Mu?"

"What about him Mo' he has been dead for almost five years now?"

"Not only is he alive, but he makes mysterious trips to hospitals to see burn victims in the intensive care unit."

"Mo'Najah, whatever you think you know about Kadir Muhammad trust me you don't. I would talk to Haneef directly!"

There would be no way in hell that I could figure out who Zylar had hired. But even I had to give the devious bitch credit. If I had actually lived there her plan would have been flawless. Kill me, destroy Lamar in the process. Not a bad plan. I guess it was time to figure out how Ms. Zylar knew so much about me? My first instinct was Mrs.

Davis but I could clearly remember her reaction in the bathroom. She had no idea that I was connected to Lamar until after the fire was already set in Philly. Which brought me back to my car getting hit. Little Ms. Zylar was not just bitter, but bright and calculating.

In order to beat this woman at a game she was very familiar with playing I needed help. Dialing Neko's number, I did not waste time with a text message.

"I need to see you as soon as possible."

"Come to my home in Staten Island, Emerson Hill."

When I arrived at the lavish estate it was everything a King Pin should have and more. The massive estate had nothing short of eight bedrooms, four baths; circular drive way and lion heads perched at the top of an arched stairway. Pulling up to the address that had been given to me I was surprised that the community was not gated. It was barely past 6 p.m. Sunday evening.

As I took the steps two at a time I was dressed for combat not a formal meeting. My green camo colored capris and my timberlands did not seem like the appropriate attire for my destination. Black shades and Eagles fitted pulled so far down you would wondered why I was hiding. When I touched the door bell the house seem to echo with the alert of a visitor. A small but stocky Hispanic woman answered the door within seconds of my arrival.

"Holla Senorita, el senor Sanchez ven a qui`."

When I entered the room which appeared to be a study. There was full four course Columbian meal prepared and waiting. With all of the chaos I could not remember the last meal I had. To my left was a desk were I placed two envelopes containing 50 grand.

"After dinner we can discuss why you are here." Neko said while gazing out of the large double doors that lead to what looked to be a garden.

Learning the difference between a question and a command in this business was key. That was an order one I was in no position to challenge. I needed him just as much as he needed me. I sat across the table from a bare chest Neko with so many questions running through my mind. Why had I been given the invitation to his million dollar sanctuary being the main one? The entire meal was devoured in silence. Afterwards a servant came into the room and removed the dishes. Another refilled the glasses leaving behind a silver tray with a cigar and a diamond incrusted lighter. Business commenced.

"If I lived in New York City, and found myself in a tight spot or in a predicament with a person I could not handle personally how would you recommend I resolve my issue? Keep in mind this person is good at what he or she does, but not excellent. If they were excellent I would not be sitting here having this conversation with you."

With the snap of his fingers one of Neko's associates enters the room. Some words are exchanged.

"Pending on the type of money you are trying to spend Mo'Najah everything and anything can be resolved. Goons are cheap."

"No, not a goon at all. Someone who has electrical knowledge, computer training and intelligence."

"Oh now you have asked a different type of question. Someone who will out think and undermine their enemy or opposition? There are no yellow pages for contract killers but someone who is good always has a name for themselves. There are six men and one woman that come to mind in this area. They can hack the flight manifest for South West airlines or wire a bomb to your car to detonate while they are 20 miles away."

"Here is 50 thousand dollars. Find out which of them have done work for Zylar Wingate. The job included a fire in a home in Philly, planting a gun in Lamar's car and uploading kiddie porn to his computer at Juicee. And make sure that is the last job he ever gets hires him for."

"How about you keep your money... I find the person Zylar hired and you owe me your silence as far as my partnership with you current lover is concerned?"

"I would prefer to pay for my services!"

"Did you not read the hustlers hand book? Always take a favor over money."

"The fire she had set almost claimed the lives of two people I would die for Neko."

"Would it not just be easier to remove her from the equation Moet?"

"No I have no idea of what the job entailed I could still be someone's target. Whether she is dead or alive. I would feel better if the worker was eliminated and I got to handle her myself."

"Dead people don't cause conflicts Moet."

"Someone who has already been paid to kill me won't stop until they have succeeded Neko."

Retrieving the envelopes from the desk I placed them back into my bag. Neko escorted me to the door of his home.

"Your home is amazing."

"This house belongs to my Amante {mistress}."

Helpless
Haneef

When I opened my eyes I was staring at a white ceiling with track lighting. Handcuffed to the bed by my left wrist and both of my feet were restrained. While an intravenous line dripped into my right arm. I was in the infirmary. A place I had been a lot lately but not for the same reason.

"Glad you are awake; I was starting to get a bit concerned."Said the little white nurse that I can't stand.

"What happened? Was I dreaming?"

"You got some really bad news and passed out in the Warden's office you have been unconscious for hours. How do you feel?"

"Like I got jumped in the Warden's office and everyone is out to get me."

Barely able to roll my neck, I feel the lump on the back of my head. Just as the sharp pains shot through my body I am reminded of the incident in the Warden's office. *My family trapped inside of a burning house both taken to a hospital with no details. I wish I was in a fuckin' comma then I would not have to deal with this shit.*

"Can you call the social worker for me please? I need to call my lawyer and find out what's going on with my fam'."

"Mrs. Adams is gone for the day, however you have permission to make three calls in private."

"Why are you being so nice usually you're the snottiest, nastiest nurse on duty?"

"I guess your fall did not affect your memory Mason. Look I was told that of all the convicts in this place you were one to befriend. That at anytime it could benefit me. I may be mean and nasty but I am no imbecile. The phone calls are yours to make, that is an order written in your folder."

With that she left my bedside taking her phony concern and fake ass smile. As I glanced to my left it was barely 7pm. I would wait until 10pm shift change. Make my calls around the nurse that I trusted. Greedy bitch you could see the devils horns a mile away.

Not having a clue as to where Mo'Najah had been was cause for concern. Her movements and attitude have me pissed all the way off. But when I talked to my son, earlier that week I realize no matter what she is still on my team. She may never fuck wit' me like that, but her love and loyalty is real.

Pay Day
Tanya

None of Kadir's people would return my calls or text messages. No cars were parked outside of the house. I had gotten my gun from out of the safe, loaded it and kept it close by. Once I got release from holding cell I took a cab to the hospital. Drove my car right back to the jail and placed a restraining order on Mo'Najah. I had no idea of what Kadir had planned as far as I was concern I did not care. The bitch could die a slow, painful death. If her little friends were not there she would be in a hospital bed right beside Momma M.

Lil Neef's condition was stable but still very, very serious. I made a call to my parents asking them to keep Taliah while I watched over my son. My father was at my home within the hour to pick up his only granddaughter.

Little Neef had been taken to Cooper's trauma center in Camden. After packing a bag I made my way to be with my son. Everything and everyone was irrelevant, until the phone began to ring.

"What do you want Tanya?" an aggrevated Kadir blurted into to the phone.

"I have a 50 thousand dollar idea?"

"Ha, ha, ha oh do you now? Were you not the same delusional woman that blamed me for the fire and told me our deal was off?"

"Oh, that deal is off the table. I have a new and improved, paid up front I don't care what happens offer for you. Since you are still on the phone I am guessing you're interested?"

"Humor me."

"For the fee mentioned I will deliver not just Sheed but also Mo'Najah to the hospital of your choice."

"Tanya, I don't need you for that. I could have taken Mo'Najah this evening when she walked on the third floor wearing a torn dress and flip flops, with her hair in large spiral curls. Pussy will always be my weakness."

"Not a problem have a nice day."

"Wait Tanya, let me think about what you're proposing and I will get back to you."

If Kadir had agreed to giving me this money. I already knew that I was leaving Philly with my children. My plan was very simple. I would be at the hospital with Momma M, I would have a nurse call Sheed and tell him things took a turn for the worst causing him to rush to her side in a panic. Which would give Kadir's people the element of surprise and time to plan. I am tired of waiting for scraps off the table. One day they will all respect me.

Love Is Labor
Lamar

I heard the door bell ring while I was in the shower immersed in my thoughts. I hoped like hell none of those reports had gotten by the door man. Controlling my temper has become impossible there would be no restraining me if they violated my personal space. Wrapping a thick grey towel around my waist, hair and body still dripping wet. When her face popped up on the television screen I was overjoyed.

As I snatched the door open with one hand, I pulled Mo'Najah in with the other. Tossed her phone, keys and shoulder bag to the floor. Removed her Eagles fitted hat and shades, I lifted her. Allowing our eyes to connect as if it were the first and last time.

"Never leave me like that again, I love you so fuckin' much my dick would not even get hard for another woman. I don't want to live this life without you beside me Mo'Najah."

Her silence weakened me. I had held in this pain and anger for close to 8 hours. The look on her face told me I could let it all go. With her I could be human. I held her suspended in midair while I buried my face into her full, firm breast. I allowed the tears to leak for the very first time. As she ran her soft hands through my locks caressing and consoling me in silence. When I raised my head from her cleavage. Her eyes told me everything her lips did not.

"Mar baby either put me down or take that towel off."

"I just want to hold you forever. This crazy world is sane when you're here."

Grabbing my hand she led me into the living room, removing the towel from my waist.

"Lay down on your stomach."

I did as I was told. She walked barefoot into the kitchen rattled some things, moved others. When she returned holding a small bowl, she placed that on the floor close to my right side. The scent of coconut and vanilla seduced me. The moment she straddled my exposed ass, I knew she was not about to feed me. Then the warmest sensation dripped slowly on my shoulders and back. Her hands started to kneed the stress and tension from my muscles, the more she rubbed, stroked and squeezed my back the more I relaxed. Then she started on my thighs and legs.

"Turn over."

My body felt so relaxed complying with her was beneficial. When I turned on my back Mo'Najah filled the cup of her hands with more of her miracle oil and slowly rubbed my left foot. Pounding her knuckles into the arch of my foot; rubbing in small circular motions from the heel to the toe, she repeated the same process to the other foot. The erection I was experiencing, totally involuntary. I was totally under her spell. If this was her remedy to a fucked up day, then I would take my misfortune like a man.

Without warning her mouth kissed the large toe on my right foot. Making my eyes snap open. Then her lips parted to suck my toes. I could have ejaculated instantly. Nerve endings and senses that I never knew existed became electric currents flowing wild through my body. Slowly planting kisses from the top of my foot, up my ankle licking my calf muscle the trail did not stop until she reached my groin.

Right before she placed her soft lips on my dick. She swung her hair to the left looked me dead in my eyes and told me she loved me. Then she commenced to proving it to my penis as she gagged and spit on the tip. Licking the pre-cum slowly making her tongue slither over the head and down the base. When I grabbed a head full of her hair, she had me so far gone. I started to stroke the base of my dick to meet her warm mouth. Guided her head just far enough to stimulate but not to cover.

"You want to taste it don't you? You want to know it's all yours? Damn Mo' mo I'm cummin' I'm cummin'"

Just when I thought the ride was over she spit the semen back onto my throbbing penis and continued to suck the life from me. My body was on an epic sexual roller coaster. Her warm mouth swept me from cool, to hot as hell. The muscles in my thighs, abdomen and buttocks contradicted as I shared my soul with her.

My heart pounded out of my chest. My lingam, limp and lifeless. She crawled up on my chest and allowed our hearts to beat in sync.

"Lamar, do you trust me?"

"Yes, Mo'Najah I do. Do you trust me is a better question?"

"I trust you with my life Lamar. Not just my heart or body but with my life."

"Zylar, is behind all of this; it started with the fire in Philly, then the fight at the club, sending Alashia to your room, the gun and having someone hack your computer. But she is only the money and the motive. Someone else is doing her dirty work."

"I'm listening this time Mo'Najah."

"Where is the spare key to your BMW? Who has access to your office? How would someone you hurt, hurt you back? Your freedom and your business. Now ask yourself, who would benefit from me being out of the picture?"

"Yes, Zylar still has the key to my car I never asked for it back. Mrs. Palmer also has access to the office but she hides the key in a potted plant outside. But only three of us know the code to deactivate the alarm."

"Ok. So what does Mrs. Palmer have to gain from your public and personal scandal?"

"Nothing she could lose her job if I lose my company."

"Ok how about your business partner?"

"He does not have the time to run Juicee. Plus he pushes million dollar investments the half a million he has in Juicee is not shit to Nicholas Sanchez trust. Devin is his financial advisor. Juicee is a tax write off probably."

"Lamar… I need you to use your head and not your heart. How can you make all of this work to your benefit?"

"Mo'Najah I have been formally charged for possession of a firearm. Sexual harassment, assault and child pornography; you tellin' me there is a silver lining to this shit cloud?"

"Not only am I telling you there is, I am going to put my half a million dollars into a trust for you if I am wrong."

"You are confusing the hell out of me."

"Look down stairs what do you see?"

"Traffic."

"AND?"

"People."

"ANDDD?"

"Cameras, reporters and anyone that can make a dollar off my misery."

"How much would it cost you to get this kind of publicity or media coverage?"

"Too much Mo'Najah."

"Exactly, look at all the people gettin' money in music right now. Everyone loves a bad boi' … Little Wayne – T.I.- Meek Mill- Wale even Chris B. they get more recognition for fucking up then they get for doing anything positive. How about you let your bad boy Paterson ways out. Make them give you for free what you could never afford to pay for paparazzi. Put Juicee Inc where it's supposed to be. Then use that college degree to keep it there. You are going to lose that nice guy image and maybe your kiddie group. But I will bet my money that if you start actin' like a Nigger they will pay you like a Gentleman and respect you for knowing when to be which."

"You're serious?"

Sorry
Sheed

I must have sat outside of my new home for thirty minutes or more. *Wondering what part of the game was this?* When you kill two young men who have nothing to do with your beef, kidnap an older man and burn down the house of woman who has done nothing but good in the community. For the first time ever Momma Mason's loving words and wisdom seemed like the perfect advice. *But was it too late? If I gave the game up now and still ended up catching a fuckin bullet what difference would it make. Dead is dead with or without money...*

I could not find the answer behind the wheel of the Chevy Impala I was sitting in so I decided to go make salat. Something I had not done but needed to. A lot of brothers believe that through prayer you gain clarity of your situation. That if you pray earnest enough a prophet will speak to you. I did not want to hear my own lame excuses, let alone Allah'. I proceeded to take a shower {ablution}. Entered into the smaller of the bedrooms I retrieve my sajjada from the closet. Placing it on the floor in the direction of Mecca. I prayed in Arabic for forgiveness. I prayed in English for Allah's mercy and strength, to watch over Momma M and Haneef. I prayed that my own son or daughter would never have to be hurt because of the choices I made as a man. This was the first humble and honest prayer I had offered in years. My eyes began to tear my body trembled. Something moved through me felt my pain and lifted it. When I stood I felt relieved. Free.

The light tap on the door broke my trance.

"Sheed, Haneef is on the phone."

"As-salam alaykum"

"Wa 'alaykum al-salaam, please give me some good news brother?"

"Nothing I have to say is positive Hanz, I wish it was. Your son is in Cooper they specialize in pediatric trauma, he is stable and out of I.C.U but sedated. Momma M is still in intensive care being monitored very closely she has third degree burns of 80 percent of her body. They are not very hopeful if she does not have a heart attack we are blessed. Haneef, Tanya and Mo' got into it at the hospital. They were both arrested. Everything that can go wrong is."

"Murphy's fuckin' Law. Sheed I love you man."

"Glad to hear dat'. Once I get done this package I just got from Miami, I plan on retiring."

"Sheed I just got a letter from Little Neef, asking if he could borrow the money to get his Mom's face fixed. He told me that he hates to see her cry. My son feels guilty because of the Wise situation. I can't lose my family in here. What man could live with that on his heart? I feel like such a fuckin' disappointment. I may have never let them down but I damn sure did not follow through in protecting them. I need to get in touch with Mom's doctor."

I rattled off the number to Momma Mason's room. I told Haneef to give me a chance to call the nurse's station so someone would be there when he called to place the phone by her ear. I know how much hearing from him would mean to her. I would have personally gone to the hospital but I was an hour away.

"Hanz, someone will be in her room in ten minutes. No one wants to lose her, but death is the only way most of us accept our mortality. God, literally has to kick you in the balls to make your respect his power and acknowledge his presence."

With a heavy heart and broken spirit I go find what little peace life has left me. I hold Fatima tighter than she can stand. But she does not protest. It's hard to have faith, when death and despair are more common than a cold. I have seen more people be defeated by life and never bounce back. How many chances would life give me or you?

Loveless
Mo'Najah

The time on my phone read 2 a.m. I was in no mind frame to sleep. Lamar however did not have the same issue. Curled up in the fetal position, naked with every lock twisted into a bun that rested on the pillow beside him. It was necessary to wake him. Time had not been my friend in weeks. However if something ever happened to me, I knew I would always want him comfortable. I tip-toed out of the bedroom and I made my way to the bathroom.

There was 5:45 am flight from LaGuardia airport on American Airlines. Which would get us to Las Vegas, in five and half hours I booked two first class seats. Took a shower and started getting dressed. After I was fully dressed I nudged Lamar.

"Babe, wake-up we have to be at the airport in two hours."

"Huh? Mo'Najah, why are you dressed and what time is it?"

"It's almost three in the morning. We need to leave while the reporters are gone."

"Leave where, what are you talking about?"

"Lamar do you trust me?"

"Yes I trust you!"

"Get dressed, please brush your teeth and let's go!"

As I watched him slide into a pair of Armani boxer briefs I wished I was his draws at that moment. Clumsily he stumbled around his room until he had everything he needed and walked into the bathroom. Ten minutes later he was fresh, dressed and ready to go. We both wore hats and sunglasses. In the middle of the night I thought it to be very conspicuous Lamar disagreed.

My rental was parked two blocks away. After a call down stairs to the doorman, Lamar insisted we take the exit in the rear of the building where the trash was located. Not aware as to where we were going but leading the way. His way actually placed us closer to the rental. Once I clicked the button the GMC Arcadia came alive. I tossed him the keys and waited as he came around the passenger side to open my door. With my crystal studded MCM back pack between my legs. I leaned over and opened the door for him.

Once we were safe inside a tinted out car. My heart started to pound. Not that I had any doubts, but I did not think he would go for this plan. All night while I was awake I knew I wanted to have a life with him for days or years. But I also knew the things I had to do in order to secure that life; would cost others that exact same thing.

"Lamar, if someone intentionally tried to hurt you or I what would you do to them?"

"Can you first tell me where we are going?"

"LaGuardia Airport."

Not a muscle twitched on his face. He placed the key in the ignition fastened his seat belt and pulled off into traffic.

"I hate when you call me Lamar! It's a dead indicator that something is not right. Mo'Najah I have never been in anything more than a fist fight. I have only fired a gun at the range. I would do everything in my power to prevent any harm from coming to you. But I already know that is not what you are asking me. Not certain I can play God and take another man's life."

He stares at the road never once glancing to the right to look at my face. He drives this SUV as if his life depends on it. I will always love him for his honesty and will respect the fact that he has a code all of his own. Once we arrive at the airport parking, I no longer have time to waist. I grab the bag from between my legs and expose the 75 grand that is inside. Along with the stun gun and two pocket knives and a change of clothing.

"Look I know who is responsible for hurting my Mother and step-son. She tried like hell to hurt me, but ended up hurting people I would die for. I don't want you to be something you're not. So I am gonna lay this shit out real plan and simple. Everything from my car getting hit, to the fire in Philly and your recent criminal charges all are a result of your ex's broken heart. I thought for a minute that Brianna, had something to do with her having such accurate information. However Brianna, has the address to the house in Ardmore not to my mother's house on Ruby Street, that is information she got out of the car another reason why it appeared to be a robbery. No one knows where I lay my head for safety reasons just like that. She will not get another chance at me. But you are her primary target. I am simply in her way."

"Mo'Najah, when I met you I knew there was mystery, pain and power that made you who and what you are. I have never had so much shit happen around me or to me in my life. I want it stop, not sure how I am supposed to make it happen."

"I booked two first class seats on American Airlines to Las Vegas the first step to solving this problem is to be on the same team."

"Okay I am game let's go."

"Lamar, we are going to Vegas to get married."

"You're fuckin' serious?"

"Here is your confirmation number. If I see you on the plane then I know your game. If not leave the car here they will come pick it up. I love you I'm out."

I, removed the weapons from the backpack filled with cash, I proceeded to find the registration desk for the flight.

My heart did not seem to beat at all. I looked around for the airline I was traveling and went full speed in that direction. If something happened to me before Neko could find the hitter Zylar had hired I would set everything up so Lamar would be the beneficiary of my estate. Accidental death insurance and the money in Cuba he could be the next Clive Davis. Plus in the event things get grimy, they can't make your husband testify against the wife or vice versa. I promised Momma M I was gonna get out. I would without wonder who or what was coming for me.

No More Lies
Sheed

I don't even know what time it was when she called. Usually the sound of the phone does not wake me up. Something made me answer. Looking to my right Fatima was sound asleep in our king-size bed. I took the phone into the same room where I had made prayer a few hours earlier.

"Mo'Money what's wrong?"

Her voice echoed. I could not tell where she was but I knew she was safe. My mind raced. Since I told her about the fire and she called me to have Goldman post her bail we had not spoken. Our imaginary, dutiful lines were drawn. Mines to Haneef and her's to freedom. Lines that I envied silently; knowing I would never be free. My hooks deeper than anything I could ever walk away from.

"Everything we know is at risk, Mom, Lil Neef, me and you. I know who is doing it. But I need you to tell me why?"

"Mo'Money your talking in riddles. You're telling me you know who is behind everything that has happened?"

"Yes. I know who but I don't have a clue as to why."

"I was instructed to talk to Haneef directly, you are the next best thing if not better."

"Mo' talk to Haneef about what? Are you drunk? Tell me our mother's birthday if you're safe?"

"Momma Mason's birthday is May 17th."

"Who is behind this Mo' I will handle it tonight!"

"Shawn Anderson, the person who we have been looking for has had everyone thinking he's dead. Snipes, Rell & Remmy, my incident at the club and the house in Ardmore. I know who the mastermind behind all of that was."

"Mo'Najah, just tell me who it was and I swear on my unborn child I will resolve this problem tonight!"

"Shawn you can't kill who you can't see. The person that is out for us has been planning this for years. Waited, plotted and planned his revenge better than we could have imagined. His name is Kadir Muhammad."

As the words left her lips my body went limp. The phone fell to the floor as my breathing caught up with my thoughts. Retrieving my phone from the carpet I stared at it in disbelief.

"Who told you about Kadir? That is a name you should have never, ever known. I personally shoveled the dirt on his casket, just as I did his older brother. Mo'Najah please."

"Kadir, is alive, standing 6 foot 3 maybe 230lbs clear mocha skin with a bald head, deep brown eyes and sunnah. I only know Kalief from the pictures. But the man that walked past me had a striking resemblance.

"Mo', Haneef loathed Kadir. Kalief and Haneef did not have the same father. Even thou Haneef is named Mason, they never found out who his real father was. The way Kalief told me the story. It did not matter Momma M loved all her boys just the same.

One night while leaving the adult literacy program, Momma Mason was attacked. Someone snatched her into an alley where she was robbed, beaten and raped. The cop on duty knew Snipes and called him instead of an ambulance. Who took the young Momma M to a friend that would patch her up, she refused to go to the hospital. Keeping the incident unreported, Kalief's father was livid. Demanding that she stop all of this Mother Theresa bull shit and stay home and take care of her own household.

During that time was when Ms. Stacey came back to town. With a three year old Kadir, demanded that Kyle Mason, take care of his responsibilities. Ms. Stacey had a bad drug habit. Leaving Kadir for days at a time with Momma M and Kyle. It did not take a DNA test for Momma M to know Kalief's brother. Just looking at the boys together she knew. Kyle Mason argued with Ms. Stacey and his wife tooth and nail. Until the welfare made him take a DNA test. Confirming what they had already known. Kalief was only a few months older which confirmed the affair, between Kyle and Stacey.

That was when Momma M found out she was pregnant again, refusing to terminate the pregnancy. Kyle, went into a rage and beat his wife into what he thought was unconsciousness and never returned. When Haneef was born, Snipes stepped up and supported that household whether he was on the streets and during his incarcerations. As Haneef got older he noticed the differences in his height and skin tone. Wondering why Kalief and Kadir looked so much alike and became resentful, jealous even. Kadir, was older by three years but he never had the anger or the aggression that Haneef possesed. Kadir's efforts to cling to Kalief angered a young Hanz. Ms. Stacey would leave Kadir for weeks at a time for Momma M to look after. With no food or clothes making the load even heavier for a single mother raising her own two boys on a C.N.A. salary.

That was when I met them. Haneef had Kadir in a corner punching him senseless. While Kalief, yelled for his younger brother to stop, but never intervened. When I rolled up I had no idea of what I was breaking up luckily for me I was strong and bigger than Haneef's anger. I was able to put him in a head lock that made him submit. I almost believed that was why Kalief became my friend. I was the only one that could control a young Haneef.

As the years went the hatered grew deeper. Kadir and Kalief both grew tall and skinny with wavy hair pretty boys. While Haneef bulged out short and brown like his mother but none of the same facial features. With a temper that would make his mother cry many a day. It had gotten so bad that Haneef, found Kadir's clothes that Momma M had washed and burned them in trash can. The beating she gave him only added to the beating Kadir would get the next time Haneef saw him.

One day I remember when Kalief attempted to stand up to Haneef. Telling him that he had two brothers and he loved them both the same. Momma M and Haneef spent four hours in the emergency room as Kalief's arm got reset and placed in a cast. "I'm the only brother you got and I will kill anyone that tries to come between us." Haneef stood over his own brother crazed with hate.

After that Kadir became a whisper. Momma M convinced Stacey with money to move to the other side of town. Where Kadir attended a different school. She would pay a tutor for Kadir when she found out he had difficulties in a subject. But to keep her home peaceful, she never allowed Kadir into her home again.

When he died she was devastated. The motorcycle accident happened in Myrtle Beach S.C. during black bike week. Stacey was in no position to go claim his body. So after seven days she finally told Momma M. Who brought him home for a proper closed casket service."

"How did he die Sheed?"

"The story that made it back to Philly was that Kadir and his boys were racing down Atlantic Beach Blvd. Kadir lost control of the bike and hit a kitted-up Chevy impala. Down Myrtle you never wear a helmet. He died instantly. Mo'Money the only person that ever saw the body was Momma M. The casket was closed but I carried that coffin and it was a body in there."

"What if the guy Kadir was racing was in the casket? Everyone probably scattered when the shit happen and

Kadir placed his I.D on the dead boy's body. If his face was not recognizable who would know?"

"Mo'Najah, I don't work for CSI I am a south Philly nigga that moved to west Philly. If you tell me a dude is dead and I never see him again. Then I believe the shit. Momma M is not the type of woman you question. By the way, before the bike accident Tanya and Kadir fucked around sending Haneef into another rage. Taliah is said to be Kadir's daughter Mo'."

"Shawn, what happen to Kalief?"

It was one thing to reveal Momma Mason's drama, telling Mo'Najah everything I had witness or knew about Kadir and the Mason family. But now she wanted my dark secret. So much shit had happened, so much shit was still happening. This guilt I did not want to be buried with.

"The night at the skating ring. We were all dressed to impress Momma M had hit the number and took us all shopping. She gave Kalief the keys to the Mercedes Benz wagon and told us to have fun. Kalief, was the pretty boi of the crew. Haneef was muscles and I was just the big black guy. I got pussy by default. I always got the ugly or the phat girl in the bunch. I did not mine because I never had to talk Kalief and Haneef made the plan and I went along with it.

Well, when we got to the skating ring in Camden. She looked like Aaliyah the singer. Light skin, long hair, pretty brown eyes and thick pink lips. Wearing white jeans and a pink top, her white skates and pink puffs on the toe made her stand out. Out of all the women in the skating ring that was the challenge I posed to Kalief. Telling him I would call him Master Kalief, from that day forth if he pulled her.

Showboat Kalief laced up his rental skates and went out on the slippery floor and started skating backwards doing all kinds of tricks I had never seen before. Impressed the hell out the young girl with the white jeans on. When it was time for couple skate. Kalief was standing next to her table guiding her to the floor. The girl with the white pants on forgot she had a boyfriend. Who approached Kalief after the couple skate song was over.

Mo'Najah, I remember it just like it happened ten minutes ago. The boy approached Kalief. Very humble Kalief ignored the boy and skated off."

In the distance I could hear the girl with the white jeans. "Scream we were just skating."

"Young boy left the skating ring. Kalief did not waste time meeting four other females that kept us busy for the rest of the night. When Kalief turned in his rental skates guess who was right there waiting? Ms. White pants asking if we could take her home because her jealous boyfriend left her.

Kalief left the skating ring with two females that night. As we all walked to the car that was when her boyfriend appeared he fired five shots. One right through my bicep, three into Kalief's chest and abdomen and one into the face of the girl with the white pants. Haneef caught the boy about three blocks from the skating ring, beat him mercilessly, until the cops showed up.

Master Kalief died in my arms Mo' all because I picked the girl in the white jeans my best friend died."

Mo', I need to wake up my fiancee'. I have never told another soul that story until just now.

"You don't have to wake me up. I was wondering why you were in here whispering." Fatima said with watery eyes from the other side of the door.

Confused
Lamar

After she got out of her own rental car, I sat there paralyzed. Staring at the lights on the dashboard as if her words were some Morse code or riddle that I had missed; expecting the dashboard to talk back. I sat still behind the wheel, clueless to what my next move should be. I pulled out my phone and called the only person I could talk to at three in the morning without getting cursed the hell out. The phone rang twice before Devin answered.

"Devin, what does it mean when you trust someone you love?"

"Lamar, it's the middle of the night and you want a damn vocabulary lesson? Hold on let me go down stairs I don't want to awaken Brianna."

Moments of silence fill the air space between my best friend, and I.

"Did you just say you don't want to wake up Bri'? Your back home?"

"When you called with your drama, it made my good news seem insignificant. That camping trip taught me more than it taught any of those boys. I have Jared & Jason in my care indefinitely. Because of the adoption process Brianna and I had been through I was granted permission to be the protective guardian. Who else better suited to help me care for two teenage boys than my loving wife?"

"Wow, I wish I had time to go into those details but I am between a rock and a bullet right now. It was brought to my attention that Zylar would be the logical suspect for my recent misfortune."

"Lamar, who else would have access to your car and your office? She knows how much your company means to you brah'. What else does she have to hurt you with?"

"Mo'Najah." I replied into the phone.

"LJ, trust is when you believe in a person or thing when there is no proof or evidence to confirm what they are saying. You have the mental and physical assurance that whatever is being done or said will not harm you. Even if it does you know that the person responsible will not rest until the problem is resolved."

"Devin find me a lawyer not a great one but decent and tell my mother to only believe half of what she will see on television. I am about to become a bad boi."

When I made it to the flight counter I was at U.S Air not American Air. They also had a direct flight going to LAS that was leaving in 35 minutes. Handing the lady my credit card and identification she was able to get me on the flight. Making my way through airport security. I needed this time to make sure I was on team no turning back.

When I stepped off the plane all of the stores were still closed with the three hour time difference I arrived in Vegas at 6a.m. Mo'Najah's flight would land a half hour later. If I did not have my company at least I would have the type of woman that would help me build six more companies. I must have pissed four times in an hour. My stomach churned as I watched flight 812 land. Wondering how many times she had cursed me during the five hour flight. When she stepped through the doors I stood behind her. Her hair still pulled back into the pony tail. Her red Phillies cap down low over her forehead. The biggest shades to cover her amazing eyes. Rime stoned backpack and Camoflauged capris. Remembering the fool I made out of myself when I wanted her attention made this gesture apropos. On one knee with a gate full of strangers surrounding.

"Mo'Najah … Excuse me."

Of course everyone walking behind, in front and the airline personal all stopped as if I was speaking to them. My heart pounded erratically. This felt nothing like the first time.

"I probably will never be worthy of the love, loyalty, respect and commitment you will give in an abundance to my life. There is a good man; provider, protector and friend inside of me. That will make you question your own sanity at times. But I knew when you walked away. That I would rather practice and fail at forever with you, than live a life of maybe's without you. So ummm would you do me the honor and become the next Mrs. James?"

Big Fish
Monajah

When I arrived in Philly all hell had broken lose. I had been served at the hospital with the restraining order Tanya had placed against me. Mother Mason was awake and mad as hell. China finally had a chance to tell me about her attack and the car that was destroyed. The two hundred grand was the only high light. In a little over ten days between Buddah and China, I was sixty thousand away from breaking even and that was with everyone being paid and the of cost of the lost Altima. The house in Washington Township was done. I placed a for sale sign on it. Calling a broker out of south jersey by the name of Stephany Watson, I was back at square one.

Since Latham did not believe Kadir Muhammad was alive I needed someone who was not close to the alleged deceased. I made a call to Neko, with the hopes that he also had some good news for me in return.

"Hola' senorita"

"Please tell me you have some good news for me?"

"Good but not great. Your girl hired a middle man. Not a hitter."

"What do you mean who subcontracts a hit?"

"Someone who knows his limitations."

"He personally handled the gun and drugs in the vehicle. The kiddie porn and the email conversations between Lamar and Alashia. He is a computer geek. The fire was someone else he is alleging."

"Let me guess he is not giving up the name?"

"Nope… I had his balls in a vice for eight hours. Beat him unconscious twice and started to pull the skin off his back. Who ever took the fire is more deadly than the pain I am dispensing."

"Find something he loves. Make it disappear. By the way how good are your people with finding someone who has pretended to be dead for over five years?"

"That maybe a challenge but my people hate easy jobs."

"Good I will send you everything I can find from the high school year book to location of the where the body is buried. Neko, don't kill him until we know I am not still on someone's list."

Being in this hospital I was a walking target. I needed to make Momma M want to move. So when her lunch came in I had a small bug placed on the tray. Within two hours the doctors had her release forms and I had a private institution, ready to admit her on arrival.

Not being able to see or talk to Lil Neef had me vexed. So much that I had Rocc start to watch Tanya. Figuring if I could not see him at least I could get up to date reports. Rocc's fee was seven thousand a week. I was already on week three. Only to get an alarming report. That Tanya had been to see her plastic surgeon twice in one week. Between Momma M, being in the hospital and me not having any contact with Little Neef. Her recent trips to the doctor was a major mystery. I know he did not take Medicad. *Did this bitch find a way to get the thirty grand*? Even if the money came from Haneef it would have gone through Goldman or Sheed.

Once Mamma M arrived at the rehabilitation clinic in Bucks county which was closer to Sheed. But far from Tanya. I placed three much needed calls one was to Sheed. Telling him not to release Momma Mason's new location. If Tanya wanted to be a bitch so could I. Then maybe I could see little Neef in the process. The second was to Goldman, who eagerly passed several messages from

Haneef. Neither of them had given Tanya any lumps sums of money and lastly was to China.

"China, I have a secret mission for you. Can you blow the dust off your medical skills and tell me why Tanya has been at the plastic surgeon on Chestnut twice in a week?"

"Bitch give me something hard to do. I will have an answer in three hours."

You Lead
Lamar

One night with my wife was all this bizarre situation would allow. We got married that day. I brought her the cheapest ring at the Pawn On Da Lawn pawn shop. She gave me the ring off of a Cuban cigar. The ceremony was nothing short of bad clip in someone's underground movie. But standing by her side, promising my life and heart to her was all I needed. Once I stood in front of her I knew she was my everything. I only hoped that I could give her the same. After the vows we checked into the Wynn Casino.

Mo'Najah is a fuckin' poker shark. Taking ten grand she quickly turned it into twenty-five. Bluffing and bulling grown men on the table. When we made it to the honeymoon suite. I only had one word. Perfection. I was distracted but my wife was on point. She had brought her tablet with her pulling up the links and access codes to her Cuban account. Mo'Najah's six figure accounts made me feel like a welfare case. Her second call was to a lawyer by the name of Goldman to find out who had her life insurance policy. Another 1.5 million in accidental death coverage, now with my name listed as the beneficiary. Property, cars and jewelry etc. she wanted her step-son to have. Someone faxed over a living wills to the concierges'. We went and got the papers notarized and placed everything in a safety deposit box along with our marriage certificate, half of the cash and the rings.

"Mo'Najah I think you should sell the house in New Jersey. What if Brianna accidentally told Zylar about it."

"The house was brought through a series of dummy companies Brianna's people help me create. I would hope she would not be that naïve or careless. But your right I can't afford to sleep on Ms. Wingate."

"Mo'Najah are you sure you want to keep so much valuable information this far away?"

"If I am dead Las Vegas, is not too far for you to be set from life. If you die that couple of dollars won't mean shit. No patterns rule number one."

When we arrived at the airport we had bags from our elaborate trip. Her skin was a ripe caramel color. Her wet wavy hair danced on her shoulders. I hated to leave. The late flight was surprising empty. I had no idea of how long it would take to make this plan work; but I knew I needed my mile high badge before it went into action. The first class stall was a sneeze bigger than the other. When I came out with the paper towel in my hand I watched as the two flight attendants catered to Mo'Najah. I removed my wallet, from my left hip pocket, I pulled out four crisp, blue hundred dollar bills. Giving both of the women a knowing look, I grabbed Mo'Najah's left hand. Once she unfastened her seat belt she knew what was about to go DOWN. I gave her the money to dispense to the attendants. Whispered in her ear to follow me.

As I opened the door to the lavatory inward I could hear one attendant say. "It happens more than you think. Thank you."

Sundresses were made for events just like this. Both of us in the compact toilet knowing hundreds of people had been in and out only added to the pornographic scene my mind had envisioned.

"Luckily this is a long flight you can take your time and suck this dick."

"For that money we could have fucked in our seats."

"The flight ain't over and my partner is ready for action." Grabbing the bulge in my jeans to confirm my statement.

Lifting up her dress Mo'Najah exposed a clean freshly waxed pussy. Grabbing five paper towels she placed them between the back of her dress and the plastic sink. Leaning back just far enough to place her right leg over my shoulder she fed me on the plane. Spreading her meaty lips apart with my tongue I devoured her clitoris like a lesbian. No fingers just licks, sucks and slurps to make her whispered sweet, nasty nothings. Glancing up at my beautiful wife her head was back, her eyes closed. Her lips formed shapes and sounds that only encouraged my mission. I wanted the flood. Darting my tongue in and out of the vaginal opening I tasted the cream but I wanted the liquid. The head grabbing, face fuckin' that I knew she could deliver. Lowering her leg I get up off the toilet, unzip my jeans and remove her best friend from my boxers.

"Are you sore from last night?"

"Fuck sore write my new last name on this pussy."

"Yes Mrs. James the pleasure is all mines."

Without further conversation I entered Mo'Najah's swollen, warm-wetness. Feeling her tightness around the circumference of my penis made it grow larger inside her. Not knowing when I would get to touch her again triggered mad man thoughts. The slow deep deliberate strokes; turned into thrust as she wrapped her legs around my bare ass. Somehow she knew where I was mentally. Pulling her left breast from the top of the dress she forced my head down. Dug her nails into my skin through the thin white sleeveless tee-shirt marked her territory. Dared me to be me.

"Yeah, that's what Daddie needed, lady in the streets and whore in the sheets. Give me that dick, give me something to remember on the nights when I am all alone and I need my husband's touch. Ain't no pussy like this Mo'Jo. Yeah beat it up."

She whispered her sultry obscenities into my ear which made my mouth water. As badly as I wanted to release I wanted her liquid joy dripping from my face. Releasing her nipple ring from my mouth. I resumed my original position. Only this time my right index and middle finger spread her smooth labia apart. So that my attack was as precise and swift all parts to that Mo'Jo needed exposure and I refused to be denied. Inserting two fingering into her vulva I found my own erection throbbing. Hooking my fingers slightly I found the ridge area. Gently sucking on her clit and stroking my fingered against her pleasure palace. Had her speaking Spanish in no time. Leaving me with a mouth full of her orgasm that I gladly consumed. Prying her hands from my locks I watched in admiration as her chest heaved. Gliding my beautiful wife off the sink. I reminded her of hard situation that she had under looked. We switched positions and she road my dick like a backwards cowgirl. Pressing me hard against the sink as she used the wall for leverage. Rotating her round perfect ass on my manhood. Begging me to please her. Daring me to cause another eruption. The verbal fuck was just as enticing as the physical. She knew how to handle me and I loved it. I grabbed her shoulders making her weight fall completely on my pelvic area. Giving her all nine and quarter inches. My right hand around her neck squeezing ever so firmly.

"Ugggghhhh."

As the plane prepared to land my fantasy was over.

"Lamar, I need you to pretend that you hate me. Like the fight we are about to have is the wrath of all the frustration you have been experiencing. When I pull off you're a C.E.O of a million dollar label and you don't give a fuck about anyone or anything. We are building a company from the time we pull up to your building play your position. No harm no foul. Any time you talk to Devin it has to be in person. Not even your Mother can know. There is a method to my madness."

A block away from the penthouse. She removed the ponytail holder from her hair shaking her head wildly. Smeared the lip stick and rubbed the eye liner. Her beautiful face now looking like a war zone. When she frantically pulled up in front of the building she startled the shit out of the doorman and at least three camera people. As the tire from the massive SUV rolled up on the curb she made the vehicle come to a screeching halt. People moved in a panic. Jumping out of the driver door leaving the car running her performance began…

"Get the fuck out, I hate you!!! You probably did order that kiddie porn you sick bastard."

Slinging the clothes we just brought onto the sidewalk like a mad woman.

"I don't need you or this bullshit. Take your ass back to that wanna be pop diva. If you can get that thing up for her."

I did not want to play this game. But I knew I had to. Slamming the passenger door of the rental the glass shattered. My drama matched hers.

"Oh word you gonna try and humiliate me strip bitch find another pole. Taking the money out of my wallet I tossed it into Mo'Najah's face.

"I brought you, I can buy another. Maybe you should take your show on the road. Become a professional I hear they make more."

"You would know, since the only pussy you get you pay for Mr. Pedophile!"

Jumping back into the driver's seat she sped off. Leaving me to now argue with reporters and camera men. Picking up the bags and the money I made my way upstairs. I am glad she is on my team. Who or whatever goes up against her will get more than they bargained for. Zylar will not be an exception.

Silent Security
Benny D

Mo'Najah, never asked for my help. But when she called to ask permission for Sheed to reach me I became alarmed. It had been some years, when old contacts want to resume business you take notice. Especially when the stakes are so high. I had to get reacquainted with the Mason group. After all everyone wants the top spot. I sent my personal best guard to handle the task. By the time Loco, arrived in Philly so much was already happening. Snipes, was the original connection between Haneef and I, his disappearance was disturbing.

Loco's primary mission was Mo'Najah's safety. But with Haneef's entire team being targeted no one was safe. Loco was an ex- Marine he served two tours in Afghanistan. Urban life was not shit to him. Bullet wounds and drug over doses he considered happy endings. I had feared that Haneef's son was the next target. So I took a gamble and had Loco, pay special attention to Tanya. After I was notified of how much security Mo' kept herself surrounded with, I was confident that she was safe.

Tanya's stunt with District Attorney Petrini, was nothing short of brilliant. Even though I had no idea as to why she would want her dead. Tanya was on someone's team. Loco, had taken the time to place a few listening devices into the home of Ms. Tanya with the hopes that we could figure out the connection to the dead D.A.; when that failed. Loco started to take high def. photos of everyone that came into contact with Tanya directly or indirectly. The man known as Kadir was a complete mystery. No positive photo I.D, no matches with FBI or any of the criminal data bases. Kadir reminded me of myself a walking, living and breathing ghost.

 "Mo'Najah it's Miami secured land line thirty minutes."

One week after Mo'Najah talked with Benny D.

Heaven or Hell
Haneef

"Mason visit."

"I don't get visits remember."

"Mason visit! Last time I am going to call you or I will go out there and talk to that fine piece myself."

Dressed to kill Mo'Najah wore an all white two piece suite with a large tan belt to show off her small waist. Tan and white wedge peak toe sandals. But the kicker was the hair cut. Her asymmetrical bob that was parted on the left side. With a touch of make-up to make her look even more exotic. When I got to the table, I was speechless.

"You look amazing Mo'."

"Thank you, Haneef your still in here stressing I see?"

"A lot to stress over would you not agree?"

"You ain't never lied."

The tension was thick. Her eyes wander around the visit hall. It's not my mother or my son. I have not seen her since we signed papers finalizing her role in my life. As badly as I wanted to know why she was here. I knew it could not be good.

"Sorry to hear about you and the music dude. You made World Star."

"Shit happens. Right?"

"I really want to thank you for being there for my family. My mother loves you like a daughter. We would not have gotten through this without you."

"Haneef, Kadir Muhammad is alive and well."

The look on my face told my thoughts. She knew me too well.

"Not only is he alive but him and Tanya have been in cahoots. Benny has photos of them together. I don't think she is reuniting him with his long lost daughter either."

"I carried his casket. I saw the college ring he wore on his middle finger. The brand from his frat on his shoulder. My mother actually had his property from Myrtle Beach police department. Mo' he is dead!"

"Tanya is getting her face repaired as we speak, thanks to Mr. Kadir's generosity. Or did you give her the money?"

"Stop saying this motherfucker's name he is dead!"

"Did you hear about District Attorney Petrini having a massive heart attack at 53 years old in her office?"

"Of course, you know I stay up on all the news in Philly. I can't say I was sorry to hear about it. She fucked up on..."

"Kalief's murder trial." Mo' finished my sentence.

"Revenge is a dish that is best served cold. Tanya, happened to be in the same WaWa the morning that D.A. Petrini died. How ironic is that? Did I mention that your mother had a visitor at the hospital? The day that Tanya and I go arrested for fighting in the emergency room. Kadir Muh, made a special bedside appearance to Momma M."

Dis' bitch is crazy. She is seeing dead people. Telling me farfetched fables, leaned all the way back in the plastic chair I stare at her. Looking for signs of drug use or dilated pupils something; darkness around her eyes and mouth. My silence does not make the story end however.

"Who else would go through such great lengths to avenge his only brother's death?"

My heart pounded as my mind started to decipher and filter everything that has happened. Kadir, Kalief, the trial, Snipes, and Mo'Najah.

"No. No. No. He would never hurt Momma M. or anything she loved. Look for Wise or Joey Black, dead men don't resurrect. He is a fucking man and men die every day Mo'Najah."

"I could not bring the photos with me. You should know I have seen him. But I had no idea of who he was. About 6'3 slender he looked like Kalief's old high school photo only with a full sunnah and Kuffi. When I leave here. I need you to call this number, its Miami. When you hear the voice and the conversation. You tell me how you want your son's mother to die?"

Three Long Months later...

Price of Fame
Lamar

Menace and I have traveled the entire country. With my recent legal issues I was not allowed to leave the U.S. but that did not stop the tour. Mohegan Sun, in Connecticut to Charlotte, Huston, Miami, Chicago, every event sold out. Every night we partied like stars, lived like kings and acted like royalty. I had never been surrounded by so many beautiful women. The cameras never stopped flashing. The bottles came in multitudes, along with the drama.

In the last quarter, Juicee Inc had made more money than the entire time my company had been established. Menace was getting calls to work with top name artist. Invitations to open at venues we would have never even seen until you had three or four multi-platinum albums under your belt. The life had become everything I dreamed of. But nothing I could not walk away from.

Waking up in a different city, with a different woman every night, was routine. I was living the life of a 'Boss'. I made sure that everyone made a video before they even came close to me. I never smashed any of them but the power of knowing I could was incredible. Usually I got off watching the chicks entertain one another.

I smoked and watch them get pissy drunk and pass out. Ducking photos and interviews being rude and arrogant. For the first time in my life I did not give a fuck who thought what. Fame came with a price, I enjoyed paying it. Being a good guy was never this easy.

All of the success Mo'Najah predicted, was coming full circle. Following the road map she laid out had me more successful than years of financial planning. Every day I wanted to call her and share something with her. But my bank statements, made following her orders that much easier.

Then the letter arrived certified from the City of New York. Possession of an unregistered weapon. Now the real show as about to begin. Mo'Najah's plan was simple but dangerous. After my first court appearance where I would act like a complete ass. I would go to the penthouse and attempt suicide. Deny all of the allegations against me and claim that my recent behavior is due to the loss of my fiance' Zylar Wingate. That I loved more than life. Not being able to handle the pressure of the false allegations and failed relationship. I took two Zannies and sprinkled the rest on the floor.

When Devin found me the morning my trail was suppose to begin. The media would have a field day with my ass.

Dear, God

I know you do not grant entrée into your kingdom this way. I don't know who I am any more. I have let everything I love be tainted and destroyed by the money and the women. I have broken the heart of the only woman that loves me unconditionally. Trampled on the feelings of my family and friends. I never touched or harassed that woman a day in my life. I don't know what's happening. But I know jail is not for me. I would rather die than live like an animal.

Zylar I am sorry.

Leaving like a man,
Lamar

Damned If You Do
Devin

The rain on this December day was close to hurricane status. The winds whipped the water around the window of my office making me wish I would have stayed home with Brianna. Now that we had three kids in the house, adult time was few and far between.

When she walked into my office I had no idea who she was. Dressed in all black wearing big Liz Taylor like glasses and bright red lipstick. My receptionist said that her name was Mrs. James. I did not think anything of it because the last name was very common. Once she removed her glasses and sat across the desk. I realized I had never actually seen her. Yes I selected her for Lamar's bachelor party from an array of photos the club had online. But I had never laid eyes on her face to face. *I see why my brother from another mother is coo-coo for coco puffs.* I tried hard not to stare.

"I was told, I could trust you Devin I hope for Lamar's sake that is true."

"I won't pretend that I agree with the parts of the plan you have me playing. But I gave my brother my word that I would do whatever was necessary."

"Good the drug is named Propofol it is used every day in emergency rooms around the world. The dosage is based on Lamar's weight. Every ten pounds you receive a .2 cc of the drug. It can be done directly into his I.V. line."

"I don't understand why he has to be in an induced coma? Why would Zylar have to think he is dying? None of this makes since. Yes the stunt show you and him put on jump started Juicee Inc's paramount climb into the industry. But what if you are wrong?"

"Devin, remember when you crashed your car a few months ago and Lamar came to your bedside and told you he was not going to marry Zylar and why?"

"Yeah I remember that entire conversation."

"When people believe this maybe their last chance at redemption they say things, do things. The human reactions and impulses are different. If Zylar loves him how I believe she does. There would be nothing that would keep her from his bedside. Just make sure the balloon with the bear inside is always pointed in the direction of his bed."

"The lawyer said that the case is beatable. They could prove his office was broken into and the same with the car. Why risk his life in the process?"

"Listen I don't have time to break this down for you. Your job is two things. Administer the Propofol in three twenty four hour doses. Make sure Zylar finds out which hospital he is in and that it does not look good."

Tossing the viles and stack of hundred dollar bills on my desk Mo'Najah left my office. Leaving the sweetest scent of Clive Christian perfume behind. Lamar was playing a deadly game of cat and mouse. I could not figure out who was the cat. If looks were a crime Mo'Najah would be first degree murder and her body made her armed and dangerous. I guess a chance to play house with her I might go to jail for a few months and play dead for my ex.

At 8a.m. I pulled my Camry up to Lamar's penthouse, there were at least ten reporters and six camera men posted out front of his building. When the door man let me in he whispers to use the back exit to leave.

When I let myself into Lamar's apartment. He was indeed unconscious partially dressed and sprawled out on his bathroom floor. If this was part of the act I was not ready for the Lamar and Mo'Najah reality show.

"911 what is your emergency?"

"My friend is passed out on the bathroom floor with an empty bottle of pills on the counter."

"Can you tell me if your friend is breathing?"

"Yes he appears to be breathing but he is not waking up!"

"Are you in a safe location?"

"Yes, I am at 555 west Harlem Drive. Penthouse 3."

"Okay sir what is your name? I am dispatching a unit to your location."

"My name is Devin Davis. His head is bleeding should I put anything on it?"

"No don't touch or attempt to move him he could have broken something during his fall. Just wait until the ambulance arrives. Stay on the line."

God Don't Like Ugly
Zylar

"Mother what would you like me to do with all of these can goods?"

"Zylar we are making baskets for the less fortunate for the holidays sort them and place the items in the basket.

Example sweet potatoes and string beans one of each should be placed in each basket."

Why did I volunteer to help? At seven months pregnant I am miserable and moody. My face is hideous with bumps and blotches. My feet are swollen and my back is sore. I have gained 23lbs with this baby. But I promised my mother that I would assist with the charity event at the social club. After all my parents have been just as charitable to me. Moving me out of the city and finding me a nearby apartment. Menace, graciously pays all of the bills however with his recent fame. I had not seen or heard much from him. Money in the bank suites me just fine.

The last few months have been lonely but calm. Drama-free and peaceful I rejoined my Pop-Pop's church I was singing in the choir again. Life after Lamar was not flashy and exciting. But I stopped crying after the first month of being back in Charleston. Menace's proposal lasted until he got the true feel of his new found fame. There were a million women that looked good, thousands that could sing. They all would fuck, suck and swallow just to be in his bed for an hour. He tried to keep his word. With me not being able to travel with him reason one because of Lamar and the other the baby. I knew it was only a matter of time. I did not love him like that so I did not faze me. Plus I got updates on Lamar.

After two hours I had packed forty basket with a can ham and vegetables. Not only had I done my charitable deed for the day but for the following year as well. My body was tired as I sat on the soft chair. Leaning my head back I started to relax. The buzzing and sound of my cell phone that was all the way on the other side of the room shattered what little peace I had found. Wobbling over to my Hermes bag I retrieved my phone. Only to find that I had three missed calls and several text messages from Brianna. Which was odd with Devin's return, Ebony's adoption and the hoodlum boys Brianna was very short on conversation lately.

As I checked my voice mail, I heard something that I never thought I would hear.

"Zylar, I really don't know how to tell you this, but Lamar attempted suicide this morning. Devin found him on the floor with a note that said he was sorry he hurt you. I know you are moving on with your life and you said not to bother you with these trivial things. But somehow this seems very important."

Payne
Mo'Najah

Getting Momma Mason back into her house was a blessing. Every therapy session, doctor's visit, all the fussin' and cussin'; was music to my ears. The holidays were fast approaching and I was more thankful than I had ever been.

Little Neef had not been to the house Tanya, refused to allow him to come over. But I made a trip to his school. It was not the time I was accustomed to, but it had to suffice. The hug he gave me when he saw me in the office was priceless.

"Where you been? I have been waiting months to tell you thank you?"

"I have been getting Momma M, back on track and I purchased the property for my daycare."

"Mo' thank you so much my mom has never been happier. Her scars are gone, everything is normal now. She still wants to move, but I don't care. I will be a good kid as long as she is smiling."

"No matter where you live I will always love you. No matter what your Dad misses you like crazy. Do me a favor and don't mention my visit here your mom would flip."

"No problem Mo' I love you."

When I left the school I was having a change of heart. Maybe I did not care that she had plotted and planed my demise. My love for her son was incredible, his touch made me soft forgiving, merciful even. Haneef had gotten a chance to listen to the recording. He knew it was Kadir, the conversation was about the party when little Neef was three. How Kadir planned to kill Haneef until Momma M walked out of the back yard holding the spatula. How Kadir's love for Momma M allowed him to let his enemy live.

Haneef was crazed on the phone. He only asked that I allow her to have an open casket. Let his son and her daughter say good- bye properly. I had agreed. To allow her death to be as payne-less as possible. Not for her but for her son. Someone that I loved more than the hurt she tried to break me with.

Pulling up to Ruby Street the hawk was out today. Early December and it was low 30's. I had on a hat, scarf and North Face. Before I got out of the car my cell phone rang. It was Buddah.

"Mo'Money let me hold something?"

"You got it all gurl I should be asking you for a loan."

"I did my weekly drive by of the crib in Ardmore you got a package from Allenwood with Haneef's name on it."

"How big?"

"Nice size box about the size of a X-box."

"Can you meet me on Ruby?"

"No doubt."

When I walked into the house the smell of fried chicken greeted me. When I walked up behind her in the kitchen Momma M was back to her old self. The scars on her face and hands were still there but she did not mind. Called them battle wounds said the devil tried to get her and she got the marks to prove it.

"Sheed's girl friend Fatima had the baby this morning Mo'. Look they sent me a pictures." She said placing her huge Galaxy Note phone on the kitchen table.

"It's a boy awww damn how big is he?"

"9lbs 4 ounces and 34 inches long she was only in labor for three hours."

"I guess so that big ass baby could have walked out the pussy."

"Get outta my kitchen. Talking that mess, you next."

"I ain't having no super-size baby come out of me."

Moments like this was why I would kill for this family. Her laughter even after enduring weeks of hell and healing. Her joy and appreciation for this life was astounding. I thank God everyday for not taking that from me. This was more love, affection, humor and bonding than I could let go of. Especially knowing there would be no one there to replace it. While I was being teased and interrogated about Lamar, thanks to Haneef. My cell phone chimed.

 I'm outside.{Puff puff pass.}

I brought the box back into the house and went into the basement to open it. Last time I had received Haneef's property I was not happy with my findings I did not expect this time to be any different. When I opened the box about forty photos fell from the inside and twice as many letters. As I shifted through the letters they had rather recent dates by the post mark. I guess Allenwood did not return the mail. The letter from LuLu caught my attention because it was in a pretty blue envelope and slightly larger than the rest. Unsealed already I decided to open it. The photo of Kayla in her school uniform looking a lot like Haneef made me smile but pissed me off. So many lies for no reason. I would have loved to have another kid to spoil. Stuffing the photo back into the envelope. I saw a letter from Tanya.

Haneef,

I never got a response from the letter and photos I sent. I want to say that I'm surprised, but I'm not. What I can't understand is how another bitch that walks, talks and bleeds just like me. Has so much control over what you do, how you think and what goes on with our family???

You think she is better because she is mixed or maybe because she was a virgin when you met her. She is a North Philly, hood rat no different and damn sure not an exception.

I will give her props for not turning into a full fledge whore however. Even after she started to get confirmation about all the bitches you fucked and tricked up on. See on the strength of that alone I may have emptied your damn accounts out. I may have even, taken your lifetime rival in the streets on an all inclusive vacation. But that's just me!

As I sit here and think, I birthed your mother fuckin' son. I was the one on the team when you were barely moving ounces. I was the one that had the cars and cribs in my name. So now that I need you most you gon' shit on me? Over a piece of pussy?

Mo'Najah, ain't even legally married to you. At anytime that bitch can jump ship. Leaving you ass out! That would be what you deserved.

But at the end of the day I am raising your son. I am cooking his food and helping with his homework. All of that is me. Your priorities and loyalties are fucked up. I know I have done some dump shit in the past. None of us are perfect. With that said, I never turned my back on you. Even after you chose to start a new life with her, I was always there, a phone call away. If you needed me to handle something you never had to ask twice. If you wanted to fuck you never had to ask at all. The bond between us was supposed to last until the grave Hanz' I guess I am dead to you now.

Since you refuse to give me this money, for the plastic surgeon to repair my face. I feel like there are too many bad memories here. My family, will be moving out of the state as soon as I can transfer my section eight. You will always be Lil' Neef's Father, but your definitely not his Dad.

Blah, blah fuckin' blah. See just when I had a change of heart. No this would not be a good Christmas. I could not let this bitch live another week and think that she could pop off anytime she did not get her fuckin' way. Throwing the rest of the mail and photos back into the box I was pissed.

Kissing Momma M on the check I asked her if she had any gum or mints.

"Look in my pocket book baby next to my bible."

Knowing that she would not be leaving the house any time soon I removed her keys from her bag. Knowing one of them was to Tanya's. I took the keys and had copies made. Less than a hour I returned her keys, without her ever realizing they were gone. There were only six keys on the ring luckily and one of them was to the house in Ardmore and two to the new locks her own door.

Tanya has always had a severe allergic reaction to peanuts called anaphylaxis. As much as I wanted to make her suffer I would find solace in watching her take her last breathes. Most people that had such allegeries carried a self-induced pin containing epinephrine. She would not be fortunate enough to find hers.

When Tanya left her house to take the kids to school. I had applied deadly doses of pure peanut extract into her tooth paste, mouth and body wash. If she drank the juice in the refrigerator she would get a dose of death. I had decided a very sneaky attack against my lifelong enemy. As soon as Tanya entered her house I would be there waiting. Silently I sat in her closet with the needle filled with her demise. Dressed like a ninja my heart pounded, not out of fear but anger and rage. She left me no choice. I would not walk uncertain steps in a city that I had planned to grow in. Wondering when the next trap or explosion would occur. No dead ex's were best.

When Tanya's maxima pulled up to the house I heard her click the auto lock. As Tanya walked through the door her cellular began to ring. China was right outside watching my back.

"Yes this is Ms. Thompson."

"Ms. Thompson this Tina Cosati from Reform & Refresh Medical Mobility. I work in the accounting department. It seems that you were charged for three sessions of therapy that you never attended. Would you like to schedule those sessions or receive a refund?"

"I had seven sessions of muscle therapy that were ordered by my surgeon. I attended every one."

"Well you were charged for ten maybe they estimated the visits and since you pre-paid for your treatment. Your entitled to a refund would you like me to mail that money to you?"

"No, can you have a check issued? I will get dressed and come down there now. How much was the over payment?"

"Three hundred a session so the check will be for $900.00."

"That will jump start Christmas shopping I will be there in an hour."

Dressed in pajama pants, UGG boots and scarf. Tanya tossed her coat and pocket book on the couch. Headed in the direction of the master bedroom I heard the water start. Music began to play from the same direction. I left my hiding place to pursue my nemesis. Needle covered in my left hand and my gun secure in my right. As Kendrick Lamar's 'Poetic Justice' blasted through the speakers of her radio. Tanya slowly undressed and sang along to the song.

"If I told that a flower bloom in a dark room would you trust it I mean I write poems and then songs. Dedicated to you when you're in the the mood for empathy is blood in my pen."

As she stood in her mirror admiring her beauty she played with her 24 inch Malian weave. The steam from the shower started to cloud the mirror. She ran water into the sink and grabbed her face cloth. The steam from the towel on her ebony skin glistened. Now it was time to administer the cream that her surgeon had given her to even out her skin tone. Which was also infused with Peanut extract. As she generously rubbed the cream into her skin in a clockwise motion. I stood motionless from six feet away. Patiently waiting to see which device would aide me in the death of my advisory. After she completed her facial treatment Tanya, reached for the Crest tooth paste and spread it along the bristles of her brush. Setting down the tooth brush she guzzles from the bottle, a mouth full of Listerine. Before she could even spit it out. Her eyes began to bulge; she began coughing and gagging violently. Just as she turned around completely naked I stood there. Poking her with the needle full of pure peanut extract. I stepped back and aimed my gun at her face.

"Do you like the way death feels Tanya? Would you like me to call Kadir to save you? Do you know how badly I wanted to pour battery acid all over your fucking body and watch you die a gruesome and painful death? No, how about how I wanted someone to stuff there dirty large dick into every orifice of your body as you screamed and begged for mercy. With everything you have allowed to happen to me, you never got the pleasure to see the pain you inflicted or the look of death. So this is my personal pleasure I am certain my pussy is wet right now. Death is a blessing you jealous, crazy bitch. I am going to stand here and watch you take your last breathes. Now let's figure out who will raise your son and Kadir's daughter. Hmmmm, let me think about it I guess that would be me and Momma M. I sure hope you have life insurance you treacherous wanna' be? Because it doesn't seem right to kill you and pay for your damn funeral."

As Tanya grasped at her own throat fighting for air she quickly fell on the bathroom floor. Struggling for any kind of air to enter her lungs. It took twenty minutes of rugged breathes that turned into vomiting before she eventually stopped moving all together. But she still had a pulse. I would wait until heart stopped beating. Removing the second needle from my pocket I injected another dose of pure peanut extract into her external iliac artery. I never let my guard down after an hour. Tanya was motionless. I removed my black gloves and placed blue latex gloves on and check her neck for a pulse. Her entire face was swollen as she laid naked on the floor her expensive hair all tangled. Life-less. I took her cell phone with me as I climbed out of little Haneef's bedroom window which is how he got out of the house without Tanya's knowledge.

Fool Me Twice
Zylar

I had to beg my mother to accompany me to New York. At seven months pregnant she refused to allow me to travel alone. Even though everything had been smooth since my little black out, several months ago. Once I told my mother that Lamar attempted to kill himself over me she reluctantly agreed to take the trip.

Visitation hours was all night at the hospital. Between friends and family there was no way I would have a moment alone with Lamar. Not to mention I did not want anyone to know I was pregnant. But I needed to see him. What if he never woke up from his coma or worse if he died? I needed to say good bye. I had to forgive him for hurting me.

Late that night while mother was sleeping. I took a taxi to the hospital. Surprisingly there was no one visiting. But just to be on the safe side, I borrowed one of the doctor lab coats. Entered the room very nonchalantly. I stood there waiting to see if he moved. The room was filled with flowers, cards and balloons. Everyone praying for Lamar's speedy recovery. How pathetic.

Even standing this close to him I still thought he was faking. I slapped his face, pinched his side and even fondle his penis. This bastard really tried to kill himself. The threat of losing his freedom was more than Mr. Music could handle.

"I guess you and little miss stripper were not evenly yoked after all? I have been reading the papers I know all about the drinking, smoking and fighting. You are just going to hell in a hand basket. See how wretched life is without a good Godly woman beside you? These things don't happen by accident God knows what we need even when you alter his plan. I came to tell you that I forgive you Lamar. You are human prone to make mistakes. Leaving this relationship was a grave mistake on your part. But I forgive you as God has forgiven. If you should die I would not want you to think I do not love you still. You will forever be a part of me in more ways than one. Even though I wished you dead on many a night. I never wanted you to not be alive. I only wanted to hurt you like you hurt me.

Oh congratulations on the going multi-platinum, I told you Menace would be everything you were looking for. See I was more than your lover; I was an amazing partner, spiritual companion and friend. I guess that is what I miss most about you or should I say us. I had made my entire life around you and your business and just like that it was gone. You never even called to see if I was okay after the incident at the album release party. It took for your strip-whore to disrespect you and countless other events to happen for you to realize exactly what I meant to you. What a tragedy we could have been like Jay-Z and Beyonce`. Men never look at the big picture your species is led by your penis. I guess I miss that too, damn that dick was astounding. I see you gained a few pounds. But the six pack is still as tight as ever. Mother sends her best, you know she is a good Baptist woman. We even pray for our enemies.

I can't stay too long this 24 hour visitation schedule. Leaves the door open for just about anyone to pop up anytime. So have a peaceful journey to where ever God destines you to be. I will be fine raising our baby with love. While you wallow in the mess, that I created. Too bad I did not wait for her to just leave you, I could have saved a lot of money on that fire in Philly. Oh well, nothing ventured even less gained."

As I leaned in to kiss Lamar on the forehead in walked two police officers.

"Zylar Wingate you are under arrest for two counts of murder, two counts of attempted murder, black mail and conspiracy charges."

Missing
Mo'Najah

"Mo'Najah I am sorry but I could not locate the man in those pictures. I wish I could fix this problem for you. Even with the phone every contact was never to him personally there was always a middle man. If I did not live my life very similar I would be impressed. When someone goes through great lengths to die, only someone close to them will ever know something different."

"He is very lucky I love children or I would use his own blood to get what he has taken from me. However I am certain he will not disappear into the night forever. His main objective is Haneef who is still alive, strong and well connected. Thank you, Benny for everything including the Cartier Necklace. I will make sure I send you photo's when I wear it.

Punishment
Zylar

"Mother, I simply need you to call Ashward. He is more than capable of getting me out of here in a few hours."

"Zylar, I now know what your father was saying to me in that hospital room. I have spoiled the soil in which you have grown. Corrupted and enabled such a devious and devilish child to evolve into a woman capable of un-godly acts. Zylar, this is how this is going to play-out. You will plead guilty to the charges you are facing and plead mental defect. You will sign over custody to either Lamar or me. You will not shame or embarrass this family with a high profile trail. Spending countless dollars on legal fees and tarnishing the name your father has worked so hard to keep prestigious. In return I will send you money every month, with current updates on your child. That is all that will happen at this point Zylar Taylor Wingate, your father supports this decision. We love you but you need professional help dear Mommy can't fix this one."

Two months later...

PROMIE
Lamar

"Mrs. Mo'Najah Maria Harrison -James, I would like you to meet Promise Lyric James. She was born three days ago in Bedford Hills women's state maximum security prison. I have full legal custody without any restrictions as long as I allow her grandparents to see her twice a year. They would not fight me for custody or visitation."

"Lamar Justin James I would like you to meet, the woman I call Mom, Henrietta Mason this is my husband Lamar. Oh and my first love Little Neef who prefers to be called Mason these days."

Thank you just does not seem like enough.

www.ingramcontent.com/pod-product-compliance
Lightning Source LLC
Chambersburg PA
CBHW051236260626
47162CB00002B/458